CONTENTS

CONTENTS

The Mystery of the Four Fingers

CHAPTER I

The Black Patch

CONSIDERING it was nearly the height of the London winter season, the Great Empire Hotel was not unusually crowded. This might perhaps have been owing to the fact that two or three of the finest suites of rooms in the building had been engaged by Mark Fenwick, who was popularly supposed to be the last thing in the way of American multi-millionaires. No one knew precisely who Fenwick was, or how he had made his money; but during the last few months his name had bulked largely in the financial Press and the daily periodicals of a sensational character. So far, the man had hardly been seen, it being understood that he was suffering from a chill, contracted on his voyage to Europe. Up to the present moment he had taken all his meals in his rooms, but it was whispered now that the great man was coming down to dinner. There was quite a flutter of excitement in the Venetian dining-room about eight o'clock.

The beautifully decorated saloon had a sprinkling of well-dressed men and women already dining decorously there. Everything was decorous about the Great Empire Hotel. No thought had been spared in the effort to keep the place quiet and select. The carpets were extra thick, and the waiters more than usually soft-footed. On the whole, it was a restful place, though, perhaps, the decorative scheme of its lighting erred just a trifle on the side of the sombre. Still, flowers and ferns were soft and feathery. The band played just loudly enough to stimulate conversation instead of drowning it. At one of the little tables near the door two men were dining. One had the alertness and vigor which bespeaks the dweller in towns. He was neatly groomed, with just the slight suspicion of the dandy in his dress, though it was obvious at the merest glance that he was a gentleman. His short, sleek hair gave to his head a certain suggestion of strength. The eyes which gleamed behind his gold-rimmed glasses were keen and steady. Most men about town were acquainted with the name of Jim Gurdon, as a generation before had been acquainted with his prowess in the athletic field. Now he was a successful barrister, though his ample private means rendered professional work quite unnecessary.

The other man was taller, and more loose-limbed, though his spare frame suggested great physical strength. He was dark in a hawk-like way, though the suggestion of the adventurer about him was softened by a pair of frank and pleasant grey eyes. Gerald Venner was tanned to a fine, healthy bronze by many years of wandering all over the world; in fact, he was one of those restless Englishmen who cannot for long be satisfied without risking his life in some adventure or other.

The two friends sat there quietly over their dinner, criticising from time to time those about them.

"After all," Gurdon said presently, "you must admit that there is something in our civilization. Now, isn't this better than starving under a thin blanket, with a chance of being murdered before morning?"

Venner shrugged his shoulders indifferently.

"I don't know," he said. "There is something in danger that stimulates me; in fact, it is the only thing that makes life worth living, I dare say you have wondered why it is that I have never settled down and become respectable like the rest of you. If you heard my story, you would not be surprised at my eccentric mode of living; at any rate, it enables me to forget."

Venner uttered the last words slowly and sadly, as if he were talking to himself, and had forgotten the presence of his companion. There was a speculative look in his eyes, much as if London had vanished and he could see the orchids on the table before him growing in their native forests.

"I suppose I don't look much like a man with a past," he went on; "like a man who is the victim of a great sorrow. I'll tell you the story presently, but not here; I really could not do it in surroundings like these. I've tried everything, even to money-making, but that is the worst and most unsatisfactory process of the lot. There is nothing so sordid as that."

"Oh, I don't know," Gurdon laughed. "It is better to be a multi-millionaire than a king to-day. Take the case of this man Fenwick, for instance; the papers are making more fuss of him than if he were the President of the United States or royalty travelling incognito."

Venner smiled more or less contemptuously. He turned to take a casual glance at a noisy party who had just come into the dining-room, for the frivolous note jarred upon him. Almost immediately the little party sat down, and the decorous air of the room seemed to subdue them. Immediately behind them followed a man who came dragging his limbs behind him, supported on either side by a servant. He was quite a young man, with a wonderfully handsome, clean-shaven face. Indeed, so handsome was he, that Venner could think of no more fitting simile for his beauty than the trite old comparison of the Greek god. The man's features were perfectly chiselled, slightly melancholy and romantic, and strongly suggestive of the early portraits of Lord Byron. Yet, all the same, the almost perfect face was from time to time twisted and distorted with pain, and from time to time there came into the dark, melancholy eyes a look of almost malignant fury. It was evident that the newcomer suffered from racking pain, for his lips were twitching, and Venner could see that his even, white teeth were clenched together On the whole, it was a striking figure to intrude upon the smooth gaiety of the dining-room, for it seemed to Venner that death and the stranger were more than casual acquaintances. He had an idea that it was only a strong will which kept the invalid on this side of the grave.

The sufferer sank at length with a sigh of relief into a large armchair, which had been specially placed for him. He waved the servants aside as if he had no further use for them, and commenced to study his *menu*, as if he had no thought for anything else. Venner did not fail to note that the man had the full use of his arms, and his eye dwelt with critical approval on the strong, muscular hands and wrists.

"I wonder who that fellow is?" he said. "What a magnificent frame his must have been before he got so terribly broken up."

"He is certainly a fascinating personality," Gurdon admitted. "Somehow, he strikes me not so much as the victim of an accident as an unfortunate being who is suffering from the result of some terrible form of vengeance. What a character he would make for a story! I am ready to bet anything in reason that if we could get to the bottom of his history it would be a most dramatic one. It regularly appeals to the imagination. I can quite believe our friend yonder has dragged himself out of bed by sheer force of will to keep some appointment whereby he can wreak his long nursed revenge."

"Not in a place like this," Venner smiled.

"Why not? In the old days these things used to be played out to the accompaniment of thunder and lightning on a blasted heath. Now we are much more quiet and gentle in our methods. It is quite evident that our handsome friend is expecting someone to dine with him. He gives a most excellent dinner to his enemy, points out to him his faults in the most gentlemanly fashion, and then proceeds to poison him with a specially prepared cigar. I can see the whole thing in the form of a short story."

Venner smiled at the conceit of his companion. He was more than half inclined to take a sentimental view of the thing himself. He turned to the waiter to give some order, and as he did so, his eyes encountered two more people, a man and a woman, who, at that moment, entered the dining-room.

THE BLACK PATCH

The man was somewhat past middle age, with a large bald head, covered with a shining dome of yellow skin, and a yellow face lighted by a pair of deep-sunk dark eyes. The whole was set off and rendered sinister by a small hook nose and a little black moustache. For the rest, the man was short and inclined to be stout. He walked with a wonderfully light and agile step for a man of his weight; in fact he seemed to reach his seat much as a cat might have done. Indeed, despite his bulk, there was something strangely feline about the stranger.

Venner gave a peculiar gasp and gurgle. His eyes started. All the blood receded from his brown face, leaving him ghastly white under his tan. It was no aspect of fear—rather one of surprise,—of strong and unconquerable emotion. At the same moment Venner's hand snapped the stem of his wine glass, and the champagne frothed upon the table.

"Who is that man?" Venner asked of the waiter. His tone was so strained and harsh that he hardly recognised his own voice. "Who is the man, I say? No, no; I don't mean him. I mean that stout man, with the lady in white, over there."

The waiter stared at the speaker in astonishment. He seemed to wonder where he had been all these years.

"That, sir, is Mr. Mark Fenwick, the American millionaire."

[13]

Venner waved the speaker aside. He was recovering from his emotion now and the blood had returned once more to his cheeks. He became conscious of the fact that Gurdon was regarding him with a polite, yet none the less critical, wonder.

"What is the matter?" the latter asked. "Really, the air seems full of mystery. Do you know that for the last two minutes you have been regarding that obese capitalist with a look that was absolutely murderous? Do you mean to tell me that you have ever seen him before?"

"Indeed, I have," Venner replied. "But on the last occasion of our meeting, he did not call himself Mark Fenwick, or by any other name so distinctly British. Look at him now; look at his yellow skin with the deep patches of purple at the roots of the little hair he has. Mark the shape of his face and the peculiar oblique slit of his eyelids. Would you take that man for an Englishman?"

"No, I shouldn't," Gurdon said frankly. "If I had to hazard a guess, I should say he is either Portuguese or perhaps something of the Mexican half caste."

"You would not be far wrong," Venner said quietly. "I suppose you thought that the appearance of that man here to-night was something of a shock to me. You can little guess what sort of a shock it has been. I promise to tell you my story presently, so it will have to keep. In the meantime, it is my mood to sit here and watch that man."

"Personally, I am much more interested in his companion," Gurdon laughed. "A daughter of the gods, if ever there was one. What a face, and what a figure! Do you mean to say that you didn't notice her as she came in?"

"Positively I didn't," Venner confessed. "My whole attention was rivetted on the man. I tell you I can see absolutely nothing but his great, yellow, wicked face, and for the background the romantic spot where we last met."

It was Gurdon's turn now to listen. He leant forward in his chair, his whole attention concentrated upon the figure of the stranger, huddled up in the armchair at the little table opposite. He touched Venner on the arm, and indicated the figure of the man who had suffered so cruelly in some form or other.

"The plot thickens," Venner murmured. "Upon my word, he seems to know this Mark Fenwick as well as I do."

The maimed crippled figure in the armchair had dragged himself almost to his feet, with his powerful, muscular arm propping him against the table. His unusually handsome face was all broken and twisted up with an expression of malignant fury. He stood there for a moment or two like a statue of uncontrollable passion, rigid, fixed, and motionless, save for the twitching of his face. Then, gradually he dropped back into his chair again, a broken and huddled heap, quivering from head to foot with the pain caused by his recent exertion. A moment later he took from his breast pocket a silk shade, which he proceeded to tie over his eyes, as if the light hurt him. Watching his every movement with intense eagerness, the two friends saw that he had also taken from his pocket a small silver case, about the same size as an ordinary box of safety matches. Indeed, the case looked not unlike the silver coverings for wood matches, which are generally to be seen in well-appointed households. Then, as if nothing interested him further, he leaned back in his chair, and appeared to give himself over entirely to his enjoyment of the orchestra. In all probability no diner there besides Venner and Gurdon had noticed anything in the least out of the common.

"This is very dramatic," Gurdon said. "Here is a melo-drama actually taking place in a comedy 'set' like this. I am glad you will be in a position later on to gratify my curiosity. I confess I should like to learn something more about this Mark Fenwick, who does not appear to be in the least like one's idea of the prosaic money spinner."

"He isn't," Venner said grimly. "Anything but that. Why, three years ago that man was as poor and desperate as the most wretched outcast who

walks the streets of London to-night. And one
thing you may be certain of—wherever you dine
from now to your dying day, you will be under the
roof of no more diabolical scoundrel than the creature who calls himself Mark Fenwick."

There was a deep note in Venner's voice that
did not fail to stimulate Gurdon's curiosity. He
glanced again at the millionaire, who appeared to
be talking in some foreign tongue with his companion. The tall, fair girl with the shining hair had
her back to the friends, so they could not see her
face, and when she spoke it was in a tone so low
that it was not possible to catch anything more than
the sweetness of her voice.

"I wonder what she is doing with him?" Gurdon said. "At any rate, she is English enough.
I never saw a woman with a more thoroughbred
air. She is looking this way."

Just for a moment the girl turned her head, and
Venner caught a full sight of her face. It was only
for an instant; then the fair head was turned again,
and the girl appeared to resume her dinner. Venner jumped from his chair and took three strides
across the room. He paused there as if struggling
to regain possession of himself; then he dropped into
his chair again, shielding his face from the light
with his hands. Gurdon could see that his companion's face had turned to a ghastly grey. Veri-
tably it was a night of surprises, quick, dra-

matic surprises, following close upon one another's heels.

"What, do you mean to say you know her, too?" Gurdon whispered.

Venner looked up with a strange, unsteady smile on his face. He appeared to be fighting hard to regain his self-control.

"Indeed, I do know her," he said "My friend, you are going to have all the surprises you want. What will you say when I tell you that the girl who sits there, utterly unconscious of my presence, and deeming me to be at the other end of the world, is no less a person than—my own wife?"

CHAPTER II

THE FIRST FINGER

GURDON waited for his companion to go on. It was a boast of his that he had exhausted most of the sensations of life, and that he never allowed anything to astonish him. All the same, he was astonished now, and surprised beyond words. For the last twenty-five years, on and off, he had known Venner. Indeed, there had been few secrets between them since the day when they had come down from Oxford together. From time to time, during his wanderings, Venner had written to his old chum a fairly complete account of his adventures. During the last three years the letters had been meagre and far between; and at their meeting a few days ago, Gurdon had noticed a reticence in the manner of his old chum that he had not seen before.

He waited now, naturally enough, for the other to give some explanation of his extraordinary statement, but Venner appeared to have forgotten all about Gurdon. He sat there shielding one side of his face, heedless of the attentions of the waiter, who proffered him food from time to time.

"Is that all you are going to tell me?" Gurdon asked at length.

"Upon my word, I am very sorry," Venner said. "But you will excuse me if I say nothing more at present. You can imagine what a shock this has been to me."

"Of course. I don't wish to be impertinent, old chap, but I presume that there has been some little misunderstanding——"

"Not in the least. There has been no misunderstanding whatever. I honestly believe that the woman over yonder is still just as passionately fond of me as I am of her. As you know, Gurdon, I never was much of a ladies' man; in fact, you fellows at Oxford used to chaff me because I was so ill at ease in the society of women. Usually a man like myself falls in love but once in his lifetime, and then never changes. At any rate, that is my case. I worship the ground that girl walks upon. I would have given up my life cheerfully for her; I would do so now if I could save her a moment's pain. You think, perhaps, that she saw me when she came in here to-night. That is where you have got the impression that there is some misunderstanding between us. You talked just now of dramatic surprises. I could show you one even beyond your powers of imagination if I chose What would you say if I told you that three years ago I became the husband of that beautiful girl yonder, and that from half-an-hour after the ceremony till the present moment I have never set eyes on her again?"

THE FIRST FINGER

"It seems almost incredible," Gurdon exclaimed.

"Yes, I suppose it does. But it is absolutely a fact all the same. I can't tell you here the romance of my life. I couldn't do it in surroundings like these. We will go on to your rooms presently, and then I will make a clean breast of the whole thing to you. You may be disposed to laugh at me for a sentimentalist, but I should like to stay here a little longer, if it is only now and again to hear a word or two from her lips. If you will push those flowers across between me and the light I shall be quite secure from observation. I think that will do."

"But you don't mean to tell me," Gurdon murmured, "that the lady in question is the daughter of that picturesque-looking old ruffian, Mark Fenwick?"

"Of course, she isn't," Venner said, with great contempt. "What the connection is between them, I cannot say. What strange fate links them together is as much a mystery to me as it is to you. I do not like it, but I let it pass, feeling so sure of Vera's innocence and integrity. But the waiter will tell us. Here, waiter, is the lady dining over there with Mr. Fenwick his daughter or not?"

"Certainly, sir," the waiter responded. "That is Miss Fenwick."

There was silence for a moment or two between the two friends. Venner appeared to be deeply immersed in his own thoughts, while Gurdon's eyes travelled quickly between the table where the millionaire sat and the deep armchair, in which the invalid lay huddled, and Venner now saw that the cripple on the opposite side of the room was regarding Fenwick and his companion with the intentness of a cat watching a mouse.

Dinner had now come pretty well to an end, and the coffee and liqueurs were going round. A cup was placed before Fenwick, who turned to one of the waiters with a quick order which the latter hastened to obey. The order was given so clearly that Gurdon could hear distinctly what it was. He had asked for a light, wherewith to burn the glass of Curaçoa which he intended to take, foreign fashion, in his coffee.

"And don't forget to bring me a wooden match," he commanded "Household matches. Last night one of your men brought me a vesta."

The waiter hurried off to execute his commission, but his intention was anticipated by another waiter who had apparently been doing nothing and hanging about in the background. The second waiter was a small, lithe man, with beady, black eyes and curly hair. For some reason or other, Gurdon noticed him particularly; then he saw a strange thing happen. The little waiter with the snaky hair glanced swiftly across the room in the direction of the cripple huddled up in the armchair.

[22]

THE FIRST FINGER

Just as if he had been waiting for a signal, the invalid stretched out one of his long arms, and laid his fingers significantly on the tiny silver box he had deposited on the table some little time before. The small waiter went across the room and deliberately lifted the silver box from the table. He then walked briskly across to where the millionaire was seated, placed the box close to his elbow, and vanished. He seemed to fairly race down the room until he was lost in a pile of palms which masked the door. Gurdon had followed all this with the deepest possible interest. Venner sat there, apparently lost to all sense of his surroundings. His head was on his hands, and his mind was apparently far away. Therefore, Gurdon was left entirely to himself, to study the strange things that were going on around him. His whole attention was now concentrated upon Fenwick, who presently tilted his glass of Curaçoa dexterously into his coffee cup, and then stretched out his hand for the silver match box by his side. He was still talking to his companion while he fumbled for a match without looking at the little case in his hand Suddenly he ceased to speak, his black eyes rivetted on the box. It fell from his fingers as if it had contained some poisonous insect, and he rose to his feet with a sudden scream that could be heard all over the room.

There was a quick hush in the conversation, and every head was turned in the direction of the millionaire's table. Practically every diner there knew who the man with the yellow head was, so that the startling interruption was all the more unexpected. Once again the frightened cry rang out, and then Fenwick stood, gazing with horrified eyes and white, ghastly face at the innocent looking little box on the table.

"Who brought this here?" he screamed. "Bring that waiter here. Find him at once. Find him at once, I say. A little man with beady eyes and hair like rats' tails."

The head waiter bustled up, full of importance; but it was in vain that he asked for some explanation of what had happened. All Fenwick could do was to stand there gesticulating and calling aloud for the production of the erring waiter.

"But I assure you, sir," the head waiter said, "we have no waiter here who answers to the description of the man you mention. They are all here now, every waiter who has entered the room to-night. If you will be so good as to pick out the one who has offended you——"

Fenwick's startled, bloodshot eyes ranged slowly over the array of waiters which had been gathered for his inspection round his table. Presently he shook his head with an impatient gesture.

"I tell you, he is not here," he cried. "The man is not here. He is quite small, with very queer, black hair."

THE FIRST FINGER

The head waiter was equally positive in his assurance. Louder rose the angry voice of the millionaire, till at length Venner was aroused from his reverie and looked up to Gurdon to know what was going on. The latter explained as far as possible, not omitting to describe the strange matter of the silver box. Venner smiled with the air of a man who could say a great deal if he chose.

"It is all part of the programme," he said. "That will come in my story later on. But what puzzles me is where that handsome cripple comes in. The mystery deepens."

By this time Fenwick's protestations had grown weaker. He seemed to ramble on in a mixture of English and Portuguese which was exceedingly puzzling to the head waiter, who still was utterly in the dark as to the cause of offence. Most of the diners had gathered round the millionaire's table with polite curiosity, and sundry offers of assistance.

"I think we had better get to our own room," a sweet, gentle voice said, as the tall, fair girl by Fenwick's side rose and moved in the direction of the door. It was, perhaps, unfortunate that Venner had risen at the same time. As he strode from his own table, he came face to face with the girl who stood there watching him with something like pain in her blue eyes. Just for an instant she staggered back, and apparently would have fallen had not Venner placed his arm about her waist. In the strange confusion caused by the unexpected disturbance, nobody had noticed this besides Gurdon, who promptly rose to the occasion.

"You had better take the lady as far as her own rooms," he said. "This business has evidently been too much for her. Meanwhile, I will see what I can do for Mr. Fenwick."

Venner shot his friend a glance of gratitude He did not hesitate for a moment; he saw that the girl by his side was quite incapable of offering any objections for the present. In his own strong, masterful way, he drew the girl's hand under his arm, and fairly dragged her from the room into the comparative silence and seclusion of the corridor beyond.

"Which way do we go?" he asked.

"The Grand Staircase," the girl replied faintly. "It is on the first floor. But you must not come with me, you must come no further. It would be madness for him to know that we are together."

"He will not come just yet," Venner replied. "My friend knows something of my story, and he will do his best to get us five minutes together. You have heard me speak of Jim Gurdon before."

"But it is madness," the girl whispered. "You know how dangerous it is. Oh, Gerald, what must you think of me when—"

"I swear to you that I think nothing of you that is unkind or ungenerous," Venner protested "By a cruel stroke of fate we were parted at the very moment when our happiness seemed most complete. Why you left me in the strange way you did, I have never yet learned. In your letter to me you told me you were bound to act as you did, and I believed you implicitly. How many men in similar circumstances would have behaved as I did? How many men would have gone on honoring a wife who betrayed her husband as you betrayed me? And yet, as I stand here at this moment, looking into your eyes, I feel certain that you are the same sweet and innocent girl who did me the happiness to become my wife."

The beautiful face quivered, and the blue eyes filled with tears. Her trembling hand lay on Venner's arm for a moment; then he caught the girl to his side and kissed her passionately.

"I thank you for those words," she whispered. "From the bottom of my heart I thank you. If you only knew what I have suffered, if you only knew the terrible pressure that is put upon me;— and it seemed to me that I was acting for the best. I hoped, too, that you would go away and forget me; that in the course of time I should be nothing more than a memory to you. And yet, in my heart, I always felt that we should meet again. Is it not strange that we should come together like this?"

"I do not see that it is in the least strange," Venner replied, "considering that I have been looking for you for the last three years. When I found you to-night, it was with the greatest difficulty that I restrained myself from laying my hands on the man who is the cause of all your misery and suffering. How long has he been passing for an Englishman? Since when has he been a millionaire? If he be a millionaire at all."

"I cannot tell you," the girl whispered. "Really, I do not know. A little time ago we were poor enough; then suddenly, money seemed to come in from all sides. I asked no questions; they would not have been answered if I had. At least, not truthfully. And now you really must go. When shall I see you again? Ah, I cannot tell you. For the present you must go on trusting me as implicitly as you have done in the past. Oh, if you only knew how it wrings my heart to have to speak to you like this, when all the time my whole love is for you and you alone. Gerald—ah, go now; go at once. Don't you see that he is coming up the stairs?"

Venner turned away, and slipped down a side corridor, till Fenwick had entered his own room. Then he walked down the stairs again into the dining-room, where a heated discussion was still going on as to the identity of the missing waiter.

"'They'll never find him," Gurdon muttered, "for the simple reason that the fellow was imported for the occasion, and, in my opinion, was no waiter at all. You will notice also that our crippled friend has vanished. I would give a great deal to know what was in the box that pretty nearly scared the yellow man to death. I never saw a fellow so frightened in my life. He had to fortify himself with two brandies before he could get up to his own room. Gerald, I really must find out what was in that box!"

"I think I could tell you," Venner said, with a smile. "Didn't you tell me that the mysterious waiter fetched it from the table where it had been placed by the handsome cripple?"

"Certainly, he did. I saw the signal pass directly Fenwick asked for a wooden match; that funny little waiter was palpably waiting for the silver box, and as soon as he placed it on Fenwick's table, he discreetly vanished. But, as I said before, I would give considerable to know what was in that box."

"Well, go and see," Venner said grimly. "Unless my eyes deceive me, the box is still lying on Fenwick's table. In his fright, he forgot all about it, and there isn't a waiter among the whole lot, from the chief downwards, who has a really clear impression of what the offence was. If you take my advice, you will go and have a peep into that box when you get the chance. Don't tell me what you find, because I will guess that."

Gurdon crossed over to the other table, and took the box up in his hand. He pulled the slide out and glanced at the contents with a puzzled expression of face. Then he dropped the box again, and came back to Venner with a look on his face as if he had been handling something more than usually repulsive.

"You needn't tell me what it is," Venner said. "I know quite as well as you do. Inside that box is a dried up piece of flesh, some three inches long —in other words a mummified human forefinger."

CHAPTER III

The Lost Mine

GURDON nodded thoughtfully. He was trying to piece the puzzle together in his mind, but so far without success. He was not in the least surprised to find that Venner had guessed correctly.

"You've got it exactly," he said. "That is just what the gruesome thing is. What does it all mean?"

By this time dinner had long been a thing of the past, and all the guests had departed. Here and there the lights were turned down, leaving half the room in semi-darkness. It was just the time and place for an exchange of confidences.

"How did you know exactly what was in that box?" Gurdon asked. "I have read things of this kind before, but they have generally taken the form of a warning previous to some act of vengeance."

"As a matter of fact, this is something of the same kind," Venner said; "though I am bound to say that my guess was somewhat in the nature of a shot. Still, putting two and two together, I felt that I could not have been far wrong. Since I have been here this evening, I have begun to form a pretty shrewd opinion as to where Fenwick gets his money."

[31]

"What shall we do with that box?" Gurdon asked.

"Leave it where it is, by all means. You may depend upon it that Fenwick will return for his lost property."

The prophecy came true quicker than Gurdon had expected, for out of the gloom there presently emerged the yellow face of Mark Fenwick. He came in with a furtive air, like some mean thief who is about to do a shabby action. He was palpably looking for something. He made a gesture of disappointment when he saw that the table where he had dined was now stripped of everything except the flowers. He did not seem to see the other two men there at all. Venner took the box from his companion's hand, and advanced to Fenwick's side.

"I think you have lost something, sir," he said coolly. "Permit me to restore your property to you."

The millionaire gave a kind of howl as he looked at Venner. The noise he made was like that of a child suffering from toothache. He fairly grovelled at Venner's feet, but as far as the latter's expression was concerned, the two might have met for the first time. Just for a moment Fenwick stood there, mopping his yellow face, himself a picture of abject misery and despair.

"Well?" Venner said sharply. "Is this little box yours, or not?"

"Oh, yes, oh yes," Fenwick whined. "You know that perfectly well—I mean, you must recognise—oh, I don't know what I mean. The fact is, I am really ill to-night. I hardly know what I am doing. Thank you, very much."

Fenwick snatched the box from Venner's fingers, and made hastily for the door.

"I believe we are allowed to smoke in here after ten," Gurdon said. "If that is the case, why not have a cigar together, and discuss the matter? What I am anxious to know at present is the inner meaning of the finger in the box."

There was no objection to a cigar in the dining-room at this late hour, and presently the two friends were discussing their Havanas together. Venner began to speak at length.

"Perhaps it would be as well," he said, "to stick to the box business first. You will remember, some three years ago, my writing you to the effect that I was going to undertake a journey through Mexico. I don't suppose I should have gone there at all, only I was attracted by the notion of possible adventures in that country, among the hills where, at one time, gold was found. There was no question whatever that gold in large quantities used to be mined in the wild district where I had chosen to take up my headquarters. Practical engineers say that the gold is exhausted, but that did not deter me in the least.

3

THE MYSTERY OF THE FOUR FINGERS

"The first man who put the idea into my head was a half-caste Mexican, who had an extraordinary grip on the history of his country, especially as far as legends and traditions were concerned. He was a well-educated man, and an exceedingly fascinating story-teller. It was he who first gave me the history of what he called the Four Finger Mine. It appears that this mine had been discovered some century or more ago by a Frenchman, who had settled down in the country and married the daughter of a native chief. The original founder of the mine was a curious sort of man, and was evidently possessed of strong miserly tendencies. Most men in his position would have gathered together a band of workers, and simply exploited the mine for all it was worth. However, this man, Le Fenu, did nothing of the kind. He kept his discovery an absolute secret, and what mining was to be done, he did himself. I understand that he was a man of fine physique, and that his disposition was absolutely fearless. It was his habit at certain seasons of the year to go up to his mine, and there work it for a month or two at a time, spending the rest of the year with his family. It is quite certain, too, that he kept his secret, even from his grown-up sons; for when he died, they had not the slightest idea of the locality of the mine, which fact I know from Le Fenu's descendants.

"And now comes the interesting part of my story.

THE LOST MINE

Le Fenu went up into the mountains early in May one year, to put in his solitary two months' mining, as usual. For, perhaps, the first time in his life, he suffered from a serious illness—some kind of fever, I suppose, though he had just strength of will enough to get on the back of a horse and ride as far as the nearest *hacienda*.

"Now, on this particular farm there dwelt a Dutchman, who, I believe, was called Van Fort. Whether or not Le Fenu partially disclosed his secret in his delirium, will never actually be known. At any rate, two or three weeks later the body of Le Fenu was discovered not very far away from the scene of his mining operations, and from the evidence obtainable, there was no doubt in the world that he was foully murdered. Justice in that country walks with very tardy footsteps, and though there was little question who the real murderer was, Van Fort was never brought to justice. Perhaps that was accounted for by the fact that he seemed to be suddenly possessed of more money than usual, and was thus in a position to bribe the authorities.

"And now comes a further development. Soon, after the death of Le Fenu, it was noted that Van Fort spent most of his time away from his farm in the mountains, no doubt prospecting for Le Fenu's mine. Whether he ever found it or not will never be known. Please to bear in mind the fact that for a couple of centuries at least Le Fenu's mysterious property was known as the Four Finger Mine. With this digression, I will go on to speak further of Van Fort's movements. To make a long story short, from his last journey to the mountains he never returned. His widow searched for him everywhere; I have seen her—a big sullen woman, with a cruel mouth and a heavy eye. From what I have heard, I have not the slightest doubt that it was she who inspired the murder of the Frenchman.

"She had practically given up all hope of ever seeing her husband again, when, one dark and stormy night, just as she was preparing for bed, she heard her husband outside, screaming for assistance. From his tone, he was evidently in some dire and deadly peril. The woman was by no means devoid of courage; she rushed out into the night and searched far and near, but no trace of Van Fort could be found, nor did the imploring cry for assistance come again. But the next morning, on the doorstep lay a bleeding forefinger, which the woman recognised as coming from her husband's hand. To make identity absolutely certain, on the forefinger was a ring of native gold, which the Dutchman always wore. Please to remember once more that this mine was known as the Four Finger Mine."

Venner paused just for a moment to give dramatic effect to his point. Gurdon said nothing; he was too deeply interested in the narrative to make any comment.

[36]

THE LOST MINE

"That was what I may call the first act in the drama," Venner went on. "Six months had elapsed, and Van Fort's widow was beginning to forget all about the startling incident, when, one night, just at the same time, and in just the same circumstances, came that wild, pitiful yell for assistance outside the Dutchman's farm. Half mad with dread and terror the woman sat there listening. She did not dare to go outside now; she knew how futile such an act would be. Also, she knew quite well what was going to happen in the morning. She sat up half the night in a state bordering on madness. I need not insult your intelligence, my dear fellow, by asking you to guess what she found on the doorstep in the daylight."

"Of course, I can guess," Gurdon said. "Beyond all question, it was the third finger of the Dutchman's hand."

"Quite so," Venner resumed. "I need not over elaborate my story or bore you by telling how, six months later, the second finger of the hand appeared in the same sensational circumstances, and how, at the end of a year, the four fingers were complete. Let me once more impress upon you the fact that this mine was called the Four Finger Mine for more than a century before these strange things happened."

"It is certainly an extraordinary thing," Gurdon muttered. "I don't think I ever listened to a weirder tale. And did the Dutch woman confess to her crime? This strikes me as being a fitting end to the story. I suppose it came from her lips."

"She didn't confess, for the simple reason that she had no mind to confess with," Venner explained. "Of course, certain neighbors knew something of what was going on, but they never knew the whole truth, because, after the appearance of the last finger, Mrs. Van Fort went stark raving mad. She lived for a few days, and at the end of that time her body was found in a waterfall close to her house. That is the story of the Four Finger Mine so far as it goes, though I should not be surprised if we manage to get to the last chapter yet. Now, you are an observant man—did you notice anything peculiar in Fenwick's appearance to-night?"

Gurdon shook his head slowly. It was quite evident that he had not noticed anything out of the common in the appearance of the millionaire. Venner proceeded to explain.

"Let me tell you this," he said. "When I married my wife, we were within an easy ride of the locality where the Four Finger Mine is situated. Mind you, our marriage was a secret one, and I presume that Fenwick is still in ignorance of it, though, of course, he was fully aware of the fact that I had more than a passing admiration for Vera. I merely mention this by way of accentuating the little point that I am going to make. It is more than probable that, when I stumbled upon Fenwick and the girl who passes for his daughter, he also was in search of the Four Finger Mine. When he came in to-night he, of course, recognised me, though I treated him as an absolute stranger whom I had met for the first time. You will see presently why I treated him in this fashion. I am glad I spoke to him, because I noticed a slight thing that throws a flood of light upon the mystery. Now, did it escape your observation, or did you notice that Fenwick took the box I gave him in his right hand?"

"Oh, dear, no," Gurdon said. "A little thing like that would be almost too trivial for the typical detective of the cheap story."

"All the same, it is very important," Venner said. "He took the box in his right hand; he made as if to extend his left, then suddenly changed his mind, and put it in his pocket. But he was too late to disguise from me that he had——"

"I know," Gurdon shouted. "He had lost all the fingers on his left hand. What an amazing thing! We must get to the bottom of this business at all costs."

"That is precisely what we are going to do," Venner said grimly. "I am glad you are so quick in taking up the point. When I noted the loss of those fingers, I was absolutely staggered for a moment. If he had been less agitated than he was,

[39]

Fenwick would have guessed what I had seen. I need not tell you that when I last saw Fenwick his left hand was as sound as yours or mine. The inference of this is, that Fenwick has fallen under the ban of the same strange vengeance that overtook Van Fort and his wife. There is not the slightest doubt that he discovered the mine, and that he has not yet paid the penalty for his temerity."

"I presume the penalty is coming," Gurdon said. "What a creepy sort of idea it is, that terrible vengeance reaching across a continent in such a sinister fashion. But don't forget that we know something as to the way in which this thing is to be brought about. Don't forget the cripple who sat at yonder table to-night."

"I am not likely to forget him," Venner observed. "All the more because he evidently knows more about this matter than we do ourselves. When he came here to-night, he little dreamed that there was one man in the room, at least, who had a fairly good knowledge of the Four Finger Mystery. We shall have to look him out, and, if necessary, force him to speak. But it is a delicate matter, and as far as I can see, one not unattended with danger."

Gurdon smoked in thoughtful silence for some little time, turning the strange thing over in his mind. The more he dwelt upon it, the more wild and dramatic did it seem.

"There is one thing in our favor," he said, presently. "The mysterious cripple is evidently a deadly enemy of Fenwick's. We shall doubtless find him ready to accept our offer, provided that we put it in the right way."

"I am not so sure of that," Venner replied. "At any rate, we can make no move in that direction without thinking the whole thing out carefully and thoroughly. Our crippled friend is evidently a fanatic in his way, and he is not alone in his scheme. Do not forget that we have also the little man who played the part of the waiter to deal with. I am sorry that I did not notice him. A man who could carry off a thing like that with such splendid audacity is certainly a force to be reckoned with."

Gurdon rose from his seat with a yawn, and intimated that it was time to go to bed. It was long past twelve now and the hotel was gradually retiring to rest. The Grand Empire was not the sort of house to cater to the frivolous type of guest, and usually within an hour of the closing of the theatres the whole of the vast building was wrapped in silence.

"I think I will go now," Gurdon said. "Come and lunch with me to-morrow, and then you can tell me something about your own romance. What sort of a night is it, waiter?"

"Very bad, sir," the waiter replied. "It's pouring in torrents. Shall I call you a cab, sir?"

CHAPTER IV

In The Lift

GURDON looked out from the shelter of the great portico to see the sheets of rain falling on the pavement. Silence reigned supreme but for the steady plash of the raindrops as they rattled on the pavements. To walk half a mile on such a night meant getting wet through; and Gurdon somewhat ruefully regarded his thin slippers and his light dust overcoat. Half a dozen times the night porter blew his whistle, but no sign of a cab could be seen.

"We sha'n't get one to-night," Venner said. "They are all engaged. There is only one thing for it—you must take a room here, and stay till the morning. I've no doubt I can fit you up in the way of pyjamas and the things necessary."

Gurdon fell in readily enough with the suggestion. Indeed, there was nothing else for it. He took his number and key from the sleepy clerk in the office, and made his way upstairs to Venner's bedroom.

"I'll just have one cigarette before I turn in," he said. "It seems as if Fate had ordained that I am to keep in close touch with the leading characters of the mystery. By the way, we never took the' trouble to find out who the handsome cripple was.",

"That is very easily done in the morning," Venner replied. "A striking personality like that is not soon lost sight of. Besides, he has doubtless been here before, for, if you will recollect, his attendants took him to the right table as if it had been ordered beforehand And now, if you don't mind, I'll turn in—not that I expect to sleep much after an exciting evening like this. Good night, old fellow."

Gurdon went on to his own room, where he slowly undressed and sat thinking the whole thing out on the edge of his bed. Perhaps he was suffering from the same suppressed excitement which at that moment was keeping Venner awake, for he felt not the slightest disposition to turn in Usually he was a sound sleeper, but this night seemed likely to prove an exception to the rule

An hour passed, and Gurdon was still sitting there, asking himself whether it would not be better to go to bed and compel sleep to come to him. Impatiently he turned out his light and laid his head resolutely on the pillow.

But it was all in vain—sleep was out of the question The room was not altogether in darkness, either; for the sleeping apartments on that landing had been arranged back to back with a large, open ventilator between them. Through this ventilator came a stream of light; evidently the occupant of

[43]

the adjoining room had not yet retired. The light worried Gurdon; he asked himself irritably why his neighbor should be permitted to annoy him in this way. A moment or two later the sound of suppressed voices came through the ventilator, followed by the noise of a heavy fall.

At any ordinary time Gurdon would have thought nothing of this, but his imagination was aflame now, and his mind was full of hidden mysteries. It seemed to him that something sinister and underhand was going on in the next room.

Usually, no one would identify the Grand Empire Hotel with crime and intrigue; but that did not deter Gurdon from rising from his bed and making a determined effort to see through the ventilator into the adjoining room. It was not an easy matter, but by dint of balancing two chairs one on top of the other the thing was accomplished. Very cautiously Gurdon pushed back the glass slide and looked through. So far as he could see, there was nothing to justify any suspicion. The room was absolutely empty, though it was brilliantly lighted; and for a moment Gurdon felt ashamed of his suspicions, and turned away, half determined to try and sleep. It was at that instant that he noticed something out of the common. To his quickened ear there came a sound unmistakably like a snore, and pushing his body half through the ventilator he managed to make out the bed in the next room.

On it lay the body of a boy in uniform, unmistakably a messenger boy or hotel attendant of that
kind. Gurdon could see the hotel name embroi-
dered in gold letters on his collar.

Perhaps there was nothing so very suspicious in
this, except that the boy was lying on the bed fully
dressed, even to his boots. It was a luxurious room;
not at all the class of apartment to which the hotel
management would relegate one of their messenger
boys, nor was it possible that the lad had had the
temerity to go into the vacant room and sleep.

"Something wrong here," Gurdon muttered.
"Hang me if I don't get through the ventilator and
see what it is."

It was no difficult matter for an athlete like Gurdon to push his way through and drop on to the
bed on the other side. Then he shook the form of
the slumbering lad without reward. The boy
seemed to be plunged in a sleep almost like death.
As Gurdon turned him over, he noticed on the
other side of the lad's collar the single word "Lift."
It began to dawn upon Gurdon exactly what had
happened. In large hotels like the Grand Empire
there is no fixed period when the lift is suspended,
and consequently, it has its attendants night and
day. For some reason, this boy had evidently been
drugged and carried into the room where he now lay
There was no doubt whatever about it, for it was
impossible to shake the lad into the slightest sem-

blance of life. Gurdon crossed to the door, and found, not to his surprise, that it was locked. His first impulse was to return to his room and call the night porter; but a strange, wild idea had come into his mind, and he refrained from doing so. It occurred to him that perhaps Mark Fenwick or the cripple had had a hand in this outrage.

"I'll wait a bit," Gurdon told himself. "It is just possible that my key will fit this door Anyway, it is worth trying."

Gurdon made his way back to his own room again, to return a minute or two later with his key. To his great delight the door opened, and he stood in a further corridor, close against the cage in which the lift worked noiselessly up and down.

It was absolutely quiet, so that anybody standing there would have been able to carry out any operation of an unlawful kind without observation. Gurdon stood, looking down the lift shaft, until he saw that the cage was once more beginning to ascend. It came up slowly and smoothly and without the least noise, until it was level with the floor on which Gurdon was standing. It was one of the open kind, so he could see inside quite clearly. To all practical purposes, the lift was empty, save for the presence of one man, who lay unconscious on the floor. The cage was ascending so leisurely that Gurdon was in a position to make a close examination of the figure before the whole structure had

risen to the next floor It did not need a second
glance to tell Gurdon that the man in the cage was
the attendant, and that he was suffering from the
same drug which had placed his boy assistant beyond all power of interfering.

"Now what does all this mean?" Gurdon muttered. "Who is there on the floor above who is interested in getting these two people out of the way?
What do they want to bring up or send down which
it is not safe to dispose of by the ordinary means?
I think I'll wait and see. No sleep for me to-night."

The lift vanished in the same silent way. It hung
overhead for some little time, and once more appeared in sight, this time absolutely empty, save for
a small square box with iron bands at the corners,
which lay upon the floor. As the cage descended,
Gurdon suddenly made up his mind what to do.
He sprang lightly on to the top of the falling cage,
and grasped the rope with both hands. A moment
later and he was descending in the darkness.

As far as he could judge, the lift went down to
the basement, where, for the time being, it remained.
There was a warm damp smell in the air, suggestive
of fungus, whereby Gurdon judged that he must be
in the vaults beneath the hotel. As his eyes became accustomed to the gloom, he could make out
just in front of him a circular patch of light, which
evidently was a coal shoot.

He had no need to wait now for the full development of the adventure. He could hear whispered voices and the clang of metal, as if somebody had opened the door of the lift. One of the voices he failed to understand, but with a thrill he recognised the fact that the speaker was talking in either Spanish or Portuguese. Instantly it flashed into his mind that this was the language most familiar to the man who called himself Mark Fenwick. Beyond doubt he was quite right when he identified this last development with the actors in the dramatic events earlier in the evening.

"Now don't be long about it," a hoarse voice whispered. "There are two more cases to send up, and two more to come down here. Has that van come along, or shall we have to wait until morning?"

"The van is there right enough," another hoarse voice said. "We have the stuff out on the pavement. Let's have the last lot here, and get it up at once."

Gurdon could hear the sound of labored breathing as if the unseen man was struggling with some heavy burden. Presently some square object was deposited on the floor of the lift. It seemed to slip from someone's hands, and dropped with a heavy thud that caused the lift to vibrate like a thing of life."

"Clumsy fool," a voice muttered. "You might have dropped that on my foot. What did you want to let go for?"

[48]

"I couldn't help it," another voice grumbled. "I didn't know it was half so heavy. Besides, the rope broke."

"Oh, are you going to be there all night?"—another voice, with a suggestion of a foreign accent in it, asked impatiently. "Don't forget you have to bring the man down yet, and see that the boy is taken to his place. Now, up with it."

Standing there, holding on to the rope and quivering with excitement, Gurdon wondered what was going to happen next. Once more he felt himself rising, and an instant later he was in the light again. He waited till the lift had reached his own floor; then he jumped quickly down, taking care as he went to note the heavy box which lay on the floor of the lift. A corner of it had been split open by the heavy jar, and some shining material like sand lay in a little heap, glittering in the rays of the electric light.

Gurdon stood there panting for a moment, and rather at a loss to know what to do next. Once more the lift came down, this time with two boxes of a smaller size. They vanished; and as the lift rose once again, Gurdon had barely time to hide himself behind the bedroom door, and thus escape the observation of two men who now occupied the cage He just caught a fleeting glimpse of them, and saw that one was an absolute stranger, but he felt his heart beating slightly faster as he recognised in the other the now familiar form of Mark Fenwick. The mystery was beginning to unfold itself.

"That was a close thing," Gurdon muttered, as he wiped his hot face. "I think I had better go back to my own room, and wait developments. One can't be too careful."

The lift-boy was still sleeping on the bed; but his features were twitching, as if already the drug was beginning to lose its effect. At least, so Gurdon shrewdly thought, and subsequent events proved that he was not far wrong. He was standing in his own room now, waiting by the ventilator, when he heard the sound of footsteps on the other side of the wall. Two men had entered the room, and by taking a little risk, Gurdon could see that they were examining the unconscious boy coolly and critically.

"I should think about five minutes more would do it," one of them said. "Better carry him out, and shove him in that little sentry box of his. When he comes to himself again he won't know but what he has fallen asleep; barring a headache, the little beggar won't be any the worse for the adventure."

"Have we got all the stuff up now?" the other man asked.

"Every bit of it," was the whispered reply. "I hope the old man is satisfied now. It was not a bad idea of his to work this little game in a great hotel of this kind. But, all the same, it is not without risks, and I for one should be glad to get away to that place in the country where we are going in a week or two."

Gurdon heard no more. He allowed the best part of half-an-hour to pass before he ventured once more to creep through the ventilator and reach the landing in the neighborhood of the lift. Everything looked quite normal now, and as if nothing had happened. The lift boy sat in his little hut, yawning and stretching himself. It was quite evident that he knew nothing of the vile uses he had been put to. A sudden idea occurred to Gurdon.

"I want you to bring the lift up to this floor," he said to the boy. "No, I don't want to use it; I have lost something, and it occurs to me that I might have left it in the lift."

In the usual unconcerned manner of his class the boy touched an electric button, and the lift slowly rose from the basement.

"Does this go right down to the cellars?" Gurdon asked.

"It can if it's wanted to," the boy replied. "Only it very seldom does. You see, we only use this lift for our customers. It's fitted with what they call a pneumatic cushion—I mean, if anything goes wrong, the lift falls into a funnel shaped well, made of concrete, which forms a cushion of air, and so breaks the fall. They say you could cut the rope and let it down without so much as upsetting a glass of water. Not that I should like to try it, sir, but there you are."

Gurdon entered the lift, where he pretended to be searching for something for a moment or two. In reality, he was scraping up some of the yellow sand which had fallen from the box to the floor of the lift, and this he proceeded to place in a scrap of paper. Then he decided that it was absolutely necessary to retire to bed, though he was still in full possession of his waking faculties. As a matter of fact, he was asleep almost as soon as his head touched the pillow. Nevertheless, he was up early the following morning, and in Venner's bedroom long before breakfast. He had an exciting story to tell, and he could not complain that in Venner he had anything but an interested listener.

"We are getting on," the latter said grimly. "But before you say anything more, I should like to have a look at that yellow sand you speak of. Bring it over near the light."

Venner let the yellow stuff trickle through his hands; then he turned to Gurdon with a smile.

"You look upon this as refuse, I suppose?" he said. "You seem to imagine that it is of no great value."

"Well, is it?" Gurdon asked. "What is it?"

"Gold," Venner said curtly. "Pure virgin gold, of the very finest quality. I never saw a better sample."

CHAPTER V

A Puzzle for Venner

Venner sat just for a moment or two with the thin stream trickling through his fingers, and wondering what it all meant. With his superior knowledge of past events, he could see in this something that it was impossible for Gurdon to follow.

"I suppose this is some of the gold from the Four Finger Mine?" Gurdon suggested. "Do you know, I have never handled any virgin gold before. I had an idea that it was more brilliant and glittering. Is this very good stuff?"

"Absolutely pure, I should say," Venner replied. "There are two ways of gold mining. One is by crushing quartz in machinery, as they do in South Africa, and the other is by obtaining the metal in what are called pockets or placers. This is the way in which it is generally found in Australia and Mexico. I should not be in the least surprised if this came from the Four Finger Mine."

"There is no reason why it shouldn't," Gurdon said. "It is pretty evident, from what you told me last night, that Mark Fenwick has discovered the mysterious treasure house, but that does not account for all these proceedings. Why should he have taken all the trouble he did last night, when he might just as well have brought the stuff in, and taken the other boxes out by the front door?"

"That is what we have to find out," Venner said. "That fellow may call himself a millionaire, but I believe he is nothing more nor less than a desperate adventurer."

Gurdon nodded his assent. There must have been something very urgent to compel Mark Fenwick to adopt such methods. Why was he so strangely anxious to conceal the knowledge that he was receiving boxes of pure gold in the hotel, and that he was sending out something of equal value? However carefully the thing might have been planned the drugging of lift attendants must have been attended with considerable risk. And the slightest accident would have brought about a revelation. As it was, everything seemed to have passed off smoothly, except for the chance by which Gurdon had stumbled on the mystery.

"We can't leave the thing here," the latter said. "For once in my life I am going to turn amateur detective. I have made up my mind to get into Fenwick's suite of rooms and see what is going on there. Of course, the thing will take time, and will have to be carefully planned. Do you think it is possible for us to make use of your wife in this matter?"

"I don't think so," Venner said thoughtfully.

[54]

A PUZZLE FOR VENNER

"In the first place, I don't much like the idea; and in the second, I am entirely at a loss to know what mysterious hold Mark Fenwick has on Vera. As I told you last night, she left me within a very short time of our marriage, and until a few hours ago I had never looked upon her again. Something terrible must have happened, or she would never have deserted me in the way she did. I don't for a moment believe that Mark Fenwick knew anything about our marriage, but on that point I cannot be absolutely certain. You had better come back to me later in the day, and I will see what I can do. It is just possible that good fortune may be on my side."

The afternoon was dragging on, and still Venner was no nearer to a practical scheme which would enable him to make an examination of Fenwick's rooms without the chance of discovery. He was lounging in the hall, smoking innumerable cigarettes, when Fenwick himself came down the stairs. Obviously the man was going on a journey, for he was closely muffled up in a big fur coat, and behind him came a servant, carrying two bags and a railway rug. It was a little gloomy in the lobby, so Venner was enabled to watch what was going on without being seen himself. He did not fail to note a certain strained anxiety that rested on Fenwick's face. The man looked behind him once or twice, as if half afraid of being followed. Venner had seen

[55]

that same furtive air in men who are wanted by the police. Fenwick stopped at the office and handed a couple of keys to the clerk. His instructions were quite audible to Venner.

"I sha'n't want those for a day or two," he said. "You will see that no one has them under any pretext. Probably, I shall be back by Saturday at the latest."

Venner did not scruple to follow Fenwick's disappearing figure as far as the street. He was anxious to obtain a clue to Fenwick's destination. Straining his ears, he just managed to catch the words "Charing Cross," and then returned to the hall, by no means dissatisfied. Obviously, Fenwick was intending to cross the Channel for a day or two, and he had said to the clerk that he would not be back before Saturday.

Here was something like a chance at last. Very slowly and thoughtfully, Venner went up the stairs in the direction of his own room. He had ascertained by this time that one part of Fenwick's suite was immediately over his own bedroom. His idea now was to walk up to the next floor, and make a close examination of the rooms there. It did not take him long to discover the fact that Fenwick's suite was self contained, like a flat. That is to say, a strong outer door once locked made communication with the suite of rooms impossible. Venner was still pondering over his problem when the master door opened, and Vera came out so hurriedly as almost to fall into Venner's arms. She turned pale as she saw him; and as she closed the big door hurriedly behind her, Venner could see that she had in her hand the tiny Yale key which gave entrance to the suite of rooms. The girl looked distressed and embarrassed, but not much more so than Venner, who was feeling not a little guilty

But all this was lost upon Vera; her own agitation and her own unhappiness seemed to have blinded her to everything else.

"What are you doing here?" she stammered.

"Perhaps I am looking for you," Venner said. He had quite recovered himself by this time. "I was in the lobby just now, when I saw that scoundrel, Fenwick, go out. He is not coming back for a day or two, I understand."

"No," Vera said with accents of evident relief. "He is gone, but I don't know where he is gone. He never tells me."

Just for a moment Venner looked somewhat sternly at his companion. Here was an opportunity for an explanation too good to be lost.

"There is a little alcove at the end of the corridor," he said. "I see it is full of ferns and flowers. In fact, the very place for a confidence. Vera, whether you like it or not, I am going to have an explanation"

The girl shrank back, and every vestige of color

faded from her face. Yet at the same time, the pleading, imploring eyes which she turned upon her companion's face were filled with the deepest affection. Badly as he had been treated, Venner could not doubt for a moment the sincerity of the woman who had become his wife. But he did not fail to realise that few men would have put up with conduct like this, however much in love they might have been. Therefore, the hand that he laid on Vera's arm was strong and firm, and she made no resistance as he led her in the direction of the little alcove.

"Now," he said. "Are you going to tell me why you left me so mysteriously on our wedding day? You merely went to change your dress, and you never returned. Am I to understand that at the very last moment you learned something that made it absolutely necessary for us to part? Do you really mean that?"

"Indeed, I do, Gerald," the girl said. "There was a letter waiting for me in my bedroom. It was a short letter, but long enough to wreck my happiness for all time."

"No, no," Venner cried; "not for all time. You asked me to trust you absolutely and implicitly, and I have done so. I believe every word that you say, and I am prepared to wait patiently enough till the good time comes. But I am not going to sit down quietly like this and see a pure life like yours wrecked

[58]

for the sake of such a scoundrel as Fenwick. Surely it is not for his sake that you——"

"Oh, no," the girl cried. "My sacrifice is not for his sake at all, but for that of another whose life is bound up with his in the strangest possible way. When you first met me, Gerald, and asked me to be your wife, you did not display the faintest curiosity as to my past history. Why was that?"

"Why should I?" Venner demanded. "I am my own master, I have more money than I know what to do with and I have practically no relations to consider. You were all-sufficient for me; I loved you for your own sake alone; I cared nothing, and I care nothing still for your past. What I want to know is, how long this is going on?"

"That I cannot tell you," Vera said sadly. "You must go on trusting me, dear. You must——"

The speaker broke off suddenly, as someone in the corridor called her name. She slipped away from Venner's side, and, looking through the palms and flowers, he could see that she was talking eagerly to a woman who had the appearance of a lady's maid. Venner could not fail to note the calm strength of the woman's face. It was only for a moment; then Vera came back with a telegram in her hand.

"I must go at once," she said "It is something of great importance. I don't know when I shall see you again——"

"I do," Venner said grimly. "You are going to dine with me to-night. Come just for once; let us imagine we are on our honeymoon. That blackguard Fenwick is away, and he will be none the wiser. Now, I want you to promise me."

"I really can't," Vera protested. "If you only knew the danger——"

However, Venner's persistency got its own way. A moment later Vera was hurrying down the corridor. It was not until she was out of sight that Venner found that she had gone away, leaving the little Yale key behind her on the table. He thrilled at the sight of it. Here was the opportunity for which he had been waiting.

Not more than ten minutes had elapsed when, thanks to the use of the telephone, Gurdon had reached the Grand Empire Hotel. In a few hurried words, Venner gave him a brief outline of what had happened. There was no time to lose.

"Of course, it is a risk," Venner said, "and I am not altogether sure that I am justified in taking advantage of this little slip on the part of my wife. What do you think?"

"I think you are talking a lot of rot," Gurdon said emphatically. "You love the girl, you believe implicitly in her, and you are desperately anxious to get her out of the hands of that blackguard, Fenwick. From some morbid idea of self sacrifice, your wife continues to lead this life of misery rather

[60]

than betray what she would probably call a trust. It seems to me that you would be more than foolish to hesitate longer."

"Come along, then," Venner said. "Let's see what we can do."

The key was in the lock at length, and the big door thrown open, disclosing a luxurious suite of rooms beyond. So far as the explorers could see at present, they had the place entirely to themselves. No doubt Fenwick's servants had taken advantage of his absence to make a holiday. For the most part, the rooms presented nothing out of the common; they might have been inhabited by anybody possessing large means. In one of the rooms stood a desk, carefully locked, and by its side a fireproof safe.

"No chance of getting into either of those," Gurdon said. "Besides, the attempt would be too risky Don't you notice a peculiar noise going on? Sounds almost like machinery."

Surely enough, from a distant apartment there came a peculiar click and rumble, followed by a whirr of wheels, as if someone was running out a small motor close by. At the same time, the two friends noticed the unmistakable odor of petrol on the atmosphere

"What the dickens can that be?" Gurdon said. "Its most assuredly in the flat, and not far off, either"

"The only way to find out is to go and see," Venner replied "I fancy this is the way."

THE MYSTERY OF THE FOUR FINGERS

They came at length to a small room at the end of a long corridor. It was evidently from this room that the sound of machinery came, for the nearer they came the louder it grew. The door was slightly ajar, and looking in, the friends could see two men, evidently engaged on some mechanical task. There was a fire of charcoal in the grate, and attached to it a pair of small but powerful bellows, driven by a small motor. In the heart of the fire was a metal crucible, so white and dazzling hot that it was almost impossible for the eye to look upon it. Venner did not fail to notice that the men engaged in this mysterious occupation were masked; at least, they wore exceedingly large smoked spectacles, which came to much the same thing. Behind them stood another man, who had every appearance of being a master workman. He had a short pipe in his mouth, a pair of slippers on his feet, and his somewhat expansive body was swathed in a frock coat. Presently he made a sign, and with the aid of a long pair of tongs, the white hot crucible was lifted from the fire. It was impossible for the two men outside to see what became of it, but evidently the foreman was satisfied with the experiment, for he gave a grunt of approval.

"I think that will do," he muttered. "The impression is excellent. Now, you fellows can take a rest whilst I go off and finish the other lot of stuff."

"He's coming out," Venner whispered. "Let

us make a bolt for it. It won't do to be caught here."

They darted down the corridor together, and stood in an angle of a doorway, a little undecided as to what to do next. The man in the frock coat passed them, carrying under one arm a square case, that bore some resemblance to the slide in which photographers slip their negatives after taking a photograph The man in the frock coat placed his burden on a chair, and then, apparently, hurried back for something he had forgotten.

"Here is our chance," Gurdon whispered. "Let's see what is in that case. There may be an important clue here."

The thing was done rapidly and neatly. Inside the case, between layers of cotton wool, lay a great number of gold coins, obviously sovereigns. They appeared to be in a fine state of preservation, for they glistened in the light like new gold.

"Put one in your pocket," whispered Venner.

"I'm afraid we are going to have our journey for our pains; but still, you can't tell. Better take two while you are about it."

Gurdon slipped the coins into his pocket, then turned away in the direction of the door as the man in the frock coat came back, thoughtfully whistling, as if to give the intruders a chance of escape. Before he appeared in sight the outer door closed softly, and Venner and Gurdon were in the corridor once more.

CHAPTER VI

A PARTIAL FAILURE

"Do you notice anything peculiar about these coins?" Venner said, when once more they were back in the comparative seclusion of the smoking-room. "Have a good look at them."

Gurdon complied; he turned the coins over in his hand and weighed them on his fingers. So far as he could see they were good, honest, British coins, each well worth the twenty shillings which they were supposed to represent.

"I don't see anything peculiar about them at all," he said. "So far as I can judge, they appear to be genuine enough. At first I began to think that our friend Fenwick had turned coiner. Look at this."

As he spoke Gurdon dashed the coin down upon a marble table. It rang true and clear.

"I'd give a pound for it," he said. "The weight in itself is a good test. No coiner yet has ever discovered a metal that will weigh like gold and ring as true. The only strange thing about the coin is that it is in such a wonderful state of preservation. It might have come out of the Mint yesterday. I am afraid we shall have to abandon the idea of laying Fenwick by the heels on the charge of making counterfeit money. I'll swear this is genuine."

"I am of the same opinion, too," Venner said. "I have handled too much gold in my time to be easily deceived. Still, there is something wrong here, and I'll tell you why. Look at those two coins again, and tell me the dates on them."

"That is very easily done. One is dated 1901 and the other is dated 1899. I don't see that you gain anything by pointing out that fact to me. I don't see what you are driving at."

"Well the thing is pretty clear. It would be less clear if those coins had been worn by use and circulation. But they are both of them Mint perfect, and they are of different dates. Do you suppose that our friend Fenwick makes a hobby of collecting English sovereigns? Besides, the man in the frock coat was going to do something with these coins; and, of course, you noticed how carefully they were wrapped up in cotton wool."

"I should like to make assurance doubly sure," Gurdon said. "Let's take these two coins to some silversmith's shop and ask if they are all right."

It was no far journey to the nearest silversmiths, where the coins were cut up, tested, and weighed. The assistant smiled as he handed the pieces back to Venner.

"We will give you eighteen and sixpence each for them, sir," he said, "which is about the intrinsic value of a sovereign; and, as you are probably aware, sir, English gold coinage contains a certain amount of alloy, without which it would speedily deteriorate in circulation, just as the old guinea used to; but there is no doubt that I have just lost you three shillings by cutting up those coins."

Venner smiled as he left the shop. As a matter of fact, he was a little more puzzled now than he had been before. He had expected to find something wrong with the two coins.

"We must suspend judgment for the present," he said. "Still, I feel absolutely certain that there is some trick here, though what the scheme is I am utterly at a loss to know. Will you come in this evening after dinner and take your coffee and cigar with me? My wife is dining with me, but it was an express stipulation that she should go directly dinner is over."

At a little after seven Venner was impatiently waiting the coming of Vera. He was not altogether sorry to notice that the dining-room was filling up more rapidly than it had done for some days past. Perhaps, on the whole, there would be safety in numbers. Venner had secured a little table for two on the far side of the room, and he stood in the doorway now, waiting somewhat restlessly and impatiently for Vera to appear. He was not a little anxious and nervous in case something should happen at the last moment to prevent his wife's appearance. As a rule, Venner was not a man who was troubled much with nerves, though he became conscious of the fact that he possessed them to-night.

Was ever a man so strangely placed as himself, he wondered? He marvelled, too, that he could sit down so patiently without asserting his rights. He was the possessor of ample means, and if money stood in the way he was quite prepared to pay Fenwick his price.

On these somewhat painful meditations Vera intruded. She was simply dressed in white, and had no ornaments beyond a few flowers. Her face was flushed now, and there was in her eyes a look of something that approached happiness.

"I am so glad you have come, dear," Venner said, as he pressed the girl's hand. "I was terribly afraid that something might come in the way. If there is any danger——"

"I don't think there is any danger," Vera whispered, "though there are other eyes on me besides those of Mark Fenwick. But, all the same, I am not supposed to know anybody in the hotel, and I come down to dinner as a matter of course. I am glad the place is so crowded, Gerald, it will make us less conspicuous. But it is just possible that I may have to go before dinner is over. If that is so, I hope you will not be annoyed with me."

"You have given me cause for greater annoyance than that," Venner smiled. "And I have borne it all uncomplainingly. And now let us forget the unhappy past, and try and live for the present. We are on our honeymoon, you understand. I wonder what people in this room would say if they heard our amazing story."

"I have no doubt there are other stories just as sad here," Vera said, as she took her place at the table. "But I am not going to allow myself to be miserable to-night. We are going to forget everything; we are going to believe that this is Fairyland, and that you are the Prince who——"

Despite her assumed gaiety there was just a little catch in Vera's voice. If Venner noticed it he did not appear to do so. For the next hour or so he meant resolutely to put the past out of his mind, and give himself over to the ecstasy of the moment. . . . All too soon the dinner came to an end, and Gurdon appeared.

"This is my wife," Venner said simply. "Dear, Mr. Gurdon is a very old friend of mine, and I have practically no secrets from him. All the same, he did not know till last night that I was married—until you came into the room and my feelings got the better of me. But we can trust Gurdon."

"I think I am to be relied upon," Gurdon said with a smile. "You will pardon me if I say that I never heard a stranger story than yours; and if at any time I can be of assistance to you, I shall be sincerely happy to do all that is in my power."

A PARTIAL FAILURE

"You are very good," Vera said gratefully. "Who knows how soon I may call upon you to fulfil your promise? But I am afraid that it will not be quite yet."

They sat chatting there for some half an hour longer, when a waiter came in, and advancing to their table proffered Vera a visiting card, on the back of which a few words had been scribbled. The girl looked a little anxious and distressed as her eyes ran over the writing on the card. Then she rose hurriedly.

"I am afraid I shall have to go," she said. "I have been anticipating this for some little time."

She turned to the waiter, and asked if her maid was outside, to which the man responded that it was the maid who had brought the card, and that she was waiting with her wraps in the corridor. Vera extended her hand to Gurdon as she rose to go.

"I am exceedingly sorry," she said. "This has been a pleasant evening for me: perhaps the most pleasant evening with one exception that I ever spent in my life. Gerald will know what evening I mean."

As she finished she smiled tenderly at Venner. He had no words in reply. Just at that moment he was filled with passionate and rebellious anger. He dared not trust himself to speak, conscious as he was that Vera's burden was already almost more than she could bear. She held out her hand to him with an imploring little gesture, as if she understood exactly what was passing in his mind

"You will forgive me," she whispered. "I am sure you will forgive me. It is nothing but duty which compels me to go. I would far rather stay here and be happy."

Venner took the extended hand and pressed it tenderly. His yearning eyes looked after the retreating figure; then, suddenly, he turned to Gurdon, who affected to be busy over a cigar.

"I want you to do something for me," he said. "It is a strange fancy, but I should like you to follow her. I suppose I am beginning to get old and nervous, at any rate, I am full of silly fancies tonight. I am possessed with the idea that my unhappy little girl is thrusting herself into some danger. You can quite see how impossible it is for me to dog her footsteps, but your case is different. Of course, if you like to refuse——"

"I am not going to refuse," Gurdon said. "I can see nothing dishonorable. I'll go at once, if you like."

Venner nodded curtly, and Gurdon rose from the table. He passed out into the street just as the slim figure of Vera was descending the steps of the hotel. He had no difficulty in recognising her outline, though she was clad from head to foot now in a long, black wrap, and her fair hair was disguised under a hood of the same material. Rather to

A PARTIAL FAILURE

Gurdon's surprise, the girl had not called a cab. She was walking down the street with a firm, determined step, as of one who knew exactly where she was going, and meant to get there in as short a time as possible.

Gurdon followed cautiously at a distance. He was not altogether satisfied in his own mind that his action was quite as straightforward as it might have been. Still, he had given his promise, and he was not inclined to back out of it now. For about a quarter of an hour he followed, until Vera at length halted before a house somewhere in the neighborhood of Grosvenor Square. It was a fine, large corner mansion, but so far as Gurdon could see there was not a light in the place from parapet to basement. He could see Vera going up the steps; he was close enough to hear the sound of an electric bell; then a light blazed in the hall, and the door was opened. So far as Gurdon could see, it was an old man who opened the door; an old man with a long, grey beard, and a face lined and scored with the ravages of time. All this happened in an instant. The door was closed again, and the whole house left in darkness.

Gurdon paused, a little uncertain as to what to do next. He would have liked, if possible, to be a little closer to Vera, for if there were any dangers threatening her he would be just as powerless to help now as if he had been in another part of the town. He walked slowly down the side of the house, and noted that there was a fine garden behind, and a small green door leading to the lane. Acting on the impulse of the moment he tried the door, which yielded to his touch. If he had been asked why he did this thing he would have found it exceedingly difficult to reply. Still, the thing was done, and Gurdon walked forward over the wide expanse of lawn till he could make out at length a row of windows, looking out from the back of the house. It was not so very easy to discern all this, for the night was dark, and the back of the house darker still. Presently a light flared out in one of the rooms, and then Gurdon could make out the dome of a large conservatory leading from the garden to the house.

"I shall find myself in the hands of the police, if I don't take care," Gurdon said to himself. "What an ass I am to embark on an adventure like this. It isn't as if I had the slightest chance of being of any use to the girl, seeing that I——"

He broke off, suddenly conscious of the fact that another of the rooms was lighted now—a large one, by the side of the conservatory. In the silence of the garden it seemed to him that he could hear voices raised angrily, and then a cry, as if of pain, from somebody inside.

Fairly interested at last, Gurdon advanced till he was close to the window. He could hear no more now, for the same tense silence had fallen over the place once more. Gurdon pressed close to the window; he felt something yield beneath his feet, and the next moment he had plunged headlong into the darkness of something that suggested an underground cellar. Perhaps he had been standing unconsciously on a grating that was none too safe, for now he felt himself bruised and half stunned, lying on his back on a cold, hard floor, amid a mass of broken glass and rusty ironwork.

Startled and surprised as he was, the noise of the breaking glass sounded in Gurdon's ears like the din of some earthquake. He struggled to his feet, hoping that the gods would be kind to him, and that he could get away before his presence there was discovered. He was still dazed and confused; his head ached painfully, and he groped in the pitch darkness without any prospect of escape. He could nowhere find an avenue. So far as he could judge, he was absolutely caught like a rat in a trap.

He half smiled to himself; he was still too dazed to grasp the significance of his position, when a light suddenly appeared overhead, at the top of a flight of stairs, and a hoarse voice demanded to know who was there. In the same dreamy kind of way, Gurdon was just conscious of the fact that a strong pair of arms lifted him from the floor, and that he was being carried up the steps. In the same dreamy fashion, he was cognisant of light and warmth, a luxurious atmosphere, and rows upon rows of beautiful flowers everywhere. He would, no doubt, awake presently, and find that the whole thing was a dream. Meanwhile, there was nothing visionary about the glass of brandy which somebody had put to his lips, or about the hands which were brushing him down and removing all traces of his recent adventure.

"When you feel quite up to it, sir," a quiet, respectful voice said, "my master would like to see you. He is naturally curious enough to know what you were doing in the garden."

"I am afraid your master must have his own way," Gurdon said grimly. "I am feeling pretty well now, thanks to the brandy. If you will take me to your master, I will try to explain matters."

The servant led the way into a large, handsome apartment, where a man in evening dress was seated in a big armchair before the fire. He looked round with a peculiar smile as Gurdon came in.

"Well, sir," he said. "And what does this mean?"

Gurdon had no voice to reply, for the man in the armchair was the handsome cripple—the hero of the forefinger.

CHAPTER VII

THE WHITE LADY

GURDON looked hopelessly about him, utterly at a loss for anything to say. The whole thing had been so unexpected, so very opposite to the commonplace ending he had anticipated, that he was too dazed and confused to do anything but smile in an inane and foolish manner. He had rather looked forward to seeing some eccentric individual, some elderly recluse who lived there with a servant or two. And here he was, face to face with the man who, at the present moment, was to him the most interesting in London.

"You can take your time," the cripple said. "I am anxious for you to believe that I am not in the least hurry. The point of the problem is this: a well dressed man, evidently a gentleman, is discovered at a late hour in the evening in my cellar. As the gentleman in question is obviously sober, one naturally feels a little curiosity as to what it all means."

The speaker spoke quite slowly and clearly, and with a sarcastic emphasis that caused Gurdon to writhe impotently. Every word and gesture on the part of the cripple spoke of a strong mind and a

[75]

clear intellect in that twisted body. Despite the
playful acidity of his words, there was a distinct
threat underlying them. It occurred to Gurdon as
he stood there that he would much rather have this
man for a friend than a foe.

"Perhaps you had better take a seat," the cripple
said. "There is plenty of time, and I don't mind
confessing to you that this little comedy amuses me.
Heaven knows, I have little enough amusement in
my dreary life; and, therefore, in a measure, you
have earned my gratitude. But there is another
side to the picture. I have enemies who are utterly
unscrupulous. I have to be unscrupulous in my
turn, so that when I have the opportunity of laying
one of them by the heels, my methods are apt to be
thorough. Did you come here alone to-night, or
have you an accomplice?"

"Assuredly, I came alone," Gurdon replied.

"Oh, indeed. You found your way into the
garden. To argue out the thing logically, we will
take it for granted that you had no intention whatever of paying a visit to my garden when you left
home. If such had been your intention, you would
not be wearing evening dress, and thin, patent
leather shoes. Your visit to the garden was either
a resolution taken on the spur of the moment, or
was determined upon after a certain discovery. I
am glad to hear that you came here entirely by
yourself."

THE WHITE LADY

There was an unmistakable threat in these latter words; and as Gurdon looked up he saw that the cripple was regarding him with an intense malignity. The grey eyes were cold and merciless, the handsome face hard and set, and yet it was not a countenance which one usually associates with the madman or the criminal. Really, it was a very noble face—the face of a philanthropist, a poet, a great statesman, who devotes his money and his talents to the interests of his country. Despite a feeling of danger, Gurdon could not help making a mental note of these things.

"Won't you sit down?" the cripple asked again. "I should like to have a little chat with you. Here are whisky and soda, and some cigars, for the excellence of which I can vouch, as I import them myself. Perhaps, also, you share with me a love of flowers?"

With a wave of his strong arm, the speaker indicated the wealth of blossoms which arose from all sides of the room. There were flowers everywhere. The luxuriant blooms seemed to overpower and dwarf the handsome furnishings of the room. At the far end, folding doors opened into the conservatory, which was a veritable mass of brilliant colors. The cripple smiled upon his blossoms, as a mother might smile on her child.

"These are the only friends who never deceive you," he said. "Flowers and dogs, and, perhaps,

[77]

little children. I know this, because I have suffered from contact with the world, as, perhaps, you
will notice when you regard this poor body of mine.
I think you said just now you came here entirely
by yourself."

"That is a fact," Gurdon replied. He was beginning to feel a little more at his ease now. " Let
me hasten to assure you that I came here with no
felonious intent at all. I was looking for somebody,
and I thought that my friend came here. You will
pardon me if I do not explain with any amount of
detail, because the thing does not concern myself
altogether. And, besides——"

Gurdon paused; he could not possibly tell this
stranger of the startling events which had led to his
present awkward situation. In any case, he would
not have been believed.

"We need not go into that," the cripple said.
"It is all by the way. You came here alone; and,
I take it, when you left your home, you had not the
slightest intention of coming here. To make my
meaning a little more clear, if you disappeared
from this moment, and your friends never saw you
again, the police would not have the slightest clue
to your whereabouts."

Gurdon laughed just a little uneasily, he began
to entertain the idea that he was face to face with
some dangerous lunatic, some man whose dreadful
troubles and misfortunes had turned him against

the world. Evidently, it would be the right policy
to humor him.

"That is quite correct," he said. "Nobody has
the least idea where I am; and if the unpleasant
contingency you allude to happened to me, I should
go down to posterity as one of the victims of the
mysterious type of crime that startles London now
and again."

"I should think," said the stranger, in a thin, dry
tone, that caused Gurdon's pulses to beat a little
faster—"I should think that your prophecy is in a
fair way to turn out correct. I don't ask you why
you came here, because you would not tell me if I
did. But you must have been spying on the place,
or you would not have had the misfortune to tread
on a damaged grating, and finish your adventure
ignominiously in the cellar. As I told you just
now, I have enemies who are absolutely unscrupulous, and who would give much for a chance of
murdering me if the thing could be done with im-
punity. Common sense prompts me to take it for
granted that you are in some way connected with
the foes to whom I have alluded."

"I assure you, I am not," Gurdon protested." I am
the enemy of no man. I came here to night—— "

Gurdon stopped in some confusion. How could
he possibly tell this man why he had come and
what he had in his mind? The thing was awkward—almost to the verge of absurdity.

"I quite see the quandary you are in," said the cripple, with a smile. "Now, let me ask you a question. Do you happen to know a man by the name of Mark Fenwick?"

The query was so straight and to the point that Gurdon fairly started. More and more did he begin to appreciate the subtlety and cleverness of his companion. It was impossible to fence the interrogation; it had to be answered, one way or the other.

"I know the man by sight," he said; "but I beg to assure you that until last night I had never seen him."

"That may be," the cripple said drily. "But you know him now, and that satisfies me. Now, listen. You see what I have in my hand. Perhaps you are acquainted with weapons of this kind?"

So saying, the speaker wriggled in his chair, and produced from somewhere behind him a small revolver. Despite its silver plated barrel and ivory handle, it was a sinister looking weapon, and capable of deadly mischief in the hands of an expert. Though no judge of such matters, it occurred to Gurdon that his companion handled the revolver as an expert should.

"I have been used to this kind of thing from a boy," the cripple said. "I could shoot you where you sit within a hair's breadth of where I wanted to hit you."

"Which would be murder," Gurdon said quietly.

"Perhaps it would, in the eyes of the law; but there are times when one is tempted to defy the mandates of a wise legislature. For instance, I have told you more than once before that I have enemies, and everything points to the fact that you are the tool and accomplice of some of them. I have about me one or two faithful people, who would do anything I ask. If I shoot you now the report of a weapon like this will hardly be audible beyond the door. You lie there, dead, shot clean through the brain. I ring my bell and tell my servants to clear this mess away. I give them orders to go and bury it quietly somewhere, and they would obey me without the slightest hesitation Nothing more would be said. I should be as safe from molestation as if the whole thing had happened on a desert island. I hope I have succeeded in making the position clear, because I should be loth to think that a little incident like this should cause inconvenience to one who might after all have been absolutely innocent."

The words were spoken quietly, and without the slightest trace of passion. Still, there was no mistaking the malignity and intense fury which underlay the well chosen and well balanced sentences.

Gurdon was silent; there was nothing for him to say. He was in a position in which he could not possibly explain; he could only sit there, looking into the barrel of the deadly weapon, and praying

6 [81]

for some diversion which might be the means of saving his life. It came presently in a strange and totally unexpected fashion. Upon the tense, nerve-breaking silence, a voice suddenly intruded like a flash of light in a dark place. It was a sweet and girlish voice, singing some simple ballad, with a natural pathos which rendered the song singularly touching and attractive. As the voice came nearer the cripple's expression changed entirely; his hard eyes grew soft, and the handsome features were wreathed in a smile. Then the door opened, and the singer came in.

Gurdon looked at her, though she seemed unconscious of his presence altogether. He saw a slight, fair girl, dressed entirely in white, with her long hair streaming over her shoulders. The face was very sad and wistful, the blue eyes clouded with some suggestion of trouble and despair. Gurdon did not need a second glance to assure him that he was in the presence of one who was mentally afflicted. She came forward and took her place by the side of the cripple.

"They told me that you are busy," she said, "Just as if it mattered whether you were busy or not, when I wanted to see you."

"You must go away now, Beth," the cripple said, in his softest and most tender manner. "Don't you see that I am talking with this gentleman?"

The girl turned eagerly to Gurdon; she crossed

the room with a swift, elastic step, and laid her two hands on him.

"I know what you have come for," she said, eagerly. "You have come to tell me all about Charles. You have found him at last; you are going to bring him back to me. They told me he was dead, that he had perished in the mine; but I knew better than that. I know that Charles will come back to me again."

"What mine?" Gurdon asked.

"Why, the Four Finger Mine, of course," was the totally unexpected reply. "They said that Charles had lost his life in the Four Finger Mine. It was in a kind of dream that I saw his body lying there, murdered. But I shall wake from the dream presently, and he will come back to me, come back in the evening, as he always used to when the sun was setting beyond the pines."

There was something so utterly sad and hopeless in this that Gurdon averted his eyes from the girl's face. He glanced in the direction of the door; then it required all his self control to repress a cry, for in the comparative gloom of the passage beyond, he could just make out the figure of Vera, who stood there with her finger on her lip as if imposing silence. He could see that in her hand she held something that looked like a chisel. A moment later she flitted away once more, leaving Gurdon to puzzle his brain as to what it all meant.

[83]

"I am sorry for all this," the cripple said. "You have entirely by accident come face to face with a phase in my life which is sacred and inviolate. Really, if I had no other reason for reducing you to silence, this would be a sufficiently powerful inducement. My dear Beth, I really must ask you——"

Whatever the cripple might have intended to say, the speech was never finished; for, at that moment, the electric lights vanished suddenly, plunging the whole house into absolute darkness. A moment later, footsteps came hurrying along in the hall, and a voice was heard to say that the fuse from the meter had gone, and it would be impossible to turn on the light again until the officials had been called in to repair the damage. At the same moment, Gurdon rose to his feet and crept quietly in the direction of the door. Here, at any rate, was a chance of escape, for that his life was in dire peril he had felt for some little time. He had hardly reached the doorway when he felt a slim hand touch his, and he was guided from the room into the passage beyond. He could give a pretty fair idea as to the owner of the slim fingers that trembled in his own, but he made no remark; he allowed himself to be led on till his feet stumbled against the stairs.

"This way," a voice whispered. "Say nothing, and make no protest. You will be quite safe from further harm."

THE WHITE LADY

Gurdon did exactly as he was told. He found himself presently at the top of a staircase, and a little later on in a room, the door of which was closed very quietly by his guide.

"I think I can guess who I have to thank for this," Gurdon murmured. "But why did you not take me to the front door, or the back entrance leading to the garden? It was lucky for me that the lights failed at the critical moment—a piece of nominal good fortune, such as usually only happens in a story. But I should feel a great deal safer if I were on the other side of the front door."

"That is quite impossible," Vera said, for it was she who had come to Gurdon's rescue. "Both doors are locked, and all the rooms on the ground floor are furnished with shutters. As to the light going out, I am responsible for it. I learned all about the electric light when I lived in a mining camp in Mexico. I had only to remove one of the lamps and apply my chisel to the two poles, and thereby put out every fuse in the house. That is why the light failed, for it occurred to me that in the confusion that followed the darkness, I should be in a position to save you. But you little realise how near you have been to death to-night. And, why, oh, why did you follow me in this way? It was very wrong of you."

"It was Venner's idea," Gurdon said. "He had a strange fear that you were going into some danger.

[85]

He asked me to follow you, and I did so. As to the manner of my getting here——"

"I know all about that," Vera said hurriedly. "I have been listening to your conversation. I dare say you are curious to know something more about this strange household; but, for the present, you will be far better employed in getting away from it. I shall not be easy in my mind till you are once more in the street."

CHAPTER VIII

MISSING

GURDON waited to hear what his companion was going to say now. He had made up his mind to place himself implicitly in her hands, and let her decide for the best. Evidently, he had found himself in a kind of lunatic asylum, where one inhabitant at least had developed a dangerous form of homicidal mania, and he had a pretty sure conclusion that Vera had saved his life. It was no time now to ask questions; that would come later on.

"I am sure I am awfully grateful to you," Gurdon said. "Who are these people, and why do they behave in this insane fashion? This is not exactly the kind of ménage one expects to find in one of the best appointed mansions in the West End."

"I can tell you nothing about it," Vera said. There was a marked coldness in her voice that told Gurdon he was going too far. "I can tell you nothing. One thing you may rest assured of—I am in no kind of danger, nor am I likely to be. My concern chiefly at the present moment is with you. I want you to get back as soon as you can to the Great Empire Hotel, and ease Gerald's mind as to myself."

"I hardly like to go, without you," Gurdon murmured.

"But you must," Vera protested. "Let me assure you once more that I am as absolutely safe here as if I were in my own room. Now, come this way. I dare not strike a light. I can only take you by the hand and lead you to the top of the house. Every inch of the place is perfectly familiar to me, and you are not likely to come to the least harm. Please don't waste a moment more of your time."

Gurdon yielded against his better judgment. A moment or two later, he found himself climbing through a skylight on to the flat leads at the top of the house. By the light of the town he could now see what he was doing, and pretty well where he was. From the leads he could look down into the garden, though, as yet, he could not discern any avenue of escape.

"The thing is quite easy," Vera explained. "The late occupant of the house had a nervous dread of fire, and from every floor he had a series of rope ladders arranged. See, there is one fixed to this chimney. I have only to throw it over, and you can reach the garden without delay; then I will pull the ladder up again and no one will be any the wiser. Please, leave me without any further delay, in the absolute assurance that I shall be back again within an hour."

A few minutes later Gurdon was in the street

again, making his way back to the hotel where Venner was waiting for him.

It was a strange story that he had to tell; a very thrilling and interesting adventure, but one which, after all, still further complicated the mystery and rendered it almost unintelligible.

"And you mean to say that you have been actually face to face with our cripple friend?" Venner said. "You mean to say that he would actually have murdered you if Vera had not interfered in that providential manner? I suppose I must accept your assurance that she is absolutely safe, though I can't help feeling that she has exaggerated her own position. I am terribly anxious about her. I have an idea which I should like to carry out. I feel tolerably sure that this picturesque cripple of ours could tell us everything that we want to know. Besides, unless I do something I shall go mad What do you say to paying the interesting cripple a visit to-morrow night, and forcing him to tell us everything?"

Gurdon shook his head; he was not particularly impressed with the suggestion that Venner had made.

"Of course, we could get into the house easily enough," he said. "Now that I have learned the secret of the cellar, there will be no difficulty about that. Still, don't you think it seems rather ridiculous to try this sort of thing when your wife is in a position to tell you the whole thing?"

"But she would decline to do anything of the kind," Venner protested. "She has told me that her lips are sealed; she has even no explanation to offer for the way in which she left me within half-an-hour of our becoming man and wife. I should almost be justified in forcing her to speak; but, you see, I cannot do that. Therefore, I must treat her in a way as if she were one of our enemies. I have a very strong fancy for paying a visit to our cripple friend, and, if the worst came to the worst, we could convince him that we are emphatically not on the side of Mark Fenwick. At any rate, I mean to have a try, and if you don't like to come in——"

"Oh, I'll come in fast enough," Gurdon said. "You had better meet me to-morrow night at my rooms, say, about eleven; then, we will see what we can do with a view to a solution of the mystery."

At the appointed time, Venner duly put in an appearance. He was clothed in a dark suit and cap, Gurdon donning a similar costume. Under his arm Venner had a small brown paper parcel.

"What have you got there?" Gurdon asked.

"A pair of tennis shoes," was the response. "And if you take my advice, you should have a pair, too. My idea is to take off our boots directly we get into the seclusion of the garden and change into these shoes Now come along, let's get it over."

It was an easy matter to reach the garden without being observed, and in a very short time the two friends were standing close to the windows of the large room at the back of the house. There was not so much as a glimmer of light to be seen anywhere within. Very cautiously they felt their way along until they came at length to the grating through which Gurdon had made so dramatic an entrance on the night before. He took from his pocket a box of vestas, and ventured to strike one. He held it down close to the ground, shading the tiny point of flame in the hollow of his hand

"Here is a bit of luck to begin with," he chuckled. "They haven't fastened this grating up again. I suppose my escape last night must have upset them. At any rate, here is a way into the house without running the risk of being arrested on a charge of burglary, and if the police did catch us we should find it an exceedingly awkward matter to frame an excuse carefully, to satisfy a magistrate."

"That seems all right," Venner said. "When we get into the cellar it's any odds that we find the door of the stairs locked. I don't suppose the grating has been forgotten You see, it is not such an easy matter to get the British workman to do a job on the spur of the moment."

"Well, come along; we will soon ascertain that," Gurdon said "Once down these steps, we shall be able to use our matches."

They crept cautiously down the stairs into the damp and moldy cellar; thence, up the steps on the other side, where Gurdon lighted one of his matches. The door was closed, but it yielded quite easily to the touch, and at length the two men were in the part of the house which was given over to the use of the servants. So far as they could judge the place was absolutely deserted. Doubtless the domestic staff had retired to bed. All the same, it seemed strange to find no signs of life in the kitchen. The stove was cold, and though the grate was full of cinders, it was quite apparent that no fire had been lighted there for the past four and twenty hours. Again, there was no furniture in the kitchen other than a large table and a couple of chairs. The dressers were empty, and the shelves deprived of their usual burden.

"This is odd," Venner murmured. "Perhaps we shall have better luck on the dining-room floor. I suppose we had better not turn on the lights!"

"That would be too risky," Gurdon said. "However, I have plenty of matches, which will serve our purpose equally well."

On cautiously reaching the hall a further surprise awaited the intruders. There was absolutely nothing there—not so much as an umbrella stand. The marble floor was swept bare of everything, the big dining-room which the night before had been most luxuriously furnished, was now stripped and empty; not so much as a flower remained; and the conservatory beyond showed nothing but wooden staging and glittering glass behind that. A close examination of the whole house disclosed the fact that it was absolutely empty.

"If I did not know you as well as I do," Venner said grimly, "I should say that you had been drinking. Do you mean to tell me that you sat in this dining-room last night, and that it was furnished in the luxurious way you described? Do you mean to tell me that you sat here, opposite our cripple friend, waiting for him to shoot you? Are you perfectly certain that we have made our way into the right house? You have no doubt on that score?"

"Of course, I haven't," Gurdon said, a little hotly "Would there be two houses close together, both of them with a broken grating over the cellar? I tell you this is the same house right enough. It was just in this particular spot I was seated when the lights went out, and your wife's fertility of resource saved my life. It may be possible that the electric fuses have not yet been repaired. At any rate, I'll see."

Gurdon laid his hand upon the switch and snapped it down. No light came; the solitary illuminating point in the room was afforded by the match which Venner held in his hand.

"There," Gurdon said, with a sort of gloomy triumph "Doesn't that prove it? I suppose that our cripple took alarm and has cleared out of the house "

"That's all very well, but it is almost impossible

to remove the furniture of a great place like this in the course of a day."

"My dear chap, I don't think it has been removed in the course of a day. Didn't you notice just now what a tremendous lot of dust we stirred up as we were going over the house? My theory is this— only three or four of the rooms were furnished, and the rest of the house was closed. When I made my escape last night, the cripple must have taken alarm and gone away from here as speedily as possible. What renders the whole thing more inexplicable is the fact that your wife could explain everything if she pleased. But after a check-mate like this, I don't see the slightest reason for staying here any longer. The best thing we can do is to get back to my rooms and discuss the matter over a whiskey and soda and cigar. But, talking about cigars, will you have the goodness to look at this?"

From the empty grate Gurdon picked up a half smoked cigar of a somewhat peculiar make and shape.

"I want you to notice this little bit of evidence," he said. "This is the very cigar that the cripple gave me last night. I can't say that I altogether enjoyed smoking it, but it was my tip to humor him. I smoked that much. When the white lady came in I naturally threw the end of the cigar into the fireplace. In the face of this, I don't think you will accuse me of dreaming."

[94]

MISSING

More than one cigar was consumed before Venner left his friend's rooms, but even the inspiration of tobacco failed to elucidate a solitary point at issue. What had become of the cripple, and where had he vanished so mysteriously? Gurdon was still debating this point over a late breakfast the following morning, when Venner came in. His face was flushed and his manner was excited. He carried a copy of an early edition of an evening paper in his hand—the edition which is usually issued by most papers a little after noon.

"I think I've discovered something," he said. "It was quite by accident, but you will not fail to be interested in something that appears in the *Comet*. It alludes to the disappearance of a gentleman called Bates, who seems to have vanished from his house in Portsmouth Square. You know the name of the Square, of course?"

Gurdon pushed his coffee cup away from him, and lighted a cigarette. He felt that something of importance was coming.

"I suppose I ought to know the name of the square," he said grimly. "Seeing that I nearly lost my life in a house there the night before last. But please go on. I see you have something to tell me that is well worth hearing."

"That's right," Venner said. "Most of it is in this paper. It appears that the aforesaid Mr Bates is a gentleman of retiring disposition, and somewhat eccentric habits. As far as one can gather, he has no friends, but lives quietly in Portsmouth Square, his wants being ministered to by a body of servants who have been in his employ for years. Of necessity, Mr. Bates is a man of wealth, or he could not possibly live in a house the rent of which cannot be less than five or six hundred a year. As a rule, Mr. Bates rarely leaves his house, but last night he seems to have gone out unattended, and since then, he has not been seen."

"Stop a moment," Gurdon exclaimed eagerly. "I am beginning to see daylight at last. What was the number of the house where this Bates lived? I mean the number of the square."

Venner turned to his paper, and ran his eye down the printed column. Then he smiled as he spoke.

"The number of the house," he said, "is 75."

"I knew it," Gurdon said excitedly. "I felt pretty certain of it. The man who has disappeared lived at No. 75, and the place where we had our adventure, or rather, I had my adventure, is No. 74. Now, tell me, who was it who informed the police of the disappearance of Mr. Bates? Some servant, I suppose?"

"Of course; and the servant goes on to suggest that Mr. Bates had mysterious enemies, who caused him considerable trouble from time to time But now I come to the interesting part of my story. At the foot of the narrative which is contained in the

Comet, that I hold in my hand, is a full description of Mr. Bates."

"Go on," Gurdon said breathlessly. "I should be little less than an idiot if I did not know what was coming."

"I thought you would guess," Venner said. "A name like Bates implies middle age and respectability. But this Bates is described as being young and exceedingly good looking. Moreover, he is afflicted with a kind of paralysis, which renders his movements slow and uncertain And now you know all about it There is not the slightest doubt that this missing Bates is no other than our interesting friend, the good-looking cripple. The only point which leaves us in doubt is the fact that Mr. Bates is a respectable householder, living at 75, Portsmouth Square, while the man who tried to murder you entertained you at No. 74, which house, now, is absolutely empty. We need not discuss that puzzle at the present moment, because there are more important things to occupy our attention. There can be no doubt that this man who calls himself Bates has been kidnapped by somebody. You will not have much difficulty in guessing the name of the culprit."

"I guess it at once," Gurdon said. "If I mention the name of Mark Fenwick, I think I have said the last word."

CHAPTER IX

A New Phase

THERE was not the slightest doubt that Gurdon had hit the mark. As far as they could see at present, the man most likely to benefit by the death or disappearance of the cripple was Mark Fenwick. Still, it was impossible to dismiss the thing in this casual way, nor could it be forgotten that the cripple had actually been present at the Grand Empire Hotel on the night when the alleged millionaire received his message by means of the mummified finger. Therefore, logically speaking, it was only fair to infer that on the night in question Fenwick had not been acquainted with the personality of the cripple. Otherwise, the latter would have scarcely ventured to show himself in a place where his experiment had been brought to a conclusion.

On the other hand, it was just possible that Fenwick had been looking for the cripple for some time past. But all this was more or less in the air, though there was a great deal to be said for the conclusion at which the two friends had arrived.

"I work it out like this," Venner said, after a long, thoughtful pause. "You know all about the

A NEW PHASE

marked. "He appears to be a workingman who got himself into trouble over a drinking bout. Two days ago he was charged before the magistrate with being drunk and disorderly, and was sentenced to a fine of forty shillings or fourteen days' imprisonment. According to his story, the money was not forthcoming, therefore he was taken to gaol At the end of two days his friends contrived to obtain the necessary cash and he was released. He writes all this to show how it was that he was entirely ignorant of the startling events which had taken place in the Bates case. This man goes on to say that on the night when Mr Bates disappeared he was passing Portsmouth Square on his way home from some public-house festivities. He was none too sober, and has a hazy recollection of what he saw. He recollects quite clearly, now that he has time to think the matter over, seeing a cab standing at the corner of the Square within three doors of No. 75. At the same time, a telegraph boy called at No. 75 with a message. It was at this point that the narrator of the story stopped to light his pipe. It was rather a windy evening, so that he used several matches in the process. Anyway, he stood there long enough to see the telegraph boy deliver his message to a gentleman who appeared to have great difficulty in getting to the door. No sooner had the telegraph boy gone than the gentleman crept slowly and painfully down the steps and walked in the di-

[103]

rection of the cab. Then somebody stepped from the cab and accosted the cripple, who, beyond all question, was the mysterious Bates. The writer of the letter says that he heard a sort of cry, then someone called out something in a language that he was unable to understand. He rather thinks it was Portuguese, because among his fellow workmen is a Portuguese artisan, and the language sounded something like his."

"We are getting on," Gurdon said. "That little touch about the Portuguese language clearly points to Fenwick."

"Of course, it does," Venner went on. "But that is not quite all. The letter goes on to say that something like a struggle took place, after which the cripple was bundled into the cab, which was driven away. It was a four-wheeled cab, and the peculiarity about it was that it had indiarubber tires, which is a most unusual thing for the typical growler. The author of all this information says that the struggle appeared to be of no very desperate nature, for it was followed by nothing in the way of a call for help. Indeed, the workman who is telling all this seemed to think that it was more or less in the way of what he calls a spree. He said nothing whatever to the police about it, fearing perhaps that he himself was in no fit state to tell a story; and, besides, there was just the possibility that he might find himself figuring before a magistrate the next morning. That is the whole of the letter, Gurdon, which though it conveys very little to the authorities, is full of pregnant information for ourselves. At any rate, it tells us quite clearly that Fenwick was at the bottom of this outrage."

"Quite right," Gurdon said. "The little touch about the Portuguese language proves that. Is there anything else in the letter likely to be useful to us?"

"No, I have given you the whole of it. Personally, the best thing we can do is to go and interview the writer, who has given his name and address. A small, but judicious, outlay in the matter of beer will cause him to tell us all we want to know."

It was somewhere in the neighborhood of the Docks where the man who had given his name as James Taylor was discovered later on in the day. He was a fairly intelligent type of laborer, who obtained a more or less precarious livelihood as a docker. As a rule, he worked hard enough four or five hours a day when things were brisk, and, in slack periods when money was scarce, he spent the best part of his day in bed. He had one room in a large tenement house, where the friends found him partially dressed and reading a sporting paper. He was not disposed to be communicative at first, but the suggestion of something in the way of liquid refreshment stimulated his good-nature.

"Right you are," he said. "I've had nothing to-day besides a mouthful of breakfast, and when I've paid my rent I shall have a solitary tanner left; but I 'ope you gents are not down here with a view of getting a poor chap into trouble?"

Gurdon hastened to reassure him on that head. He was balancing a half-sovereign thoughtfully on his forefinger.

"We are not going to hurt you at all," he said. "We want you to give us a little information. In proof of what I say you can take this half-sovereign and obtain what liquid refreshment you require. Also, you can keep the change. If you don't like my proposal, there is an end of the matter."

"Don't be short, guv'nor," Taylor responded. "I like that there proposition of yours so well that I'm going to take it; 'alf-sovereigns ain't so plentiful as all that comes to. If you just wait a moment, I'll be back in 'alf a tick. Then I'll tell you all you want to know."

The man was back again presently, and professed himself ready to answer any questions that might be put to him. His manner grew just a little suspicious as Venner mentioned the name of Bates.

"You don't look like police," he said. "Speaking personally, I ain't fond of 'em, and I don't want to get into trouble."

"We have no connection whatever with the police," Venner said. "In fact, we would rather not have anything to do with them. It so happens that we are both interested in the gentleman that you saw getting into the cab the other night. I have read your letter in the paper, and I am quite prepared to believe every word of it. The only thing we want to know is whether you saw the man in the cab——"

"Which one?" Taylor asked. "There were two blokes in the cab."

"This is very interesting," Venner murmured. "I shall be greatly obliged to you if you will describe both of them."

"I couldn't describe the one, guv'nor," Taylor replied. "His back was to me all the time, and when you come to think of it, I wasn't quite so clear in the head as I might have been. But I caught a glimpse of the other man's face; as he looked out of the cab the light of the lamp shone on his face. He'd a big cloak on, as far as I could judge, with the collar turned up about his throat, and a soft hat on his head. He knocks the hat off looking out of the cab window, then I see as 'is head was bald like a bloomin' egg, and yellow, same as if he had been painted. I can't tell you any more than that, not if you was to give me another 'alf-sovereign on the top of the first one."

"Just another question," Gurdon said. "Then we won't bother you any more. About what age do you suppose the man was?"

Taylor paused thoughtfully for a moment before he replied.

"Well, I should think he was about fifty-five or sixty," he said. "Looked like some sort of a foreigner."

"That will do, thank you," Venner said. "We will not detain you any longer. At the same time I should be obliged if you would keep this information to yourself; but, of course, if the police question you, you will have to speak. But a discreet silence on the subject of this visit of ours would be esteemed."

Taylor winked and nodded, and the friends departed, not displeased to get away from the stuffy and vitiated atmosphere of Taylor's room On the whole, they were not dissatisfied with the result of their expedition. At any rate, they had now proof positive of the fact that Fenwick was at the bottom of the mysterious disappearance of the man called Bates.

"I don't quite see what we are going to do next," Venner said. "So far, we have been exceedingly fortunate to find ourselves in possession of a set of clues which would be exceedingly valuable to the police. But how are we going to use these clues is quite another matter. What do you suggest?"

"Keeping a close eye upon Fenwick at any rate. For that purpose it would not be a bad idea to employ a private inquiry agent. He need know nothing of what we are after."

Thereupon it was decided that Gurdon was to dine with Venner that night and go fully into the matter.

CHAPTER X

THE SECOND FINGER

IT was, perhaps, fortunate for all concerned that, though Venner was so closely identified by the irony of Fate with the movements of Mark Fenwick, he was not known to the latter personally, though they had been almost side by side three years previous in Mexico. Therefore, it was possible for Venner to get a table in the dining-room quite close to that of the alleged millionaire. It was all the more fortunate, as things subsequently turned out, that Fenwick had returned to town that afternoon and had announced his intention of dining at the hotel the same evening. This information Venner gave to Gurdon when the latter turned up about half-past seven. Then the host began to outline the plan of campaign which he had carefully thought out.

"Fenwick is dining over there," he said. "He generally sits with his back to the wall, and I have had our table so altered that we can command all his movements. Vera, of course, will dine with him. Naturally enough, she will act as if we were absolute strangers to her That will be necessary."

THE SECOND FINGER

"Of course," Gurdon admitted. "But isn't it a strange thing that you should be an absolute stranger to Fenwick?"

"Well, it does seem strange on the face of it. But it is capable of the easiest explanation You see, when I first met Vera, she was at school in a town somewhere removed from the Four Finger Mine I saw a good deal of her there, and when finally she went up country, we were practically engaged. At her urgent request the engagement was kept a secret, and when I followed to the Mines it was distinctly understood that I should not call at Fenwick's house or make myself known to him except in the way of business. As it happens, we never did meet, and whenever I saw Vera it was usually by stealth. The very marriage was a secret one, and you may charge me fairly with showing great weakness in the matter. But there, I have told you the story before, and you must make the best of it. On the whole, I am glad things turned out as they did, for now I can play my cards in the game against Fenwick without his even suspecting that he has me for an opponent. It is certainly an advantage in my favor."

Venner had scarcely ceased speaking before Fenwick and Vera appeared. She gave one timid glance at Venner; then, averting her eyes, she walked demurely across to her place at the table. Fenwick followed, looking downcast and moody, and altogether unlike a man who is supposed to be the happy possessor of millions. His manner was curt and irritable, and he seemed disposed to find fault with everything. Venner noticed, too, that though the man ate very little he partook of far more champagne than was good for anyone. Thanks no doubt to the wine, the man's dark mood lifted presently, and he began chatting to Vera. The two men at the other table appeared to be deeply interested in their dinner, though, as a matter of fact. they were listening intently to every word that Fenwick was saying. He was talking glibly enough now about some large house in the country which he appeared to have taken for the winter months. Vera listened with polite indifference.

"In Kent," Fenwick was saying. "Not very far from Canterbury. A fine old house, filled with grand furniture, just the sort of place you'd like. I've made all arrangements, and the sooner we get away from London the better I shall be pleased."

"It will be rather dull, I fear," Vera replied. "I don't suppose that I shall get on very well with county people——"

"Hang the county people," Fenwick growled. "Who cares a straw for them? Not but what they'll come along fast enough when they hear that Mark Fenwick, the millionaire, is in their midst. Still, there is a fine park round the house, and you'll be able to get as much riding as you want."

THE SECOND FINGER

Venner watching furtively saw that Vera was interested for the first time. He had not forgotten the fact that she was an exceedingly fine horsewoman; he recollected the glorious rides they had had together. Interested as he was in the mysterious set of circumstances which had wound themselves into his life, he was not without hope that this change would enable him to see more of Vera than was possible in London. In the lonely country he would be able to plan meetings with her; indeed, he had made up his mind to leave London as soon as Vera had gone. Moreover, in this instance, duty and inclination pointed the same way. If the mystery were to be solved and Vera freed from her intolerable burden, it would be essential that every movement of Fenwick's should be carefully watched. The only way to carry out this plan successfully would be to follow him into Kent.

"You heard that?" he murmured to Gurdon. "We must find out exactly where this place is, and then look out some likely quarters in the neighborhood. I must contrive to see Vera and learn her new address before she goes."

"No reason to worry about that," Gurdon said. "It will all be in the papers. The doings of these monied men are chronicled as carefully now as the movements of Royalty. It is any odds when you take up your *Morning Post* in the morning that you will know not only exactly where Fenwick is going

8 [113]

to spend the winter, but get an exact history of the house. So far as I can see we might finish our dinner and go off to a theatre. We are not likely to hear any more to-night, and all this mystery and worry is beginning to get on my nerves. What do you say to an hour or two at the Gaiety?"

Venner pleaded for a few moments' delay. So far as he was personally concerned he felt very unlike the frivolity of the typical musical comedy; but still, he had finished his dinner by this time and was not disposed to be churlish. Fenwick had completed his repast also, and was sipping his coffee in an amiable frame of mind, heedless apparently of business worries of all kinds.

At the same moment a waiter came into the room and advanced to the millionaire's table with a small parcel in his hand.

"A letter for you, sir An express letter which has just arrived. Will you be good enough to sign the receipt?"

" Confound the people," Fenwick growled. "Can't you leave me alone for half an hour when I am having my dinner? Take the thing up to my room. You sign it, Vera."

"I'll sign it, of course," Vera replied. "But don't you think you had better open the parcel? It may be of some importance. People don't usually send express letters at this time of night unless they are urgent. Or, shall I open it for you?"

THE SECOND FINGER

The waiter had gone by this time, taking the receipt for the letter with him. With a gesture Fenwick signified to Vera that she might open the parcel. She cut the string and opened the flat packet, disclosing a small object in tissue paper inside. This she handed to Fenwick, who tore the paper off leisurely. Then the silence of the room was startled by the sound of an oath uttered in tones of intense fury.

"Curse the thing!" Fenwick cried. His yellow face was wet and ghastly now. The big purple veins stood out like cords on his forehead. "Am I never to be free from the terror of this mystery? Where did it come from? How could it be possible when the very man I have most reason to dread is no longer in a position——"

The speaker broke off suddenly, as if conscious that he was betraying himself. The little object in the tissue paper lay on the table in such a position that it was impossible for Venner or Gurdon to see what it was, but they could give a pretty shrewd guess. Venner looked inquiringly at his friend.

"Well, what do you suppose it is?" he asked.

"Personally, I have no doubt whatever as to what it is," Gurdon said. "I am as sure as if I held the thing in my hand at the present moment. It is the second finger which at some time or another was attached to Fenwick's hand."

"You've got it," Venner said. "Upon my word,

[115]

the farther we go with this thing the more complicated it becomes. No sooner do we clear up one
point than a dozen fresh ones arrive. Now, is not
this amazing? We know perfectly well that the
man whom we have to call Bates has been kidnapped
by our interesting friend opposite, and yet here the
second warning arrives just as if Bates were still
free to carry out his vengeance. What can one
make of it?"

"Well, the logical conclusion is that Bates has
an accomplice. I fail to see any other way of
accounting for it."

Fenwick still sat there mopping his heated face
and turning a disgusted eye upon the little object
on the table. He seemed to be terribly distressed
and upset, though there was nothing like the scene
on the previous occasion, and, doubtless, few diners
besides Venner and Gurdon knew that anything
out of the common was taking place there. But
they were watching everything carefully; they noted
Fenwick's anxious face, they could hear his sterto-
rous breathing. Though he had dined so freely he
called for brandy now, a large glass of which he
drank without any addition whatever. Then his
agitation became less uncontrollable and a little
natural color crept into his cheeks. Without
glancing at it he slipped the little object on the
table into his pocket and rose more or less unsteadily
to his feet.

THE SECOND FINGER

"I have had a shock," he muttered. "I don't deny that I have had a terrible shock. You don't understand it, Vera, and I hope you never will. I wish I had never touched that accursed mine. I wish it had been fathoms under the sea before I heard of it, but the mischief has been done now, and I shall have to go on to the end. You can stay here if you like—as to me, I am going to my own room. I want to be alone for a bit and think this matter out."

Fenwick lurched across the room with the air of a man who is more or less intoxicated, though his head was clear enough and his faculties undimmed. Still, his limbs were trembling under him and he groped his way to the door with the aid of a table here and there. It was perhaps rather a risky thing to do, but Venner immediately crossed over and took the seat vacated so recently by Fenwick. Vera welcomed him shyly, but it was palpable that she was ill at ease. She would have risen had not Venner detained her.

"Don't you think you are very imprudent?" she said. "Suppose he should change his mind and come back here again?"

"I don't think there is much chance of that," Venner said, grimly. "Fenwick will only be too glad to be by himself for a bit. But tell me, dear, what was it that gave him such a shock?"

"I don't understand it at all," Vera said. "It

was something to do with that dreadful mine and
the vengeance connected with it. This is the second
time the same thing has happened within the last
few days, and I fear that it will culminate sooner
or later in some fearful tragedy. I have some hazy
idea of the old legend, but I have almost forgotten
what it is."

"I don't think you need worry about that,"
Venner said. "Though it will have to be spoken
of again when the whole thing is cleared up; but
now I wish to talk to you on more personal matters.
Did I not understand Fenwick to say to-night that
he was taking a large house somewhere in Kent?"

"That is his intention, I believe," Vera replied.
"I understand it is a large, dull place in the heart
of the country. Personally I am not looking forward to it with the least pleasure. Things are bad
enough here in London, but there is always the comfortable feeling that one is protected here, whereas
in a lonely neighborhood the feeling of helplessness
grows very strong."

"You are not likely to be lonely or neglected,"
Venner smiled. "As soon as I have definitely ascertained where you are going, Gurdon and myself
will follow. It is quite necessary that we should
be somewhere near you; but, of course, if you
object—"

But Vera was not objecting. Her face flushed
with a sudden happiness. The knowledge that

the man she loved was going to be so near her filled her with a sense of comfort.

"Don't you think it will be dangerous?" she asked.

"Not in the least," Venner said. "Don't forget that I am a stranger to Mark Fenwick, which remark applies with equal force to Gurdon. And if we take a fancy to spend a month or two hunting in the neighborhood of Canterbury, surely there is nothing suspicious in that. I am looking forward to the hunting as a means whereby we may manage to get some long rides together. And even if Fenwick does find it out, it will be easy to explain to him that you made my acquaintance on the field of sport."

"I am glad to near you say that," Vera whispered. "I may be wrong, of course, but I feel that strange things are going to happen, and that I shall need your presence to give me courage."

Vera might have said more, but a waiter came into the room at the same moment with an intimation to the effect that Mr. Fenwick desired to speak to her. She flitted away now, and there was nothing for it but for Venner to fall in with Gurdon's suggestion of a visit to the theatre.

It was not long after breakfast on the following morning that Venner walked into Gurdon's rooms with a new proposal.

"I have been thinking out this confounded

thing," he said. "I have an idea; as you know, the house where you had your adventure the other night is empty, it has occurred to me that perhaps it may be to let. If so, we are going to call upon the agent in the characters of prospective tenants. What I want to do is to ascertain if possible the name of the owner of the premises."

"I see," Gurdon said thoughtfully. "I am ready for you now."

It was some little time before the friends got on the right track, but they found the right man at length. The agent was not quite sure whether he was in a position at present to make any definite arrangements on the part of the owner.

"I presume he wants to let the house," he said, "though I have no instructions, and it is some considerable time since I have heard from my client. You see, he lives abroad."

"Can't you give us his address," Venner asked, "and let us write to him direct? It would save time."

"That I fear is equally impossible," the agent explained. "My client wanders about from place to place, and I haven't the remotest idea where to find him. However, I'll do my best."

"You might tell us his name," Venner said.

"Certainly. His name is Mr. Le Fenu."

"What do you make of it?" Venner said, when once more he and Gurdon were in the street. "I

see you have forgotten what the name of Le Fenu
implies. Don't you remember my telling you that
the original owner of the Four Finger Mine who
was murdered by the Dutchman, Van Fort, was called Le Fenu?"

CHAPTER XI

An Unexpected Move

On the whole the discovery was startling enough. It proved to demonstration that the man who called himself Bates must have been in some way connected with the one-time unfortunate owner of the Four Finger Mine. There was very little said as the two friends walked down the street together. Venner paused presently, and stood as if an idea had occurred to him.

"I have a notion that something will come of this," he said. "I had a great mind to go back to the agent's and try to get the key of the empty house under some pretext or another."

"What do you want it for?" Gurdon asked.

"I am not sure that I want it for anything," Venner admitted "I have a vague idea, a shadowy theory, that I am on the right track at last, but I may be wrong, especially as I am dealing with so unscrupulous an opponent as Fenwick All the same, I think I'll step round to that agent's office this afternoon and get the key. Sooner or later, I shall want a town house, and I don't see why that Portsmouth Square place shouldn't suit me very well."

AN UNEXPECTED MOVE

Venner was true to his intention, and later in the afternoon was once more closeted with the house-agent.

"Do you really want to let the place?" he asked.

"Well, upon my word, sir, I'm not quite sure," the agent replied. "As I said before, it is such a difficult matter to get in contact with the owner."

"But unless he wanted to let it, why did he put it in your hands?" Venner asked. "Still, you can try to communicate with him, and it will save time if you let me have the keys to take measurements and get estimates for the decorating, and so on. I will give you any references you require."

"Oh, there can be no objection to that," the agent replied. "Yes, you can have the keys now, if you like. You are not in the least likely to run away with the place."

Venner departed with the keys in his possession, and made his way back to the hotel. He had hardly reached his own room before a waiter came in with a note for him. It was from Vera, with an urgent request that Venner would see her at once, and the intimation that there would be no danger in his going up to the suite of rooms occupied by Mark Fenwick. Venner lost no time in answering this message. He felt vaguely uneasy and alarmed. Surely, there must be something wrong, or Vera would not

have sent for him in this sudden manner. He could
not quite see, either, how it was that he could call
at Fenwick's rooms without risk. However, he
hesitated no longer, but knocked at the outer door
of the self-contained rooms, which summons was
presently answered by Vera herself.

"You can come in," she said. "I am absolutely
alone. Mr. Fenwick has gone off in a great hurry
with all his assistants, and my own maid will not be
back for some little time."

"But is there no chance of Fenwick coming back?"
Venner asked. "If he caught me here, all my plans
would be ruined. My dear girl, why don't you
leave him and come to me? I declare it makes me
miserable to know that you are constantly in contact
with such a man as that. It isn't as if you were any
relation to him."

"Thank goodness, I am no relation at all,"
Vera replied. "It is not for my own sake that I
endure all this humiliation."

"Then, why endure it?" Venner urged.

"Because I cannot help myself. Because there
is someone else whom I have to look after and shield
from harm. Some day you will know the whole
truth, but not yet, because my lips are sealed. But
I did not bring you here to talk about myself. There
are other and more urgent matters. I am perfectly
sure that something very wrong is going on here.
Not long after breakfast this morning, Mr. Fenwick

was sitting here reading the paper, when he suddenly rose in a state of great agitation and began sending telegrams right and left. I am certain that there was terribly disturbing intelligence in that paper; but what it was, I. of course, cannot say. I have looked everywhere for a clue and all in vain. No sooner were the telegrams dispatched than the three or four men here, whom Mr. Fenwick calls his clerks, gathered all his papers and things together and sent them off by express vans. Mr. Fenwick told me that everything was going to the place that he had taken at Canterbury, but I don't believe that, because none of the boxes were labelled. Anyway, they have all gone, and I am instructed to remain here until I hear from Mr. Fenwick again. "

Venner began to understand; in the light of his superior knowledge it was plain to him that these men had been interrupted in some work, and that they feared the grip of the law. He expressed a wish to see the paper which had been the cause of all the trouble. The news-sheet lay on the floor where Fenwick had thrown it, and Venner took it up in his hands.

"This has not been disturbed?" he asked.

"No," Vera replied. "I thought it best not to. I have looked at both sides of the paper myself, but I have not turned over a leaf. You see, it must have been on one side or another of this sheet that the disturbing news appeared, and that

[125]

is why I have not looked further. Perhaps you will
be able to pick out the particular paragraph? There
is plenty of time "

Very carefully Venner scanned the columns of
the paper. He came at length to something that
seemed to him to bear upon the sudden change of
plans which appeared to have been forced upon
Fenwick. The paragraph in question was not a
long one, and emanated from the New York correspondent of the *Daily Herald*.

"We are informed," the paragraph ran, "that
the police here believe that at length they are on
the track of the clever gang of international swindlers
who were so successful in their bank forgeries two
years ago. Naturally enough, the authorities are
very reticent as to names and other details, but they
declare that they have made a discovery which em-
braces what is practically a new crime, or, at any
rate, a very ingenious variant upon an old one. As
far as we can understand, the police were first put on
the track by the discovery of the fact that the head
of the gang had recently transported some boxes
of gold dust to London. Quite by accident this
discovery was made, and, at first, the police were
under the impression that the gold had been stolen.
When, however, they had proved beyond the shadow
of a doubt that the gold in question was honestly
the property of the gang, they naturally began to
ask themselves what it was intended for. As the

[126]

metal could be so easily transferred into cash, what was the object of the gang in taking the gold to Europe? This question the Head of the Criminal Investigation Department feels quite sure that he has successfully solved. The public may look for startling developments before long. Meanwhile, two of the smartest detectives in New York are on their way to Europe, and are expected to reach Liverpool by the *Lusitania* to-day."

"'There is the source of the trouble," Venner said. "I hardly care about telling you how I know, because the less information you have on this head the better. And I don't want your face to betray you to the sharp eyes of Mark Fenwick. But I am absolutely certain that that paragraph is the source of all the mischief."

"I daresay it is," Vera sighed. "I feel so terribly lonely and frightened sometimes, so afraid of something terrible happening, that I feel inclined to run away and hide myself. What shall I do now, though I am afraid you cannot help me?"

"I can help you in a way you little dream of," Venner said through his teeth. "For the present, at any rate, you had better do exactly as Fenwick tells you. I am not going to leave you here all alone, when we have a chance like this; after dinner, I am going to take you to a theatre. Meanwhile, I must leave you now, as I have much work to do, and there is no time to be lost. It will be no fault of mine if you are not absolutely free from Mark Fenwick before many days have passed "

Venner sat alone at dinner, keeping a critical eye open for whatever might be going on around him. He had made one or two little calculations as to time and distance, and, unless his arithmetic was very far out, he expected to learn something useful before midnight.

The meal had not proceeded very far when two strangers came in and took their places at a table close by. They were in evening dress and appeared to be absolutely at home, yet, in some subtle way, they differed materially from the other diners about them. On the whole, they might have passed for two mining engineers who had just touched civilisation after a long lapse of time. Venner noticed that they both ate and drank sparingly, and that they seemed to get through their dinner as speedily as possible. They went off to the lounge presently to smoke over their coffee, and Venner followed them. He dropped into a seat by their side.

"You have forgotten me, Mr. Egan," he said to the smaller man of the two. "Don't you remember that night on the Bowery when I was fortunate enough to help you to lay hands on the notorious James Daley? You were in rather a tight place, I remember."

"Bless me, if it isn't Mr. Venner," the other cried. "This is my friend, Grady. I daresay you have heard of him."

"Of course I have," Venner replied. "Mr. Grady is quite as celebrated in his way as you are yourself. But you see, there was a time when I took a keen interest in crime and criminals, and some of my experiences in New York would make a respectable volume. When I heard that you were coming over here——"

"You heard we were coming here?" Egan exclaimed. "I should very much like to know how you heard that."

"Oh, you needn't be alarmed," Venner laughed. "Nobody has betrayed your secret mission to Europe, though, strangely enough, I fancy I shall be in a position to give you some considerable assistance. I happened to see a paragraph in the *Herald* to-day alluding to a mysterious gang of swindlers who had hit upon a novel form of crime—something to do with gold dust, I believe it was. At the end of the paragraph it stated that two of the smartest detectives in the New York Force were coming over here, and, therefore, it was quite fair to infer that you might be one of them. In any case, if you had not been, I could have introduced myself to your colleagues and used your name."

Egan looked relieved, but he said nothing.

"You are quite right to be reticent," Venner said. "But, as I remarked before, I think I can help you in this business. You hoped to lay hands on the man you wanted in this hotel."

"I quite see you know something," Egan replied. "As a matter of fact, we are a long way at present from being in a position to lay hands on our man with a reasonable hope of convicting him. There will be a great deal of watching to do first, and a lot of delicate detective work. That is the worst of these confounded newspapers. How that paragraph got into the *Herald*, I don't know, but it is going to cause Grady and myself a great deal of trouble. To be quite candid, we did expect to find our man here, but when he had vanished as he did, just before we arrived, I knew at once that somebody must have been giving him information."

"Do I know the name of the man?" Venner asked.

"If you aon't, I certainly can't tell you," Egan said. "One has to be cautious, even with so discreet a gentleman as yourself."

"That's very well," Venner sa.d. "But it so happens that I am just as much interested in this individual as yourself. Now let me describe him. He is short and stout, he is between fifty and sixty years of age, he has beady black eyes, and a little hooked nose like a parrot. Also, he has an enormous bald head, and his coloring is strongly like that of a yellow tomato If I am mistaken, then I have no further interest in the matter."

"Oh, you're not mistaken," Egan said. "That is our man right enough But tell me, sir, do you happen to know what his particular line is just at present?"

"I have a pretty good idea," Venner said; "but I am not quite sure as yet. I have been making a few inquiries, and they all tend to confirm my theory, but I am afraid I cannot stay here discussing the matter any longer, as I have an important appointment elsewhere. Do you propose to stay at the Empire Hotel for any time?"

Egan replied that it all depended upon circumstances. They were in no way pressed for time, and as they were there on State business they were not limited as to expenses. With a remark to the effect that they might meet again later on in the evening, Venner went on his way and stood waiting for Vera at the foot of the stairs. She came down presently, and they entered a cab together.

"We won't go to a theatre at all," Venner said. "We will try one of the music halls, and we shall be able to talk better there; if we have a box we shall be quite secure from observation."

"It is all the same to me," Vera smiled. "I care very little where I go so long as we are together. How strange it is that you should have turned up in this extraordinary way!"

"There is nothing strange about it at all," Venner said. "It is only Fate making for the undoing of the criminal. It may be an old-fashioned theory of mine, but justice always overtakes the rogue sooner or later, and Fenwick's time is coming. I have been the instrument chosen to bring about his downfall, and save you from your terrible position. If you would only confide in me——"

"But I can't, dear," Vera said. "There is somebody else. If it were not for that somebody else, I could end my troubles to-morrow. But don't let us talk about it. Let us have two delightful hours together and thank Providence for the opportunity."

The time passed all too quickly in the dim seclusion of one of the boxes; indeed, Vera sat up with a start when the orchestra began to play the National Anthem. It seemed impossible that the hour was close upon twelve. As to the performance itself, Vera could have said very little. She had been far too engrossed in her companion to heed what was taking place upon the stage.

"Come along," Venner said. "It has been a delightful time, but all too brief. I am going to put you in a cab and send you back to the hotel, as I have to go and see Gurdon."

Vera made no demur to this arrangement, and presently was being conveyed back to the hotel, while Venner thoughtfully walked down the street. Late as it was, the usual crop of hoarse yelling newsboys were ranging the pavement and forcing their wares on the unwilling passers-by.

"Here you are, sir. 'Late Special.' Startling

development of the Bates Case. The mystery solved."

"I'll take one of those," Venner said. "Here's sixpence for you, and you can keep the change. Call me that cab there."

CHAPTER XII

THE HOUSE NEXT DOOR

VENNER lost no time in reaching the rooms of his friend Gurdon, and was fortunate enough to find the latter at home. He was hard at work on some literary matter, but he pushed his manuscript aside as Venner came excitedly into the room.

"Well, what is it?" he asked. "Anything fresh? But your face answers that question. Have you found Bates?"

"No, I haven't," Venner said; "but he seems to have been discovered. I bought this paper just now in Piccadilly, but I have not been able to look at it yet. It is stated here that the mystery has been solved."

"Hand it over," Gurdon cried excitedly. "Let's see if we can find it. Ah! here we are. The Press Association has just received a letter which appears to come from Mr. Bates himself. He says he is very much annoyed at all this fuss and bother in the papers, about his so-called kidnapping. He goes on to say that he was called to the Continent by pressing business, and that he had not even time to tell his servants he was going, as it was imperatively necessary that he should catch the midnight boat to Dieppe. The correspondent of the Press Assooiation says that Mr. Bates has been interviewed by a foreign journalist, who is absolutely certain as to his identity. Moreover, an official has called at Mr. Bates' residence and found that his servants have had a letter from their master instructing them to join him at once, as he has let his house furnished for the next two months. Well, my dear man, that seems to be very satisfactory, and effectually disposes of the idea that Mr. Bates has been mysteriously kidnapped. I am rather sorry for this in a way, because it upsets all our theories and makes it necessary to begin our task all over again."

"I don't believe a word of it," Venner said "I believe it's a gigantic bluff. I was coming to see you to-night in any case, but after buying that paper I came on here post haste. Now that story of the Press Association strikes me as being decidedly thin. Here is a man living comfortably at home who suddenly disappears in a most mysterious manner, and nothing is heard of him for some time. Directly the public began to regard it as a fascinating mystery and the miscreants realising what a storm they were likely to stir up, the man himself writes and says that it is all a mistake. Now, if he had come back and shown himself, it would have been quite another matter. Instead of doing that, he writes a letter from abroad, or sends a telegram or something of that kind, saying that he has been called away on urgent business. That might pass easily enough, but mark what follows. He writes to his servants asking them to join him at once in some foreign town because he has let his house for two months, and the new tenant wishes to get in without delay. Did ever anybody hear anything so preposterous? Just as if a man would let a house in that break-neck fashion without giving his servants due warning. The thing is not to be thought of."

"Then you think the servants have been lured away on a fools' errand?" Gurdon asked. "You don't think there is anybody in the house?"

"Oh, yes, I do," Venner said drily. "I have a very strong opinion that there *are* people in the house, and I also have a pretty shrewd idea as to who they are. It happens, also, that I am in a position to test my theory without delay."

"How do you propose to do that?" Gurdon asked.

"Quite easily. After I left you this afternoon I went back to the agent and succeeded in obtaining possession of the keys of the empty house in Portsmouth Square. My excuse was that I wanted to go into detail and to take measurements and the like I need not remind you that Bates' house is next door to the empty one. In fact, there is no question that both houses belong to the same person. You will remember, also, the mysterious way in which that furniture vanished from the scene of your adventure."

"I remember," Gurdon said grimly. "But all the same I don't quite see what you are driving at·

"The thing is quite plain. That furniture did not vanish through the prosaic medium of a van, nor was it carted through the front door from one house to the other. The two houses communicated in some way, and it will be our business to find the door. As I have the keys and every legitimate excuse for being on the premises, we can proceed to make our investigations without the slightest secrecy, and without the least fear of awkward questions being asked. Now do you follow me?"

"I follow you fast enough. I suppose your game is to try and get into the next house by means of the door?"

"You have hit it exactly," Venner said. "That is precisely what I mean to do. We shall find it necessary to discover the identity of Mr Bates' tenant."

"When are we going to make the experiment?" Gurdon asked.

"We are going to make it now," Venner replied. "We will have a cab as far as the Empire Hotel, so that I can get the keys. After that, the thing will be quite easy. Come along, and thank me for an exciting evening's adventure. I shall be greatly surprised if it is not even more exciting than the last occasion."

They were in the empty house at last. The windows were closed and shuttered, so that it was possible to use matches in the various rooms without attracting attention from the outside. But search how they would, for upwards of two hours, they could find no trace whatever of a means of communication between the two houses. They tapped the walls and sounded the skirtings, but without success. Venner paced the floor of the drawing-room moodily, racking his brains to discover a way out of the difficulty.

"It must be here somewhere," he muttered. "I am sure all that furniture was moved backwards and forwards through some door, and a wide one at that."

"Then it must be on the ground floor," Gurdon remarked. "When you come to think of it, some of that furniture was so heavy and massive that it would not go through an ordinary doorway, neither could it have been brought upstairs without the assistance of two or three men of great strength. We shall have to look for it in the hall; if we don't find it there, we shall have to give it up as a bad job and try some other plan."

"I am inclined to think you are right," Venner
said. "Let us go down and see. At any rate, there
is one consolation. If we fail to-night we can come
again to-morrow."

Gurdon did not appear to be listening He strode
resolutely down the stairs into the hall and stood
for some moments contemplating the panels before
him. The panels were painted white; they were
elaborately ornamented with wreaths of flowers
after the Adams' style of decoration. Then it
seemed to Gurdon that two pairs of panels, one above
and one below, had at one time taken the formation
of a doorway. He tapped on one of the panels,
and the drumming of his fingers gave out a hollow
sound. Gurdon tapped again on the next panel,
but hardly any sound came in response. He looked
triumphantly at Venner.

"I think we have got it at last," he said. "Do
you happen to have a knife in your pocket?
Unless I am greatly mistaken, the decorations
around these panels come off like a bead. If
you have a knife with you we can soon find
out."

Venner produced a small knife from his pocket,
and Gurdon attempted to insinuate the point of
the blade under the elaborate moulding. Surely
enough, the moulding yielded, and presently came
away in Gurdon's hands.

"There you are," he said. "It is exactly as I

told you. I thought at first that those mouldings were plaster, but you can see for yourself now that they are elaborately carved wood."

Venner laid the ornament aside and stood watching Gurdon with breathless interest while the latter attacked another of the mouldings. They came away quite easily, pointing to the fact that they must have been removed before within a very short period. Once they were all cleared away, Gurdon placed the point of the knife behind one of the panels, and it came away in his hands, disclosing beyond a square hole quite large enough for anybody to enter. Here was the whole secret exposed.

"Exactly what I thought," Gurdon said. "If I removed all the mouldings from the other three panels there would be space enough here to drive a trap through. I think we have been exceedingly lucky to get to the bottom of this. How clever and ingeniously the whole thing has been managed! However, I don't think there is any occasion for us to worry about moving any more of the panels, seeing that we can get through now quite easily. Wouldn't it be just as well to put all the lights out?"

"I haven't thought of that," Venner muttered. "On the whole, it would be exceedingly injudicious not to extinguish all the lights. We had better go on at once, I think, and get it over."

THE HOUSE NEXT DOOR

The house was reduced to darkness, and very quietly and cautiously the two adventurers crept through the panel. They were in the hall on the other side, of which fact there was no doubt, for they stepped at once off a marble floor on to a thick rug which deadened the sound of their footsteps. They had, naturally enough, expected to find the whole place in darkness, and the tenant of the house and his servants in bed. This, on the whole, would be in their favor, for it would enable them to take all the observations they required with a minimum chance of being disturbed.

A surprise awaited them from the first. True, the hall was in darkness, and, as far as they could judge, so was the rest of the house. But from somewhere upstairs came the unmistakable sound of a piano, and of somebody singing in a sweet but plaintive soprano voice. Gurdon clutched his companion by the arm.

"Don't you think it is just possible that we have made a mistake?" he whispered. "Isn't it quite on the cards that this is a genuine affair, and that we are intruding in an unwarrantable manner upon some respectable private citizen? I am bound to say that that beautiful voice does not suggest crime to me."

"We must go on now," Venner said, impatiently. "It won't do to judge by appearances. Let us go up the stairs and see what is going on for ourselves.

If we are intruding, we will get away as speedily as possible."

Gurdon made no further objection, and together they crept up the stairs. There was no chance of their being surprised from behind by the servants, for they had taken good care to notice that the basement was all in darkness. They were getting nearer and nearer now to the sound of the music, which appeared to come from the drawing-room, the door of which was widely enough open for the brilliant light inside to illuminate the staircase. A moment later the music ceased, and someone was heard to applaud in a hoarse voice.

"Sing some more," the voice said. "Now don't be foolish, don't begin to cry again. Confound the girl, she makes me miserable."

"Do you recognise the voice?" Venner whispered.

"Lord! yes," was Gurdon's reply. "Why, it's Fenwick. No mistaking those tones anywhere. Now, what on earth does all this mean?"

"We shall find out presently," Venner said. "You may laugh at me, but I quite expected something of this kind, which was one of the reasons why I obtained the keys of the house."

"It's a most extraordinary thing," Gurdon replied. "Now isn't this man—Fenwick—one of the last persons in the world you would credit with a love of music?"

"I don't know," Venner said. "You never can

tell. But don't let's talk. We are here more to listen than anything else. I wish we could get a glimpse of the singer."

"I am going to," Gurdon declared. "Unless I am greatly mistaken, I have made a discovery, too. Oh, I am not going to take any risk. Do you see that mirror opposite the door? It strikes me if I get close enough to look into it that I shall be able to see who is in the room without betraying my presence."

So saying, Gurdon crept forward till he was close enough to the mirror to get a very good idea of the room and its occupants. He could see a pale figure in white standing by a piano; he could see that Fenwick was sprawling in a big armchair, smoking a large cigar. Then he noticed that the girl crossed the floor and laid a slim hand half timidly, half imploringly, on Fenwick's shoulder.

"Why are you so unkind to me?" she said. "Why so cruel? How many times have you promised me that you will bring him back to me again? I get so tired of waiting, I feel so sad and weary, and at times my mind seems to go altogether."

"Have patience," Fenwick said. "If you will only wait a little longer he will come back to you right enough. Now go to the piano and sing me another song before I go to bed. Do you hear what I say?"

The last words were harshly uttered; the girl

reeled back as if fearing a blow. Gurdon standing there clenched his fists impulsively; he had considerable difficulty in restraining himself.

"Very well," she said; "just one more, and then I will go to bed, for I am so tired and weary."

Once more the sweet pathetic voice rang out in some simple song; the words gradually died away, and there was silence. Gurdon had barely time to slip back to the head of the stairs before the girl came out and made her way to the landing above. Standing just below the level of the floor, Venner gazed eagerly at the pretty tired face and mournful blue eyes. He grasped his companion by the arm in a grip that was almost painful.

"We are getting to it," he said. "It was a good night's work coming here to-night. Do you mean to say you don't notice the likeness? Making due allowance for the difference in height and temperament, that poor girl is the image of my wife."

"I must have been a dolt not to have noticed it before," Gurdon said. "Now that you mention it, the likeness is plain enough. My dear fellow, can't you see in this a reason for your wife's reticence in speaking of the past?"

There was no time to reply, for the sinister evil face of Fenwick appeared in the doorway, and he called aloud in Spanish some hoarse command, which was answered from above by someone, in the same language. Gurdon whispered to his companion, with a view to ascertaining what had been said.

"You will see for yourself in a minute," Venner said in an excited whisper. "You are going to have another surprise. You wanted to know just now what had become of Bates. Unless I am greatly mistaken, you will be able to judge for yourself in a few moments. I believe the man to be a prisoner in his own house."

CHAPTER XIII

THE WHITE LADY AGAIN

IT was perhaps an imprudent thing for the two friends to remain there, exposed as they were to the danger of discovery at any moment; but, so completely were they fascinated by what was going on about them, that they had flung caution to the winds. One thing was in their favor, however; there was not much likelihood of their being attacked from below, seeing that all the servants had gone to bed; unless, perhaps, some late comer entered the house. Still, the risk had to be run, and so they stood there together, waiting for the next move. It was Venner who spoke first.

"I cannot get over the extraordinary likeness of that girl to my wife," he said. "Is she anything like the woman you saw next door? I mean the poor half-demented creature who happened to come into the room when you were talking with the owner?"

"Why, of course, it is the same girl," Gurdon replied.

"Then I am sure she is Vera's sister. I'll ask her about it the first time I have an opportunity.

THE WHITE LADY AGAIN

Be silent and get a little lower down the stairs. There is somebody coming from the top of the house. We can see here without being seen."

Assuredly there were sounds emanating from the top of the house. A voice was raised in angry expostulation, followed by other voices morose and threatening. As far as the listeners could judge, two men were dragging a third down the stairs against his will. But for that, the house was deadly silent; the watchers could hear the jingle of a passing cab bell, a belated foot passenger whistled as he went along. It seemed almost impossible to believe that so close to light and law and order and the well-being of the town a strange tragedy like this should be in progress; hidden from the eye of London, by mere skill of brick and mortar, this strange thing was going on. Venner wondered to himself how many such scenes were taking place in London at the same moment.

But he had not much time for his meditation, for the shuffling of feet came closer. There were no more sounds of expostulation now; only the heavy breathing of three people, as if the captive had ceased to struggle and was making but a passive resistance. Then there emerged on the landing the figure of the handsome cripple with a guardian on either side. His face was no longer distorted with pain; rather was it white with an overpowering anger—his eyes shone like points of flame. On his right side Venner and Gurdon recognised the figure of the man in the list slippers—the man who had been handling the sovereigns in Fenwick's rooms. His comrade was a stranger, though of the same type, and it seemed to Venner that anyone would have been justified in repudiating either of them as an acquaintance. It was perfectly evident that the cripple came against his will, though he was struggling no longer. Probably the condition of his emaciated frame had rendered the task of his captors an easy one. They dragged him, limp and exhausted, into the drawing-room where Fenwick was seated and they stood in the doorway awaiting further instructions.

"You needn't stay there," Fenwick growled. "If I want you I can call. You had better go back to your cards again."

The two men disappeared up the stairs, and just for a moment there was silence in the drawing-room. It was safe for Venner and his companion now to creep back to the drawing-room door and take a careful note of what was going on. With the aid of a friendly mirror on the opposite side of the room, it was possible to see and note everything. The cripple had fallen into a chair, where he sat huddled in a heap, his hand to his head, as if some great physical pain racked him. His heavy breathing was the only sound made, except the steady puffing of Fenwick's cigar. A fit of anger gripped

Venner for the moment; he would have liked to step in and soundly punish Fenwick for his brutality. Doubtless the poor crippled frame was racked with the pain caused by the violence of his late captors.

But under that queer exterior was a fine spirit. Gradually the cripple ceased to quiver and palpitate; gradually he pulled himself up in his chair and faced his captor. His face was still deadly white, but it was hard and set now; there was no sign of fear about him. He leaned forward and stared Fenwick between the eyes.

"Well, you scoundrel," he said in a clear, cold voice, "I should like to know the meaning of this. I have heard of and read of some strange outrages in my time, but to kidnap a man and keep him prisoner in his own house is to exceed all the bounds of audacity."

"You appear to be annoyed," Fenwick said. "Perhaps you have not already learned who I am?"

"I know perfectly well who you are," the cripple responded. "Your name is Mark Fenwick, and you are one of the greatest scoundrels unhung. At present, you are posing as an American millionaire. Fools may believe you, but I know better. The point is, do you happen to know who I am?"

"Yes, I know who you are," Fenwick said with a sardonic smile. "You elect to call yourself Mr. Bates, or some such name, and you pretend to be a recluse who gives himself over to literary pursuits.

As a matter of fact, you are Charles Le Fenu, and your father was, at one time, the practical owner of the Four Finger Mine."

"We are getting on," Venner whispered. "It may surprise you to hear this, but I have suspected it for some little time The so-called absent owner of these houses is the man sitting opposite Fenwick there. Now do you begin to see something like daylight before you? I wouldn't have missed this for worlds."

"We have certainly been lucky," Gurdon replied.

There was no time for further conversation, for the cripple was speaking again. His voice was still hard and cold, nor did his manner betray the slightest sign of fear.

"So you have found that out," he said. "You know that I am the son of the unfortunate Frenchman who was murdered by a rascally Dutchman at your instigation. You thought that once having discovered the secret of the mine you could work it to your own advantage. How well you worked it your left hand testifies."

The jeer went home to Fenwick, his yellow face flushed, and he half rose from his chair with a threatening gesture.

"Oh, you can strike me," the cripple said. "I am practically helpless as far as my lower limbs are concerned, and it would be just the sort of cowardly act that would gratify a dirty little soul like yours.

It hurts me to sit here, helpless and useless, knowing that you are the cause of all my misfortunes; knowing that, but for you, I should be as straight and strong as the best of them. And yet you are not safe—you are going to pay the penalty of your crime. Have you had the first of your warnings yet?"

Fenwick started in his seat; in the looking-glass the watchers could see how ghastly his face had grown.

"I don't know what you mean," he muttered.

"Liar!" the cripple cried. "Paltry liar! Why, you are shaking from head to foot now—your face is like that of a man who stands in the shadow of the gallows."

"I repeat, I don't know what you mean," Fenwick said.

"Oh, yes, you do. When your accomplice Van Fort foully murdered my father, you thought that the two of you would have the mine to yourselves; you thought you would work it alone as my father did, and send your ill-gotten gains back to England. That is how the murdered man accomplished it, that is how he made his fortune—and you were going to do the same thing, both of you. When you had made all your arrangements you went down to the coast on certain business, leaving the rascally Dutchman behind. He was quite alone in the mine, there was no one within miles of that secret spot. And yet he vanished. Van Fort was never heard of again. The message of his fingers was conveyed to his wife, for she was implicated in the murder of my father, and how she suffered you already know. But you are a brave man—I give you all the credit for that. You went back to the mine again, determined not to be deterred by what had happened. What happened to you, I need not go into. Shall I tell the story, or will you be content with a recollection of your sufferings? It is all the same to me."

"You are a bold man," Fenwick cried. He was trembling with the rage that filled him. "You are a bold man to defy me like this. Nobody knows that I am here, nobody knows that you are back in your own house again. I could kill you as you sit there, and not a soul would suffer for the crime."

The cripple laughed aloud; he seemed to be amused at something.

"Really!" he sneered. "Such cheap talk is wasted upon me. Besides, what would you gain by so unnecessary a crime, and how much better off would you be? You know as well as I do, disguise it as you will, that the long arm has reached for you across five thousand miles of sea, and that, when the time comes, you will be stricken down here in London as surely and inevitably as if you had remained in Mexico under the shadow of the mountains. The dreadful secret is known to a few, in its entirety it is even unknown to me. I asked you just now if you had received the first of your messages, and you denied that you knew what I meant. You actually had the effrontery to deny it to me, sitting opposite to you as I am, and looking straight at the dreadful disfigurement of your left hand. For over three centuries the natives of Mexico worked the Four Finger Mine till only two of the tribe who knew its secret remained. Then it was that my father came along. He was a brave man, and an adventurer to his finger tips. Moreover, he was a doctor. His healing art made those rough men his friends, and when their time came, my father was left in possession of the mine. How that mine was guarded and how the spirit of the place took its vengeance upon intruders, you know too well. Ah, I have touched you now."

Fenwick had risen, and was pacing uneasily up and down the room. All the dare-devil spirit seemed to have left the man for a moment; he turned a troubled face on the cripple huddled in his chair. He seemed half inclined to temporise, and then, with a short laugh, he resumed his own seat again.

"You seem to be very sure of your ground," he sneered.

"I am," the cripple went on. "What does it matter what becomes of a melancholy wreck like myself? Doctors tell me that in time I may become my old self again, but in my heart I doubt it, and as sure as I sit here the mere frame-work of a human being, my injuries are due to you. I might have had you shot before now, or I might even have done it myself, but I spared you. It would have been a kindness to cut your life short, but I had another use for you than that. And now, gradually, but surely, the net is closing in around you, though you cannot yet see its meshes, and you are powerless to prevent the inevitable end."

"You seem to have mapped it all out," Fenwick replied. "You seem to have settled it all to your own satisfaction, but you forget that I may have something to say in the matter. When I discovered, as I did quite by accident, that you were in London, I laid my plans for getting you into my hands. It suits me very well, apart from the criminal side of it, to hide myself in your house, but that is not all. I am in a position now to dictate terms, and you have nothing else to do but to listen. I am prepared to spare your life on one condition. Now kindly follow me carefully."

"I am listening," the cripple said, coldly. "If you were not the blind fool you seem to be you would know that there could be no conditions between us; but go on. Let me hear what you have to say."

"I am coming to that. I want you to tell me where I can find Felix Zary."

Suddenly, without the slightest premonition, the cripple burst into a hearty laugh. He rocked backward and forward in a perfect ecstasy of enjoyment;

for the moment, at any rate, he might have been on the very best of terms with his companion.

"Oh, that is what you are driving at?" he said. "So you think that if you could get Felix Zary out of the way you would be absolutely safe? Really, it is marvellous how an otherwise clever man could be so blind to the true facts of the case. My good sir, I will give you Zary's address with pleasure."

Fenwick was obviously puzzled. Perhaps it was beginning to dawn upon him that he had a man of more than ordinary intellect to grapple with. He looked searchingly at the cripple, who was leaning back with eyes half closed.

"Hang me, if I can understand you," he muttered. "I am in imminent danger of my life, though I should be safe enough if Felix Zary and yourself were out of the way."

"And you are quite capable of putting us out of the way," the cripple said, gently. "Is not that so, my friend?"

"Aye, I could, and I would," Fenwick said in a fierce whisper. "If you were both dead I could breathe freely; I could go to bed at night feeling sure that I should wake in the morning. Nothing could trouble me then. As to that accursed mine, I have done with it. Never again do I plant my foot in Mexico."

"Fool that you are!" the cripple said in tones of infinite pity. "So you think that if Zary and myself were out of the way you might die eventually in your bed honored and respected of men? I tell you, never! The vengeance is upon you, it is following you here, it is close at hand now. You have already had your warning. Perhaps, for all I know to the contrary, you may have had your second warning; that you have had one, your face told me eloquently enough a few moments ago. I am quite sure that a little quiet reflection will show you the absurdity of keeping me a prisoner in my own house. Of course, I know I am entirely in your hands, and that you may keep me here for weeks if you choose. It will be very awkward for me, because I have important business on hand."

"I know your important business," Fenwick sneered. "Everything that goes in your favor will naturally spell disaster to me. As I told you before, it was only an accident that told me where you were; indeed, so changed are you that I should not have recognised you if I had met you in the street. No, on the whole, you will stay where you are."

At this point Venner clutched Gurdon's arm and dragged him hurriedly across the landing down to the half staircase. So quickly was this done that Gurdon had no time to ask the reason for it all.

"Someone coming down the stairs," Venner whispered. "Didn't you hear a voice? I believe it is the girl in white again."

Surely enough, looking upward, they could see

the slim white figure creeping down the stairs. The girl was crooning some little song to herself as she came along. She turned into the drawing-room and called aloud to the cripple in the chair. With an oath on his lips, Fenwick motioned her away.

CHAPTER XIV

MASTER OF THE SITUATION

"WHAT have you come back here for?" Fenwick demanded. "You said you were tired, and that you were going to bed, long ago."

The girl looked dreamily about her; it was some little time before she appeared to appreciate the significance of Fenwick's question. She was more like one who walks in her sleep than a human being in the full possession of understanding.

"I don't know," she said, helplessly. She rubbed her eyes as if there had been mist before them. "I was so tired that I lay on the bed without undressing, and I fell fast asleep. Then I had a dream. I dreamed that all the miserable past was forgotten, and that Charles was with me once more. Then he seemed to call me, and I woke up. Oh, it was such a vivid dream, so vivid, that I could not sleep again! I was so restless and anxious, that I made up my mind to come downstairs, and, as I was passing a door just now, it opened, and the face of Charles looked out. It was only for a moment, then two men behind him dragged him back and the door closed once more."

"A foolish fancy," Fenwick growled.

"It was not," the girl cried almost passionately. "I tried the door a moment later, and it was locked. I tell you that Charles is in that room. I cannot go to bed again until I am certain of the truth. Oh, why do you keep me in suspense like this?"

"Mad," Fenwick muttered. "Mad as a March hare. Why don't you send her to an asylum?"

"She is not mad," the cripple said in a curiously hard voice. "Something tells me that she has made a discovery. You rascal, is it possible that you have Charles Evors under this roof?"

Fenwick laughed, but there was something uneasy and strained about his mirth. He glanced defiantly at the cripple, then his eyes dropped before the latter's steady gaze.

"Why should I worry about Evors?" he asked. "The man is nothing to me, and if by chance——"

The rest of Fenwick's sentence was drowned in a sudden uproar which seemed to break out in a room overhead. The tense silence was broken by the thud of heavy blows as if someone were banging on a door, then came muttered shouts and yells of unmistakable pain. Hastily Fenwick rose from his seat and made in the direction of the door. He had hardly advanced two steps before he found himself confronted with the rim of a silver-plated revolver, which the cripple was holding directly in the line of his head.

"Sit down," the latter said tersely. "Sit down, or, as sure as I am a living man, I'll fire. I could say that I fired the shot in self-defence, and when the whole story comes to be told I have no fear that a jury would disbelieve me. Besides, there is nothing to be afraid of. Those sounds don't come from the police trying to force their way into the house. On the contrary, it seems to me that some of your parasites are having a misunderstanding over their cards. At any rate, you are not to move. If you do, there will be an end once and for all of the millionaire Mark Fenwick. Sit down, my child—you are trembling from head to foot."

"It was his voice," the girl cried. "I am certain that it was Charles who called out just now."

Once more the shouts and cries broke out, once more came that banging on the panels, followed by a splitting crash, after which the uproar doubled. Evidently a door had given way and the conflict was being fought out on the stairs.

"Shall we go and take a hand?" Gurdon whispered excitedly. "Murder might be going on here."

"I think we had better risk it a little longer," was Venner's cautious reply. "After all is said and done, we must not make ourselves too prominent. If necessary we will take a hand, but, unless I am greatly mistaken, the prisoner upstairs has got the better of his captors. Ah, I thought so."

The sound of strife overhead suddenly ceased

after two smashing blows, in which evidently a man's clenched fist had come in contact with naked flesh. There was a groan, the thud of a falling body, and the man in the list slippers came rolling down the stairs. He was followed a moment later by a young clean-shaven man dressed in a grey Norfolk suit. His frame suggested power and strength, though his face was white like that of one who is just recovering from a long illness. He was breathing very hard, but otherwise he did not appear to have suffered much in the struggle out of which he had emerged in so victorious a fashion. He made his way direct to the drawing-room, and immediately a woman's voice uprose in a long wailing cry.

"I'd give something to see that," Venner whispered. "Only I am afraid we can't do anything until the man in the list slippers comes to his senses and takes himself off. There is another one coming now. He doesn't look much better off than his colleague."

Another man crept down the stairs, swaying as he came and holding on to the balusters. He had a tremendous swelling over his left eye and a terrible gash in his lip, from which the blood was flowing freely. Altogether he presented a terrible aspect as he bent over the prostrate form of his unconscious companion.

"Here, get up, wake up," he said. "What are

11   [161]

you lying there for? He'll be out of the house before we can turn round, and what will the governor say then?"

The man in the slippers gradually assumed a sitting position and stared stupidly about him. A hearty kick in the ribs seemed to restore him to some measure of consciousness.

"Don't ask me," he said. "I never saw anything like it. Here's a chap who has been in bed on and off for months coming out in this unexpected manner and knocking us about as if we had been ninepins. What's become of him, I should like to know?"

"What are you two ruffians doing there?" came Fenwick's voice from the drawing-room. "Go back to your room, and I will send for you when I want you."

The men slunk back again, probably by no means sorry to be out of further trouble. No sooner had they disappeared than the two friends stood in the entrance to the door of the drawing-room once more. The friendly mirror again stood them in good stead, for by its aid they watched as dramatic and thrilling a picture as ever was presented on any stage.

The young man in the Norfolk suit stood there side by side with the girl in white. He had his arm about her waist. She clung to him, with her head upon his shoulder; there were words of endearment on her lips. Just for the moment she seemed to have forgotten that they were not alone; all the world might have been made for herself and her lover. For the moment, too, the dreamy look had left her face, and she no longer conveyed the impression to a stranger's eyes that she was suffering from some form of insanity. She was alert and vigorous once more.

"Oh, I knew that you would come back to me," she said. "I knew that you were not dead, for all they told me so. How cruel they were to tell me these things——"

"Stop," the cripple cried. "It sounds cruel and heartless for me to have to interfere just now, but I must insist that you go back to your room, Beth. Back at once."

"Can't I stay a little longer?" the girl pleaded. "It is such a long time since Charles and I——"

"No, no, you must do as I tell you. It will be far better in the long run. We are only two men against three, and there may be others concealed in the house for all I know. For myself, I am perfectly helpless, and Charles looks as if he had just come from the grave. Evidently his struggles have tried him."

"Well, I must confess, I am feeling rather down," Charles Evors said. "I could not stand it any longer, and I made a dash for liberty. Goodness knows how long I have been in the hands of those men; and how long they have kept me under the influence of drugs. I suppose the supply fell short. Anyway, I had just sense enough to take advantage of my first opportunity. You can explain all to me presently, but the mere fact of Fenwick being here is enough to tell me who is at the bottom of this business."

Fenwick placed his fingers to his lips and whistled shrilly. Almost immediately sounds of footsteps broke out overhead, and a door opened somewhere with a loud crash The cripple turned to the girl, who had crept reluctantly as far as the doorway.

"Now listen to me," he said quickly. "Listen and act quickly. Go downstairs into the street and bring here the first policeman you can find. Tell him a violent quarrel has broken out between Mr. Bates and some of his guests, and say you fear that some mischief will be done. Do you understand me?"

The girl nodded quickly. Evidently she quite understood. She disappeared so suddenly that Venner and Gurdon had barely time to get out of her way. They heard the street door open—they were conscious of the sudden draught rushing up the stairs; the sound of passing cabs was distinctly audible.

The girl had hardly time to get outside before three or four men came down the stairs. They rushed headlong into the drawing-room, where they seemed to pause, no doubt deterred in their violence for a moment by the sight of the cripple's revolver.

"Here's our chance," Gurdon whispered. "The girl will be back with the police in two minutes, and we have heard quite enough to know the ingenious scheme which is uppermost in the cripple's mind. Let's lock them in. Don't you see that the key is in on this side of the door? Turn it quickly."

"Good business," Gurdon chuckled as he snapped the key in the lock. "Now they can fight as long as they like. At any rate, they can't do much mischief so long as they are caged in there."

A din of mingled voices came from the other side of the door, followed quickly by the whiplike crack of a revolver shot. Then someone tried the door and yelled aloud that it was locked. Fists battered violently on the panels, and just as the din was at its height the helmets of two policemen appeared mounting the stairs. Venner stepped coolly forward as if he had every right to be there.

"I'm glad you officers have come," he said. "There seems to be something in the nature of a free fight going on here. We took the liberty of turning in as the door was open to see what had happened. You had better go in yourself."

The policeman tried the door, which, naturally, did not yield to his hand, and he called out to those inside to open in the name of the law. A voice on the other side pleaded that the door was locked. Venner turned the key in the door.

[165]

Probably the young lady had the sense to lock them in," he said. "You had better go inside, officer. No, there is no reason why we should accompany you. As a matter of fact our presence here is more or less an intrusion."

The policemen stepped into the room and demanded to know what was the matter. They could see the master of the house sitting there in his chair, with a tall young man in a Norfolk suit by his side, and opposite him Fenwick, flushed and sullen, with his satellites behind him. There were four of them altogether, and the appearance they made was by no means attractive, seeing that two at least of them were showing unmistakable signs of violence.

It was the cripple who first recovered his self-possession.

"I am sorry to trouble you," he said, "but I am afraid we have rather forgotten ourselves. You know me, of course?"

"Oh, yes, sir," the first officer replied. "You are Mr. Bates, the gentleman who is supposed to have been kidnapped the other night; the inspector told me that you were still on the Continent."

"Well, I am not," the cripple said curtly. "I am back home again, as you can see with your own eyes. The gentleman over there with the yellow face is Mr. Mark Fenwick, the well-known millionaire. I daresay you have heard of him."

MASTER OF THE SITUATION

Both officers touched their hats respectfully; they had probably come here prepared to make more than one arrest and thus cover themselves with comparative glory; but the mere mention of Fenwick's name settled that point once and for all.

"As you are probably aware," the cripple went on, "until quite recently Mr. Fenwick was staying at the Great Empire Hotel, but the place was too public for one of his gentle and retiring disposition, and so he made arrangements to take my house furnished, though the understanding was that nobody should know anything about it, and nobody would have known anything about it but for the fact that in the way of business Mr. Fenwick had to consult these other gentlemen. Perhaps they don't look in the least like it, but they are all American capitalists, having made their money by gold mining. They don't look a very attractive lot, officer, but if you knew them as well as I do you would learn to love them for their many engaging qualities, and their purity of heart."

The officers touched their helmets again, and appeared to be undecided in their minds as to whether the cripple was chaffing them or not. But though his voice had a certain playfulness of tone, his face was quite grave and steadfast.

"Very well, sir," the foremost of the constables said. "I understand that neither of you gentlemen desires to make any charge against the other. I shall have to make a note of this."

"Of course you will," the cripple said sweetly. "Now I appeal to Mr. Fenwick and his companions as to whether or not the whole thing has not been a silly misunderstanding. You see, officer, gold mining is rather a thirsty business, and occasionally leads to rather more champagne than is good for one. I can only apologise to my tenant, Mr. Fenwick, for losing my temper, and I will at once rid him of my presence. It is getting very late, and I can come round in the morning and make my peace here. As I am a little lame, I will ask one of you officers to give me your arm. Charles, will you be good enough to give me your arm also? I wish you good-night, Mr. Fenwick. In fact, I wish all of you good-night. I shall not fail to call round in the morning——"

"But you are not going," Fenwick cried in dismay. "You are not going away from your own house at this time of night?"

"You forget," the cripple said, gravely, "that for the time being you are my tenant, and that I have no more right in this house, indeed, not so much right, as one of these policemen. I have sent my servants away, and I am at present staying—in fact, it does not matter much where I am staying. Come along."

The trap was so neatly laid and so coolly worked

that Fenwick could only sit and gasp in his chair, while his two victims walked quietly away in the most natural manner in the world.

"We had better be off," Gurdon whispered. "There is no occasion for us to stay any longer. Let us follow the cripple. By Jove, I never saw anything done more neatly than that!"

CHAPTER XV

FELIX ZARY

IT would have been a comparatively easy matter for the two friends to have slipped out of the house before the cripple came down the stairs accompanied by the young man who called himself Charles Evors. The front door was still open, and there was no one to bar their way. Then it suddenly occurred to Gurdon that by so doing they would betray the secret of the moveable panel which communicated with the house next door.

"It would never do to go away like this," he said, hurriedly. "Besides, it is more than likely that we shall want to use that entrance again. We shall have to run the risk of losing sight of the cripple; anything is better than leaving that panel open for the servants to discover in the morning."

Venner could see for himself at once that there was no help for it, so without any further discussion on the matter, the two men hurried down the stairs, their feet making no noise on the thick carpet, and then they darted through the hole into the house next door. It was only the work of a moment to re-place the panel, but hardly had they done so before

[170]

they heard a confused murmur of voices on the other side. Gurdon pressed his back to the panel until the noise of the voices ceased.

"That was a pretty close call," he said. "Give me the mouldings and I will try to make them secure without any unnecessary noise. I daresay we can get the nails to fit the same holes. Anyway, there must be no hammering, or we shall be pretty sure to rouse the suspicions of the people next door."

It was perhaps fortunate that the mouldings fitted so well, for Gurdon managed to work the nails into the original holes and complete a more or less workmanlike job to his own satisfaction. Certainly, anybody who was not in the secret would never have detected anything wrong with the panels or imagined for a moment that they had been so recently moved.

"That's a good job well done," Venner said.

"Yes, but what do you do it for? In fact, what are you two gentlemen doing here at all?"

The voice came with a startling suddenness. It was an exceedingly clear, melodious voice, yet with a steely ring in it. The two friends wheeled round sharply to find themselves face to face with an exceedingly tall individual, whose length was almost grotesquely added to by the amazing slimness of his figure. In that respect he was not at all unlike the type of human skeleton which one generally expects to find in a travelling circus, or some show of that kind. The man, moreover, was dressed in deep black, which added to his solemnity. He had an exceedingly long, melancholy face, on both sides of which hung a mass of oily-looking black hair; his nose, too, was elongated and thin, and a long drooping moustache concealed his mouth. On the whole his appearance was redeemed from the grotesque by an extraordinary pair of black eyes, which were round and large as those of a Persian cat. Despite the man's exceeding thinness, he conveyed a certain suggestion of strength. At that moment he had a handkerchief between his fingers, and Gurdon could see that his wrists were supple and pliable as if they had been made of indiarubber. Gurdon had heard that sort of hands before described as conjurer's hands. As he looked at them he half expected to see the handkerchief disappear and an orange or apple or something of that kind take its place. Then the stranger coolly walked across the hall and turned up another of the lights. He seemed to be perfectly at home, and conveyed a curious impression to the visitors that he expected to find them there.

"I beg to remind you that you have not yet answered my question," he said. "What are you doing here?"

"Let me answer your question with another," Venner said. "Who are you, and what may you be doing here?"

The man smiled in a peculiar fashion. His big black eyes seemed to radiate sparks; they were luminous and full of vivid fury, though, at the same time, the long horse-like face never for a moment lost its look of profound dejection. They might have been eyes gleaming behind a dull, painted mask.

"We will come to that presently," he said. "For the moment the mention of my name must content you It is just possible that you might have heard the name of Felix Zary."

Venner and Gurdon fairly started. The name of Felix Zary was familiar to them, but only during the last three-quarters of an hour. In fact, that was the name of the man as to whose whereabouts Fenwick had been so anxious to hear. Here was another element in the mystery, which, up to this moment, had not advanced very far towards solution.

"I have heard the name before," Venner said, "but only quite recently—within the last hour, in fact."

"Oh, yes," the stranger said, "I know exactly what you mean. You probably heard it next door when you were listening so intently to the conversation between my friend Charles Le Fenu, the cripple, and that scoundrel who calls himself Fenwick He is exceedingly anxious to know where I am, though without the smallest intention of benefitting me.

Before long, his curiosity will be gratified; but not in the way he thinks."

The latter words came from the speaker's lips with a spitting hiss, such as a cat emits in the presence of a dog. The great round black eyes added intensity to the threat, and rendered the feline simile complete. The prophecy boded ill for Fenwick when at length he and Felix Zary came face to face.

"I see my conjecture is quite right," the stranger went on. "And as to you gentlemen, I have asked your names merely as a matter of courtesy. As a matter of fact I know perfectly well who you are— you are Mr. Gerald Venner and Mr. James Gurdon. But there is one thing I don't know, and that is why you have thrust yourself into this diabolical business. You must be brave men, or absolutely unconscious of the terrible danger you are running. If either of you are friends of Fenwick's——"

"Not for a moment," Venner cried. "You pay us a poor compliment indeed if you take us to be in any way friendly with that scoundrel."

"And yet you are here," Zary went on. "You are spying on the movements of my friend, Le Fenu. You have contrived to obtain possession of the keys of his house for no other purpose. Why?"

Venner paused before he answered the question. He did not recognise the right of this man to put him through a cross-examination. Indeed, it seemed to him, the less he said the better. Perhaps

[174]

FELIX ZARY

Zary saw something of what was going on in his mind, for his big black eyes smiled, though the dejected visage remained the same.

"I see, you do not trust me," he said. "Perhaps you are right to be cautious. Let me ask you another question, assuring you at the same time that I am the friend of Charles Le Fenu and his sisters, and that if necessary I will lay down my life to save them from trouble. Tell me, Mr. Venner, why are you so interested in saving the girl who passes for Fenwick's daughter from her miserable position? Tell me."

Zary came a step or two closer to Venner and looked down into his face with a searching yearning expression in those magnetic black eyes. The appeal to Venner was irresistible. The truth rose to his lips; it refused to be kept back.

"Because," he said slowly, "because she is my wife."

A great sigh of relief came from Zary.

"I am glad of that," he said. "Exceedingly glad. And yet I had suspected something of the kind. It is good for me to know that I am with friends, and that you two are only actuated by the best motives. For some days now I have had you under close observation. I followed you here to-night; indeed, I was in the house when you removed those panels. As a matter of fact, Mr. Gurdon's first involuntary visit here absolutely ruined a carefully laid plan of

mine for getting Mark Fenwick into my hands.
But I will tell you later on all about the mystery of
the furnished dining-room and how and why the
furniture vanished so strangely. When I followed
you here to-night I was quite prepared to shoot you
both if necessary, but some strange impulse came
over me to speak to you and ask you what you were
doing. I am rather glad I did, because I should not
like to have a tragedy on my hands. Now would
you like to come with me as far as my own rooms,
where I shall be in a position to throw a little light
upon a dark place or two?"

Venner and Gurdon clutched eagerly at the suggestion. Without further words, they passed into
the street, and would have walked down the steps
had not Zary detained them.

"One moment," he whispered. "Hang back in
the shadow of the portico. Don't you see that there
are two or three men on the steps of the house next
door? Ah, I can catch the tones of that rascal Fenwick. If only that vile scoundrel knew how close
to him I was at the present moment! But let us
listen. Perhaps we may hear something useful."

It was very still and quiet in the Square now, for
the hour was late, and therefore the voices from the
portico came clear and distinct to the listeners' ears.

"What is the good of it?" one of the voices said.
"Why on earth can't you wait till morning? Le
Fenu has got clear away, and there isn't much chance

of catching him again in a hurry. It was one of the coolest things I have seen for a long time."

"Oh, he doesn't lack brains, or pluck either," Fenwick said. "I should have been proud of a trick like that myself. I ought to have poisoned him when I had the chance. I ought to have got him out of the way without delay. But it seemed such a safe thing to kidnap him and hide him in his own house, where we could go on with our work without the slightest danger or interruption from those accursed police. And then, when Fate played into our hands and we got hold of Evors as well, it looked as if everything was going our way. How you fools ever contrived to let him get the upper hand of you is more than I can understand."

"It was Jones's fault," another voice growled. "He forgot the drug, and we ran clean out of it. Then, I suppose, we got interested over a game of cards, and one way and another, Evors managed to get six or seven hours' sleep without having any of that stuff inside him. Bless me, if it wasn't all like a dream, guv'nor. There we were, interested in our cards, and before we knew where we were our heads were banged together, and I was lying on the floor thinking that the end of the world had come. That fellow has got the strength of the very devil itself."

"Poor weak creature," Fenwick sneered.

"Weak-minded, perhaps, and easily led," the

12   [177]

first speaker said. "But there is not much the matter with him when it comes to fists."

"We can't stop chattering here all night," Fenwick cried. "It is all very well for you men, who don't care so long as you have something to eat and drink. You would be quite satisfied to sit like a lot of hogs in a sty in Le Fenu's house, but he'll certainly be back in the morning with some infernal scheme or other for getting the best of us. Don't you see it is impossible for me any longer to play the part of a tenant of a furnished house, now that the owner of the house is at large again? It is a very fortunate thing, too, in a way, that I can pass all you people off as my servants. Now get away at once and do as I tell you. As for me, I am going to take a cab as far as the old place by the side of the river. In an hour's time I hope to be on my way to Canterbury. Now, you are quite sure you all know what to do? It's confoundedly awkward to have one's plans upset like this, but a clever man always has an alternative scheme on hand, and I've got mine. There, that will do. Be off at once."

"That's all very well, guv'nor," another voice said. "It is easy enough to put the door on the latch and turn out of the crib, leaving it empty, but what about the girl in the white dress? I ain't very scrupulous as a rule, but it seems rather cruel to leave the poor kid behind and she not more than half right in her head."

"Devil fly away with the girl," Fenwick said passionately. "We can pick her up at any time we want to. Besides, I think I can see a way to arrange for her and a method of getting her out of the house within the next hour. It was no bad thing for men who get their living as we do when some genius invented motor cars. Now do go along or we shall never finish."

The little group on the portico steps melted away, and one by one the slouching figures vanished into the darkness. Zary stepped on to the pavement, and proceeded to open the front door of the next house. It yielded to his touch.

"I am glad of this," he said; "and, really, we owe quite a debt of gratitude to the tender-hearted ruffian who was averse to leaving a poor girl in this house all alone. We will spare Fenwick the trouble of any inconvenience so far as she is concerned."

So saying, Zary proceeded to walk up the stairs, turning up the lights as he went. He called the name of Beth softly three or four times, and presently a door opened overhead and a girl in a white dress came out. A pleased smile spread over her face as she looked over the balusters and noted the caller.

"Felix," she said softly, "is it really you? I have been hiding myself in my room because I was terrified, and after Charles had gone those men quarrelled so terribly among themselves! I suppose Charles forgot all about me in the excitement of the moment."

[179]

"Oh, no, he didn't, dear one," Zary said very gently. "He would have come back to you in any case. But I am going to take you away from this house where you have been so miserable; I am going to see that you are not molested in the future."

"That is all very well," Venner interposed, "but where can the young lady go? She is quite alone and helpless, and unless you have some reputable female relation——"

"It is not a matter of my relations," Zary smiled. ' Miss Beth will go to one who is her natural protector, and one who will watch over her welfare with unceasing care. To put it quite plainly, Miss Beth is going to the Great Empire Hotel, and you are going to take her. To-night she will sleep under the same roof as her sister."

Venner was just a little startled by the suddenness of the proposal, yet, on the whole, the suggestion was an exceedingly natural one, for who was better capable of looking after the unfortunate Beth than her own sister? True, the hour was exceedingly late; but then a huge place like the Great Empire Hotel was practically open night and day, and a request at one o'clock in the morning that a guest in the house should be awakened to receive another guest would be nothing in the way of a novelty.

' Very well," Venner said. "Let her put on her hat and jacket, and she can come with me at once."

CHAPTER XVI

FENWICK MOVES AGAIN

BETH raised no objection to the programme; indeed, the suggestion seemed to fill her with delight. She would not be a moment, she said. She would put certain necessaries in a handbag, and come back for the rest of her wardrobe on the morrow. Venner had expressed a desire that Zary should accompany him, but the latter shook his head emphatically.

"No, no," he said; "you are going alone. As for me, I have important business on hand which will not brook the slightest delay. Mr. Gurdon had best return to his own rooms; and, for his own sake, I would advise him to keep in the middle of the road. You two little know the danger you incurred when you decided to thrust your head into this hornet's nest. Now I will see you both off the premises and put out all the lights. I may mention in passing that I have a latchkey to this place."

A few minutes later Venner found himself walking down the deserted streets with his fair little companion hanging on his arm. She chattered to him very prettily and daintily, but there was a great deal in her remarks which conveyed nothing to him at all. She constantly alluded to matters of which he was entirely ignorant, apparently taking it for granted that he was *au fait* with what she was saying. It struck Venner that though not exactly mentally deficient, she was suffering from weakness of intellect, brought about, probably, by some great shock or terrible sorrow. On the whole, he was not sorry to find himself in the great hall of the hotel, the lights of which were still burning, and where several guests were lounging for a final cigar.

"I know it is exceedingly late," Venner said to the clerk, "but it is quite imperative that this young lady should see Miss Fenwick. Will you be good enough to send up to her room and tell her how sorry I am to disturb her at this time of night, but that the matter is exceedingly urgent?"

"Miss Fenwick is not in, sir," came the startling response. "She went out shortly after eleven o'clock, and she told me that she might not be back for some considerable time. You see, she wanted to be quite sure that she could get back into the hotel at any time she returned. Oh, no doubt she is returning, or I don't suppose for a moment that she would have asked me all those questions."

The information was sufficiently disturbing, but there was no help for it. All they had to do was to sit down and wait patiently till Vera came back. They were not in the least likely to attract any attention, seeing that several men in evening dress together with their wives were seated in the hall for a final chat after the theatre or some party or reception. In her long white frock, partially concealed by a cloak and hood, Beth would have easily passed for a girl fresh from a theatre or a dance. It was a long weary wait of over an hour, and Venner was feeling distinctly anxious, when the big folding doors at the end of the hall opened and Vera's tall, graceful figure emerged.

"Here is your sister," Venner said. There was just a stern suggestion in his voice. "Now, you are not to cry or make any scene, you are not to attract any attention to yourself, but take it all for granted. You can be as emotional as you please when you are alone together in your room."

Vera came across the hall in a jaded, weary way, as if she were thoroughly tired out. Her face flushed a little as she recognised Venner. Then she looked at his companion and almost paused, while the blood ebbed from her face, leaving it deadly pale.

"Gerald," she whispered. "Gerald and Beth. What does it mean? What strange thing has happened to bring you both together here."

"Don't make a scene, for goodness' sake," Venner said. "Take it as calmly as you can. Unless you are self-possessed, your sister is sure to give way, and that is the last thing in the world to be desired. I cannot possibly stop now to tell you all the extraordinary things which have happened to-night.

[183]

Let it be sufficient to say that it is absolutely imperative that you give your sister shelter, and that nobody but yourself should know where she is."

"But how did you find her?" Vera asked. "And who was it suggested that you should bring her to me?"

"Let me just mention the name of Zary," Venner replied. "Oh, I can come round here to-morrow and tell you all about it. If you think that there is any possible danger——"

"Of course there is danger," Vera said. "Mr. Fenwick may be back at any moment. He does not know that I am aware that my sister is even alive. If he became acquainted with the fact that we had come together again, all my plans would be absolutely ruined, and my three years of self-sacrifice would be in vain."

"I am afraid you must run the risk now," Venner said. "At any rate, your sister will have to stay here till the morning. It is perhaps a good thing that she does not understand what is going on."

Apparently the girl had no real comprehension of all the anxieties and emotions of which she was unconsciously the centre. She was holding her sister's hand now and smiling tenderly into her face, like a child who has found a long-lost friend.

"You may rest assured on one point," Venner went on. "For the present there is not the slightest reason to fear Fenwick. He has had a great shock to-night; all his plans have been upset, and he finds himself in a position of considerable danger. I know for a fact that he is going straight away to Canterbury, and probably by this time he is on his way there. According to what your mysterious friend Zary said, he had some plan cut and dried for providing for your sister's safety to-morrow. Now take the poor child to bed, for she is half asleep already, and when once you have made her comfortable I want you to come down again and have a few words with me. You need not hesitate; surely a man can talk to his wife whenever he pleases—and, besides, there are several people here who show not the slightest signs of going to bed yet."

"Very well," Vera said. "Come along, dear, I see you are dreadfully sleepy—so sleepy that you do not appear to recognise the sister you have met for the first time for three years."

Venner had time to smoke the best part of a cigar before Vera reappeared. They took a seat in a secluded corner of the hall, where it was possible to talk without interruption.

"Now, please, tell me everything," the girl said.

"I am afraid that is impossible," Venner replied. "This is one of the most extraordinary and complicated businesses that I ever heard of. In the first place, I came to England, weary and worn out with my search for you, and half inclined to abandon it altogether. In the very last place in the world where I expect to meet you, I come in contact with you in this hotel. I find that you are being passed off as the daughter of one of the greatest scoundrels who ever cheated the gallows. But that does not check my faith in you. I had kept my trust in you intact. Ever since you left me on the day of our marriage I have had nothing but a few words to explain your amazing conduct; and now here am I doing my best to free you from the chains that bind you, and all the while you seem to be struggling to hug those chains about you and to baffle all my efforts. Why do you do this? What is the secret that you conceal so carefully from the man who would do anything to save you from trouble, from the man you profess to love? If you do care for me——"

"Oh, I do indeed," Vera whispered. There were tears in her eyes now and her cheeks were wet. "It is not for my own sake—it is for the sake of the poor girl upstairs. I had promised to say nothing of that to anyone—to try and save her—and I left you and ran the risk of for ever forfeiting your affection. But if Beth is better in the morning I will try to get her to absolve me from my promise and induce her——"

"She is not capable of giving a promise of rescinding it," Venner said. "Don't you think it would be far better if, instead, you discussed the matter with your brother, Charles Le Fenu?"

FENWICK MOVES AGAIN

"So you know all about that?" Vera cried.

"Yes, I do. I have seen him to-night. Gurdon has already had an interview with him—an interview that almost cost him his life. We have been having some pretty fine adventures the last two or three days—but if it all ends in saving you and lifting this cloud from your life I shall be well content. I am not going to ask you to go into explanations now, because I see they would be distasteful to you, and because you have given some foolish promise which you are loth to break. But tell me one thing. You said just now that you had not seen your sister for three years, though she has been living with your brother, whom you visited quite recently."

"That is easily explained," Vera said. "It was deemed necessary to tell Beth one or two fictions with a view to easing her mind and leaving her still with some slight shadow of hope, which was the only means of preventing her reason from absolutely leaving her. These fictions entailed my keeping out of the way. Beth is exceedingly different from me, as you know."

"Indeed, she is," said Venner, smiling for the first time. "But does it not strike you as an extraordinary thing that I should be fighting in this fierce way in your behalf, and that you should be placing negative obstacles in my way all the time? I won't worry you any more to-night, dearest— you look tired and worn out. You had better go to your own room, and we can discuss this matter further in the morning."

It was dark enough and sheltered enough in that secluded corner of the hall for Venner to draw the girl towards him and kiss her lips passionately. Just for a brief moment Vera lay in her husband's arms; then, with a little sigh, she disengaged herself and disappeared slowly up the stairs.

She had placed Beth in her own room, which they would share together for that night, at any rate. The younger girl was sleeping placidly; there was a smile on her face—her lips were parted like those of one who is utterly and entirely happy. She made a fair picture as she lay there, with her yellow hair streaming over her shoulders. She just murmured something in her sleep, as Vera bent over her and brushed her forehead lightly with her lips.

"Oh, I wonder how long this cloud will last!" Vera murmured—"how much longer I shall be till I am free! How terrible it is to have the offer of a good man's love, and be compelled to spoil it as I do, or, at least, as I appear to do. And yet I should be a happy woman if I could only throw off these shackles——"

Vera paused, unable to say more, for something seemed to rise in her throat and choke her. She was utterly tired and worn out, almost too tired to undress and get into bed—and yet once her head was on the pillow she could not sleep; she tossed and

turned wearily. All London seemed to be transformed into one noisy collection of clocks. The noise
and the din seemed to stun Vera and throb through
her head like the beating of hammers on her brain.
She fell off presently into a troubled sleep, which
was full of dreams. It seemed to her that she was
locked in a safe, and that somebody outside was
hammering at the walls to let her free. Then she
became conscious of the fact that somebody really
was knocking at the door. As Vera stumbled out
of bed a clock somewhere struck three. She flicked
up the light and opened the door. A sleepy-looking
chambermaid handed her a note, which was marked
"Urgent" on the envelope. With a thrill, she recognised the handwriting of Mark Fenwick. What
new disaster was here? she wondered.

"Is there anybody waiting for an answer?"
she asked tremblingly. "Is the messenger downstairs?"

"Yes, miss," the sleepy chambermaid replied.
"It was brought by a gentleman in a motor. I told
him you were in bed and fast asleep, but he said it
was of the greatest importance and I was to wake
you. Perhaps you had better read it."

With a hand that trembled terribly, Vera tore open
the envelope. There were only two or three lines
there in Fenwick's stiff handwriting; they were curt
and discourteous, and very much to the point.
They ran as follows—

"I am writing you this from Canterbury, where I have been for the last hour, and where I have important business. I have sent one of the cars over for you, and you are to come back at once. Whatever happens, see that you obey me."

"You will tell the gentleman I will be down in a few moments," Vera said. "I will not detain him any longer than I can help."

"What is to be done?" the girl wondered directly she was alone. She felt that she dared not disobey this command; she would have to go at all costs. She knew by bitter experience that Fenwick was not the man to brook contradiction. Besides, at the present moment it would be a fatal thing to rouse his suspicions. And yet, she felt how impossible it was for her to leave Beth here in the circumstances. Nor could she see her way to call up Venner at this hour and explain what had happened. All she could do was to scribble a short note to him with a view to explaining the outline of the new situation. Ten minutes later she was downstairs in the hall, where she found the man awaiting her. He was clad in furs, his motor cap was pulled over his eyes as if he shrank from observation; but all the same Vera recognised him.

"So it is you, Jones," she said. "Do you know that you have been sent all the way from Canterbury to fetch me at this time in the morning? It is perfectly monstrous that I should be dragged out of bed like this, perfectly disgraceful!"

"I don't know anything about that, miss," the man said sullenly. "It is the guv'nor's orders, and he gave me pretty plainly to understand that he would want to know the reason why if I came back without you. Don't blame me."

"I'm not blaming you at all," Vera said, coldly. "Nor am I going to stand here bandying words with you. I will just go to my room and put on a fur coat—then I shall be ready."

"Very well, miss. That's the proper way to take it. But where is the other young lady?"

Vera's heart fairly stood still for a moment. Fenwick's note had said nothing about her sister, though this man seemed to be aware of the fact that she was here. There was only one thing for it, and that was to lie boldly and without hesitation. She looked the speaker in the face in blank astonishment.

"I fail to understand you," she said. "There is nobody here but me; there could be nobody here but me. And now I have nothing further to say. One moment and I will be with you."

CHAPTER XVII

Merton Grange

VERA came down a few moments later ready for her journey. Now that she had had time to think matters over, she was looking forward with some dread to her forthcoming interview with Mark Fenwick. Surely something out of the common must have taken place, or he would never have sent for her at such an extraordinary time, and Vera had always one thing to contend with; she had not forgotten, in fact, she could not forget, that for the last three years she had been engaged in plotting steadily against the man by whose name she was known. Moreover, she was not in the least blind to Fenwick's astuteness, and there was always the unpleasant feeling that he might be playing with her. She had always loathed and detested this man from the bottom of her soul; there were times when she doubted whether or not he was a relation of hers. As far as Vera knew, he was supposed to be her mother's half-brother, and so much as this she owed the man— he had come to her at the time when she was nearly destitute, and in no position to turn her back on his advances. That it suited Fenwick to have a well-bred and graceful girl about him, she knew perfectly well. But long before would she have left him, only she was quite certain that Fenwick was at the bottom of the dreadful business which had resulted in Beth's deplorable state of mind.

But as to all this, Vera could say nothing at the moment. All she had to do now was to guard herself against a surprise on the part of Fenwick. She had been startled by the mere suggestion on the part of her companion that she had not been alone at the Great Empire Hotel. Much as she would have liked illumination on this point, she had the prudence to say nothing. Silently she stepped into the car, a big Mercedes with great glaring eyes; silently, too, she was borne along the empty streets. It wanted yet three hours to daylight, and Vera asked how long they would be in reaching their destination. Her companion put on speed once the outskirts of town were reached. Vera could feel the cold air streaming past her face like a touch of ice.

"Oh, about an hour and a half," the driver said carelessly. "I suppose it is about fifty-five miles. With these big lamps and these clear roads we'll just fly along."

The speaker touched a lever, and the car seemed to jump over the smooth roads. The hedges and houses flew by and the whole earth seemed to vibrate to the roar and rattle of the car. It was Vera's first experience of anything like racing, and she held her breath in terror.

13   [193]

"What would happen if a wheel gave way?" she asked. She had muffled her face in her veil, so that she could breathe more freely now. "Surely a pace like this is dangerous."

"You have to take risks, miss," the driver said coolly. "We are moving at about five and forty miles an hour now. I'm very sorry if it makes you nervous, but my instructions were to get back as quickly as possible."

"I don't feel exactly nervous," Vera said.

"Oh, no, you are getting over it. Everybody does after the first few moments. When you get used to the motion you will like it. It gives you a feeling like a glass of champagne when your're tired. You'll see for yourself presently."

Surely enough Vera did see for herself presently. As the feeling of timidity and unfamiliarity wore off she began to be conscious of a glow in her blood as if she were breathing some pure mountain air. The breeze fairly sang past her ears, the car ran more smoothly now with nothing to check its movement, and Vera could have sung aloud for the very joy of living. She began to understand the vivid pleasure of motoring; she could even make an excuse for those who travelled the high roads at top speed. Long before she had reached her destination she had forgotten everything else beside the pure delight of that trip in the dark.

"Here we are, miss," the driver said at length,

as he turned in through a pair of huge iron gates. "It's about a mile up the avenue to the house—but you can see the lights in front of you."

"Have we really come all that way in this short time?" Vera asked. "It only seems about ten minutes since we started."

The driver made no reply, and Vera had little time to look curiously about her. So far as she could judge, they were in a large park, filled with magnificent oak trees. Here and there through the gloom she seemed to see shadowy figures flitting, and these she assumed to be deer. On each side of the avenue rose a noble line of elm trees, beyond which were the gardens; then a series of terraces, culminating in a fine house of the late Tudor period. Beyond question, it was a fine old family mansion in which Fenwick had taken up his quarters for the present.

"What do you call the place?" Vera asked.

"This is Merton Grange, miss," the driver explained. "It belongs to Lord Somebody or another, I forget his name. Anyway, he has had to let the house for a time and go abroad. You had better get out here, and I'll take the car to the garage. I wouldn't ring the bell if I were you, miss. I'd just walk straight into the house. You'll find the door open and the guv'nor ready to receive you. He is sure to have heard the car coming up the drive."

[195]

Vera descended and walked up the flight of steps which led to a noble portico. Here was a great massive oak door, which looked as if it required the strength of a strong man to open it, but it yielded to Vera's touch, and a moment later she was standing in the great hall.

Tired as she was and frightened as she was feeling now, she could not but admire the beauty and symmetry of the place. Like most historic mansions of to-day, the place had been fitted with electric light, and a soft illuminating flood of it filled the hall. It was a magnificent oak-panelled apartment, filled with old armor and trophies, and lined with portraits of the owner's ancestors. It seemed to Vera that anybody might be happy here. It also seemed strange to her that a man of Fenwick's type should choose a place like this for his habitation. She was destined to know later what Fenwick had in his mind when he came here.

Vera's meditations were cut short by the appearance of the man himself. To her surprise she noted that he was dressed in some blue material, just like an engineer on board ship. His hands were grimy, too, as if he had been indulging in some mechanical work. He nodded curtly to the girl.

"So you've come at last," he said. "I daresay you wonder why I sent for you. There is a little room at the back yonder, behind the drawing-room, that I have turned into a study. Go in there and wait for me, and I'll come to you as soon as I have washed my hands I hope you have brought all you want with you; for there is precious little accommodation for your sex here at present. You can take your choice of bed-rooms—there are enough of those and to spare. I have something serious to say to you."

With a sinking at her heart Vera passed into the little room that Fenwick had pointed out to her. At any other time she would have admired the old furniture and the elegant refined simplicity of it all; now she had other things to think of. She stood warming her hands at the fire till Fenwick came in and carefully closed the door behind him.

"Now we can get to business," he said. "I daresay you wonder why I sent for you instead of leaving you in London for the present. Up to now I have always regarded you as perfectly safe—indeed, I thought you were sufficiently grateful to me for all my kindness to you. I find I am mistaken."

Vera looked up with a challenge in her eyes. She knew that she had something to face now, and she meant to see it through without showing the white feather. She was braced up and ready, now that the moment for action had come.

"Have you ever really been kind to me?" she challenged. "I mean, have you really been kind to me for my own sake, and out of pure good-nature? I very much doubt it."

"'This is your gratitude," Fenwick sneered. "I
think we had better understand one another."

"I would give a great deal to understand you,"
the girl said boldly. "But we are wasting time
fencing here like this, and I am very tired. You
sent for me at this extraordinary hour, and I came.
I have every right to know why you asked me to
come here."

"Sit down," Fenwick growled. "I sent for you
because I did not trust you. I sent for you because
you have betrayed your promise. You are doing
something that you told me you would not do."

"And what is that?" Vera asked.

"Just as if you did not know. Let us go back
a bit, back three years and a half ago. Your father
was alive in those days; it was just before he met
his death in Mexico."

"I remember perfectly well," Vera said, quietly.
"I am not likely to forget the time. Pray continue"

"Have patience please, I am coming to it all in
time. Your father died more or less mysteriously,
but there is not the shadow of a doubt that he was
murdered. Nobody knows how he was murdered,
but a good many people behind the scenes can guess
why. The thing was hushed up, possibly because
the tragedy took place in so remote a corner of the
world—possibly because the authorities were bribed.
Tell me the name of the man, or, at least, tell me

the name of the one man who was with your father at the time of his death."

Vera's face paled slightly, but she kept her eyes steadily fixed on her companion's face. She began to understand where the point of the torture was coming in.

"I will not affect to misunderstand you," she said. "The man who was with my father at that time was Mr. Charles Evors. He was a sort of pupil of my father's, and had more than once accompanied him on his excursions. You want to insinuate that my father met his death at the hands of this young man, who, overcome by certain temptation and a desire to obtain the secret of the Four Finger Mine, murdered his master?"

"I am in a position to prove it," Fenwick said sternly. "I have given you practical proof of it, more than once. Why should I have interfered in the way I did, unless it was that I desired to save you pain? I could have brought the whole thing into the light of day, but I refrained from doing so because, it seemed to me, nothing could be gained by bringing the criminal to justice. I had another reason, too, as you know."

"Yes, I am aware of that," Vera said. "I could never make it out—I could never really believe that Charles Evors was guilty of that dreadful crime. He was so frank and true, so kind to everybody! I know he was weak—I know that he had been sent away from England because he had fallen into bad company; I know, too, that he was a little fond of drink. There was only one point on which he was reticent—he never spoke much about his people; but I rather gathered that they were in a high position."

"They were," Fenwick grinned. "You'd be surprised if you knew how high a position. But go on."

"I was saying that I could not credit Charles Evors with such a crime. A man who is so fond of children, so sympathetic to things weaker than himself, could not have taken the life of a fellow-creature. He was fond of my father, too, but that was not the strangest feature of the mystery. Do you suppose for a moment that the man who was engaged to be married to my sister could have laid violent hands on her father?"

"But he did do it," Fenwick cried impatiently. "Otherwise why did he vanish so mysteriously? Why did he go away and leave us to infer that he had perished at sea? It was the kindest thing we could do to let your sister think that her lover was dead, though the shock seems to have deprived her of her reason; and, though I acted all for the best, your brother chose to proclaim me an abandoned scoundrel, and to say that your father's death lay at my door. You know why it became necessary for you to remain with me and treat your brother henceforth as a stranger. You volunteered to do it, you volunteered to turn your back on your family and remain with me. Why did you do so?"

No reply came from Vera's lips. It seemed to her that her safest course lay in silence. To her great relief, Fenwick went on without waiting for an answer.

"Now I am coming to my point," he said. "You have broken faith with me. Three or four times since we came to England you have seen your brother. You have seen him by stealth; you know all about that strange household in Portsmouth Square where he chooses to hide himself under the name of Bates. I want to know why it is that you have chosen to break your word with me? I have had you watched to-night, and I have learned all your movements by means of the telephone. You will stay down here during my pleasure. If you fail to do so, or if you try to deceive me again, as sure as I stand here at the present moment I will betray Charles Evors into the hands of the police. Now look me in the face and answer my question truthfully. Do you know where that young man is?"

It was fortunate for Vera that she could reply in the negative. A few more hours, perhaps, and she might have been able to afford the information; but, luckily for her, the startling events that had recently taken place in Portsmouth Square were not known to her in their entirety. She could look Fenwick in the face.

"I don't," she said. "I have never seen him since that fateful morning—but I don't care to go into that. I admit that I have seen my brother. I admit, too, that I have seen my sister; the temptation to find them and see them once more was too strong for me. You will not be surprised to find that I have some natural feelings left. It is not so very extraordinary."

Fenwick shot a suspicious glance at Vera, but she was gazing into the fire with a thoughtful look. She was acting her part splendidly; she was deceiving this man who, as a rule, could read the thoughts of most people.

"Perhaps you are right," he said doubtfully. "But to make assurance doubly sure you are going to help me out of a difficulty. I suppose you have not forgotten Felix Zary?"

"No," Vera said, in a curiously low voice. "I have not forgotten my father's faithful companion. I should very much like to see him again. If you know where he is——"

"Oh, I know where he is," Fenwick said with a laugh. "We will have him down here as a pleasant surprise. That is all I want you to do—I want you to write a letter to Zary, telling him that you are in great trouble, and asking him to come down here and see you at once. I should like you to write that letter now."

CHAPTER XVIII

A Couple of Visitors

SOMETHING in the tone of Fenwick's voice caused Vera to look up hastily. Perhaps it was her imagination that in the unsteady light of the flickering fire his face seemed to have changed almost beyond recognition. The features were dark and murderous and the eyes were full of a lust for vengeance. It was only just for a moment—then the man became his normal self again, just as if nothing had happened. A violent shudder passed over Vera's frame, but Fenwick appeared to notice nothing of this.

"You want me to write that letter now?" she asked.

"At once," Fenwick responded. "I don't mind telling you that I am in great trouble over business matters; there is a conspiracy on foot amongst certain people to get me into trouble. I may even find myself inside the walls of a prison. The man who can save me from all this is your friend, Felix Zary. Unfortunately for me, the man has the bad taste to dislike me exceedingly. He seems to think that I was in some way responsible for your father's death. And, as you know, he loved your father with a devotion that was almost dog-like. If I could get Zary down here I should have no difficulty in convincing him that he was wrong. But he would not come near the place so long as he knew that I was present; so, therefore, I want you to write to him and conceal the fact that I am on the premises. Directly he gets your letter he will come at once."

"I have not the slightest doubt of it," Vera said slowly. "There is nothing that Zary would not do for one of us, if you will assure me that you mean no harm by him——"

"Harm?" Fenwick shouted. "What harm could I do the man? Didn't I tell you just now that I want him to do me a service? One does not generally ill-treat those who are in a position to bestow favors. Now sit down like the good girl that you are, and write that letter at once. Then you can go to bed."

"I will write it in the morning," Vera said. "Surely there cannot be all this desperate hurry. If the letter is written before the post goes out to-morrow afternoon it will be in good time. I am much too tired to do it now."

Just for a moment Fénwick's eyes blazed angrily again. It seemed to Vera that the man was about to burst forth into a storm of passion The hot words did not come, however, for Fenwick restrained himself. Perhaps he was afraid of going a little too far; perhaps he was afraid of arousing Vera's suspicions, and thus defeating his own object by a refusal on her part to write the letter. He knew from past experience that she could be as firm of purpose as himself if she chose.

"Very well," he said, with an almost grotesque attempt at good-humor. "You look very tired to-night, and I daresay you have had a fatiguing journey —and, after all, there is no great hurry. I will show you up to the room which I have set apart for your use."

Vera was only too glad to get away. Despite her strange surroundings, and despite the sense of coming danger, she threw herself on the bed and slept the sleep of utter exhaustion. It was getting towards noon before she came back to herself, invigorated and refreshed by her long rest.

So far as the girl could see, there were no servants in the house at present besides an old retainer of the family and her husband. Fenwick had made some excuse about the staff of domestics who were to follow later on; but up to now he only had about him the men whom Vera had known more or less well for the last two years. The meals appeared to be served in a remarkably irregular fashion; even the lunch was partaken of hurriedly by Fenwick, who pleaded the pressure of business.

"I can't stop a minute," he said. "I have more to do now than I can manage. I should just like to have a look at that letter that you have written to Zary. There is no excuse for not doing it now, and I want to put it in the post-bag."

"Very well," Vera said serenely. "If you will come with me to the library you will see exactly what I write. I know you are a suspicious man and that you don't trust anybody, therefore I shall be very glad for you to know that I have carried out your request to the letter."

Fenwick laughed as if something had pleased him. Nevertheless, he looked over Vera's shoulder until she had penned the last word. She slowly folded up the communication and sealed it.

"How am I to address the envelope?" she said. "I have not the slightest idea where Zary is to be found. For all I know to the contrary, he may not even be in England."

"Oh, yes, he is," Fenwick chuckled. "He is in London at the present moment. If you address that letter, 17, Paradise Street, Camberwell, Zary will be in receipt of it to-morrow morning."

Vera wrote the address boldly and firmly, and handed the letter with more or less contempt to her companion. She wanted him to feel that she held his suspicions with scorn. She wanted him to know that so far as she was concerned here was an end of the matter. Nevertheless, she followed him carelessly from the room and saw him place the letter, together with others, on the hall table. A moment later he had vanished, and she was left alone to act promptly. She did not hesitate for a moment; she made her way back to the drawing-room and addressed a second envelope to the house in Paradise Street, into which envelope she slipped a blank sheet of notepaper. Then she stamped the envelope and made her way back cautiously to the hall. There was a chance of being discovered, a chance that she was being watched, but she had to run the risk of that. She was crossing the hall freely and carelessly now, and so contrived as to sweep the mass of letters with her sleeve to the floor, exclaiming at her own clumsiness as she did so. Like a flash she picked out the one letter that she needed and swiftly exchanged it for the other. A moment later she was out of doors, with the danger-ous communication in her pocket.

So far as she could see, she had succeeded be-yond her wildest expectations. It was only a simple ruse, but like most simple things, generally success-ful. Vera was trembling from head to foot now, but the fresh air of the park and the broad, beautiful solitude of it soothed her jarred nerves, and brought back a more contented frame of mind. Her spirits rose as she walked along.

"I am glad I did that," she told herself, "I may be mistaken, but I firmly believe that I have saved Zary's life. Had he come down here he would never have left the place again. And yet there is danger for him still, and I must warn him of it.

I must manage to communicate in some way with Gerald. I wonder if it would be safe to send him a telegram from the village. I wonder, too, in what direction the village lies. Still, I have all the afternoon before me, and a brisk walk will do me good."

With a firm, elastic step, Vera walked across the grass in the direction of a wood, beyond which she could see the slope of the high road. She had hardly entered the wood before she heard a voice calling her name, and to her intense delight she turned to find herself face to face with Venner.

"Oh, this is glorious," she said, as she placed both her hands in his. "But do you think that it is quite safe for you to come here so soon? For all I know, I may be followed.

"I don't think so," Venner said. "Now let me take you in my arms and kiss you. Let us sit down here in this snug corner and try to imagine that we are back in the happy days when no cloud loomed between us, and we were looking forward to many joyous years together. We will talk mundane matters presently."

Vera yielded to the ecstasy of the moment. Everything was so dark and melancholy that it seemed a sin to lose a gleam of sunshine like this. But the time crept on and the November sun was sinking, and it was borne in upon Vera that she must get back to the house again. Very gently, she disengaged herself from Venner's embrace.

A COUPLE OF VISITORS

"We must be really practical now," she said. "Tell me what has happened since I left the hotel last night?"

"So far as I can see, nothing," Venner replied. "I asked for you this morning, and to my surprise I found that you had vanished in the dead of the night with a mysterious chauffeur and a Mercedes car. By great good luck I found a policeman who had made a note of the number of the car, after which I went to the makers, or rather the agents of the makers, and it was quite easy to find out that the Mercedes in question had recently been delivered to Mr. Mark Fenwick's order at Merton Grange near Canterbury. After that, you will not be surprised to find that I came down here as soon as possible, and that I have been hiding here with a pair of field-glasses trying to get a glimpse of you."

"That was very interesting," Vera laughed. "But tell me about my sister. I am so anxious over her."

"No reason to be," said Venner. "I have seen to that. She has gone back to your brother."

"Oh, I am so glad. Now listen to me carefully."

She went on with some detail to tell the story of her last night's experiences. She spoke of Felix Zary and the letter which she had been more or less compelled to write to him. Also, she described the ruse by which the letter had been regained.

"Now you must go and see this Zary," she said.

"Tell him that you come from me, and tell him all about the letter. Mind, he must reply to my letter just as if it had reached him in the ordinary way through the post, because, as you see, I shall have to show the answer to Mr. Fenwick, and I want to lull his suspicions to rest entirely. You may find Zary a little awkward at first."

"I don't think I shall," Venner smiled. "In fact, he and I are already acquainted. But I am not going to tell you anything about that; you prefer to keep your secrets as far as I am concerned, and I am going to guard mine for the present. I am working to put an end to all this mystery and bother, and I am going to do it my own way. Anyway, I will see Zary for you and tell him exactly what has happened. In fact, I will go to town this evening for the express purpose. Then I will come back in the morning and meet you here the same time to-morrow afternoon "

They parted at that, and Vera made her way back to the house. She saw that the letters were no longer on the hall table, and therefore she concluded that they had been posted. She assumed a quiet, dignified manner during the rest of the evening. She treated Fenwick more or less distantly. as if she were still offended with his suspicions. Fenwick, on the other hand, was more than usually amiable. Something had evidently pleased him, and he appeared to be doing his best to wipe out the unpleasant impression of the morning. Vera felt quite easy in her mind now; she knew that her ruse had been absolutely successful. All the same, she ignored Fenwick's request of a little music, professing to be exceedingly tired, which, indeed, was no more than the truth.

"I am going to bed quite early to-night," she said. "I have been sleeping very indifferently of late."

It was barely ten before she was in her room, and there she lay, oblivious of all that was taking place around her, till she woke presently with an idea that she could hear the sound of hammering close by. As she sat up in bed with all her senses about her, she could hear the great stable clock strike the hour of three. Her ears had not deceived her; the sound of metal meeting metal in a kind of musical chink came distinct and clear. Then from somewhere near she could hear voices. The thing was very strange, seeing that Fenwick was a business man pure and simple, and that he had never confessed to any knowledge of mechanics. It came back to her mind now, that directly she had entered the house Fenwick had greeted her in a suit of blue overalls which she understood men who followed mechanical pursuits generally wore. She recollected, too, that his hands were black and grimy. What could be going on, and why had she seen nothing of this during the day-time? She could comprehend men sitting up all night and working in a factory, but surely there could be no occasion for a thing like this in a private house, unless, perhaps, Fenwick and his satellites were engaged in some pursuit that needed careful concealment from the eyes of the law.

'It would be well, perhaps, Vera thought, if she could find out what was going on. The discovery might be the means of putting another weapon into her hands. She rose from her bed and partially dressed herself. Then, with a pair of slippers on her feet and a dark wrap round her shoulders, she stole into the corridor. A dim light was burning there, so that she had no fear of being discovered, especially as the walls were draped with tapestry, and here and there armored figures stood, which afforded a capital means of concealment. As Vera sidled along she noticed that at the end of the corridor was a small room down a flight of steps. From where she stood she could see into the room, the door of which was open. Fenwick stood there apparently engaged in superintending the melting of metal in a crucible over a fire, which was driven to white heat by a pair of bellows. The rest of his gang seemed to be doing something on an iron table with moulds and discs. Vera could see the gleam of yellow metal, then somebody closed the door of the room and she could learn no more. It was all very strange and mysterious, and there was a furtive air about it which did not suggest honesty of purpose. There was nothing more for it now except for Vera to return to her room, with a determination to see the inside of that little apartment the first time that the coast was clear.

She hurried along back to her own room, and had almost succeeded in reaching it, when she came face to face with a man who had stepped out of a doorway so suddenly that the two figures came almost in contact. A fraction of a second later a hand was laid over Vera's mouth, while another grasped her wrist; then she saw that the intruder had been joined by a companion.

"Please don't say a word, miss; and, whatever you do, don't call out," one of the men whispered. "We know all about you and who you are. Believe me, we are here to do you the greatest service in our power. My colleague will tell you the same"

"But who are you?" Vera asked, as the man removed his hand from her mouth. Her courage had come back to her now. "Why do you come in this fashion?"

"My name is Egan," the stranger said, "and this is my companion, Grady. We are New York detectives, over here on important business. The man we are after is Mark Fenwick."

CHAPTER XIX

PHANTOM GOLD

VERA had entirely recovered her self-possession by this time. She was able to regard the men coolly and critically. There was nothing about them that suggested anything wrong or underhand; on the contrary, the girl rather liked their appearance. All the same it was a strange and unique experience; and though Vera had been through a series of trials and tribulations, she thrilled now as she recognised how near she had been to the man who was thus running himself into the hands of justice.

"But how can you know anything about me?" she said. "You surely do not mean to say that you suspect——"

"Not at all, miss," Egan said, civilly. "Only, you see, it is always our business to know a great deal more than people imagine. I hope you won't suppose that we are going to take any advantage of our position here, or that we want you to betray Mr. Fenwick into our hands; but since we have been unfortunate enough to be discovered by you, we will ask you to go so far as to say nothing to Mr.

Fenwick. If you tell him, you will be doing considerable harm to a great many deserving people who have suffered terribly at that man's hands. I think you understand."

Vera understood only too well, and yet her delicate sense of honor was slightly disturbed at the idea of continuing there without warning Fenwick of the danger that overshadowed him. Personally, she would have liked to have told him exactly how he stood, and given him the opportunity to get away. Perhaps Egan saw something of this in Vera's face, for he went on to speak again.

"I know it isn't very nice for you, miss," he said, "and I am not surprised to see you hesitate; but seeing that Mr. Fenwick has done you as much harm as anybody else——"

"How do you know that?" Vera exclaimed.

"Well, you see, it is our business to know everything. I feel quite certain that on reflection you will do nothing to defeat the ends of justice."

"No," Vera said, thoughtfully. "In any case, it cannot much matter. You are here to arrest Mr. Fenwick, and you probably know where he is to be found at the present moment."

"There you are wrong, miss," Grady said. "We are not in a position at present to lay hands on our man. We came here prepared to take a few risks—but I don't suppose you would care to hear anything about our methods. It will be a great favor to us if you will retire to your room and stay there till morning."

Vera went off without any further ado, feeling that once more the current of events had come between her and the sleep that she so sorely needed. But, in spite of everything, she had youth and health on her side, and within a few minutes she was fast asleep. It was fairly late when she came down the next morning, and she was rather surprised to find that Fenwick had not finished his breakfast. He sat there sullen and heavy-eyed, and had no more than a grunt for Vera in response to her morning greeting. He turned over his food with savage disapproval. Evidently, from the look of him, he had not only been up late overnight, but he had also had more wine than was good for him.

"Who can eat rubbish like this?" he growled. "The stuff isn't fit to feed a dog with Look at this bacon."

"You can expect nothing else," Vera said, coldly. "If you choose to try and run a large house like this with practically no servants beyond a caretaker and his wife, you must put up with the consequences. You are an exceedingly clever man, but you seem to have overlooked one fact, and that is the amount of gossip you are providing for the neighbors. It isn't as if we were still in town, where the man next door knows nothing of you and cares less. Here peole apie interested in their neighbors. It will cause quite a scandal when it becomes known that you are occupying Lord Merton's house with nothing more than a number of questionable men. As far as I can see, you are far worse off here than if you had stayed in London. I may be wrong, of course."

"I begin to think you are quite right," Fenwick grunted. "I must see to this. It will never do for all these chattering magpies to pry into my business. You had better go into Canterbury this morning and see if you can't arrange for a proper staff of servants to come. Well, what's the matter now?"

One of the men had come into the room with a telegram in his hand. He pitched it in a contemptuous way upon the table and withdrew, whistling unconcernedly. The man's manner was so flippant and familiar that Vera flushed with annoyance.

"I wish you would keep your subordinates a little more under your control," she said. "One hardly expects a man of your wealth to be treated in this way by his clerks."

But Fenwick was not listening. His brows were knotted in a sullen frown over the telegram that he held in his hand. He clutched the flimsy paper and threw it with a passionate gesture into the fire. Vera could see that his yellow face had grown strangely white, and that his coarse lips were trembling. He rose from the table, pushing his plate away from him.

"I've got to go to town at once," he said. "How strange it is that everything seems to have gone wrong of late! I shall be back again in time for dinner, and I shall be glad if you are good enough to see that I have something fit to eat. Perhaps you had better telephone to town for some servants. It doesn't much matter what you pay them as long as they are good."

Fenwick walked rapidly from the room, and a few moments later Vera could see his car moving swiftly down the drive. On the whole, she was not sorry to have Fenwick out of the house. She was pleased, also, to know that he had made up his mind over the servant question. Already the house was beginning to look shabby and neglected; in the strong morning sunshine Vera could see the dust lying everywhere. Her womanly instincts rebelled against this condition of things; she was not satisfied until she had set the telephone in motion and settled the matter as far as the domestic staff was concerned.

Then a sudden thought flashed into her mind. Here was the opportunity for examining the little room where Fenwick and his satellites had been busy the previous evening. Vera had not failed to notice the fact that three of the men had gone off with Fenwick in his car, so that, in all probability, they meant to accompany him to town. If this turned out to be correct, then there was only one man to be accounted for. Possibly with the assistance of Gerald, the fourth man might be got out of the way.

It was nearly three o'clock in the afternoon before Vera managed to see her husband. Eagerly and rapidly she told him all that had taken place the previous evening, though she was rather surprised to find him manifesting less astonishment than she had expected. Venner smiled when Vera mentioned this.

"Oh, that's no new thing to me," he said. "I saw all that going on in your suite of rooms at the Great Empire Hotel, though I haven't the least notion what it all means. I should have thought that your interesting guardian was manufacturing counterfeit coins. But we managed to get hold of one of them, and a jeweller pronounced at once that it was a genuine sovereign. Still, there is no question of the fact that some underhand business is going on, and I am quite ready to assist you in finding out what it is. The point is whether the coast is clear or not."

"There is only one man left behind," Vera explained. "All the rest have gone to London with Mr. Fenwick, who received a most disturbing telegram at breakfast this morning. Of course, the old caretaker and his wife count for nothing; they are quite innocent parties, and merely regard their stay here as temporary, pending the arrival of our staff of servants."

"In that case, I don't see why it shouldn't be managed," Venner said. "You had better go back to the house, and I will call and see you. There is not the slightest reason why I shouldn't give my own name, nor is there the slightest reason why you should not show me over the house when I come. I daresay all this sounds a bit cheap, but one cannot be too careful in dealing with these people."

It was all arranged exactly as Venner had suggested, and a little later Vera was shaking hands with her own husband as if he were a perfect stranger. They proceeded presently to walk up the grand staircase and along the corridor, Vera doing the honors of the place and speaking in a manner calculated to deceive anybody who was listening. She stopped presently and clutched Venner's arm excitedly. She pointed to a doorway leading to a little room down the steps at the end of the corridor.

"There," she whispered, "that is the room, and, as far as I can see, it is absolutely empty. What do you say to going in there now? The coast seems to be quite clear."

Venner hesitated for a moment; it would be just as well, he thought, to err on the side of caution. A casual glance from the corridor disclosed nothing, except that on the table there stood a bottle apparently containing wine, for a glass of some dark ruby liquid stood beside it. Very rapidly Venner ran down the flight of stairs and looked into the room.

"There is nobody there for the moment," he said, "but that bulldog of Fenwick's can't be far off, for there is a half-smoked cigarette on the end of the table which has not yet gone out. I think I can see my way now to working this thing without any trouble or danger. Do you happen to know if that rheumatic old caretaker uses snuff?"

"Really, I don't," Vera said with a smile. "But what possible connection is there between the caretaker and his snuff——?"

"Never mind about that at present. Go down and ask the old man for his snuff box. By the look of him, I am quite sure he indulges in the habit. Tell him you want to kill some insects in the conservatory Tell him anything, so long as you egt possession of the box for a few minutes."

Vera flew off on her errand. She was some moments before she could make the old man understand what she needed; then, with the air of one who parts with some treasure, he handed over to her a little tortoiseshell box, remarking, at the same time, that he had had it for the last sixty years and would not part with it for anything A moment later, Vera was back again at the end of the corridor. Venner had not moved, a sure sign that no one had approached in the meantime. Taking the box from Vera's hand, and leaving her to guard the corridor, he stepped into the little room, where he proceeded to stir a little pellet of snuff into the glass of wine. This done, he immediately hurried Vera away to the other end of the corridor.

"I think that will be all right now," he said. "We have only got to wait till our man comes back and give him a quarter of an hour. Snuff is a very strong drug, and within a few minutes of his finishing his wine he will be sound asleep on the floor."

It all fell out exactly as Venner had prophesied. The man came back presently, passing Vera and her companion without the slightest suspicion of anything being wrong. Then he turned into the little room and closed the door behind him. Half an hour passed before Vera knocked at the door on some frivolous pretext, but no answer came from the other side. She knocked again and again, after which she ventured to open the door. The wine-glass was empty, a half-finished cigarette smouldered on the floor, and, by the side of it, lay the man in a deep and comatose sleep. Venner fairly turned him over with his foot, but the slumbering form gave no sign. The thing was safe now.

"We needn't worry ourselves for an hour or so," Venner said. "And now we have to see if we can discover the secrets of the prison house. Evidently nothing is going on at present. I should like to know what the table is for. It is not unlike a modern gas stove—I mean a gas stove used for cooking purposes, and here is a parcel on the table, just the same sort of parcel that the mysterious new sovereigns were wrapped up in."

"Oh, let me see," Vera said eagerly as she pulled the lid off the box. "See, this stuff inside is just like asbestos, and sure enough here is a layer of sovereigns on the top. How bright and new they look. I have never seen gold so attractive before. I——"

Vera suddenly ceased to speak, and a sharp cry of pain escaped her as she dropped to the floor one of the coins which she had taken in her hand. She was regarding her thumb and forefinger now with some dismay, for they were scorched and swollen.

"Those coins are red hot," she said. "You try— but look out you don't get burned."

Surely enough, the coins were almost at white heat; so much so, that a wax match placed on the edge of one flared instantly. Venner looked puzzled; he could not make it out. There was no fire in the room, and apparently no furnace or oven in which the metal could have been heated. Then he suddenly recollected that Vera must be in pain.

"My poor child," he said. "I am so sorry. You must go down to the old housekeeper at once and get her to put something on your hand. Meanwhile, I will stay here and investigate, though I don't expect for a moment that I shall make any further discoveries."

Vera's hand was dressed at length, and the pain of the burn had somewhat abated when Venner came down the stairs again. He shook his head in response to the questioning glance in Vera's eyes.

"Absolutely nothing," he said. "I found a safe there let into the wall, but then, you see, the safe has been built for years, and no doubt has been used by Lord Merton to store his plate and other valuables of that kind. It is just possible, of course, that Fenwick has the key of it, and that the safe had been cleared out for his use. I am afraid we shall never solve this little puzzle until Fenwick is in the hands of those detectives who gave me such a fright last night."

"But there must have been some means of heating those coins," Vera protested. "They must have come straight from a furnace."

"Of course," Venner said. "The trouble is where to find the furnace. I am perfectly sure, too, that the sovereigns were genuine. Now what on earth can a man gain by taking current coins of the realm and making them red hot? The only chance of a solution is for me to find Egan and Grady and tell them of my discovery. I shall be at the same spot to-morrow afternoon at the same time, and if I find anything out I will let you know."

There was nothing more for it than this, whereupon Venner went away and Vera returned thoughtfully to the dining-room. She was just a little bit in doubt as to whether the man upstairs would guess the trick played upon him, but that she had to risk.

[224]

CHAPTER XX

The Prodigal's Return

MONEY can do most things, even in the matter
of furnishing a large house with competent servants,
and by six o'clock Vera had contrived for the domestic machine to run a little more smoothly. At any
rate, she was in a position now to provide Fenwick
with something in the shape of a respectable dinner
on his return from town.

It was about a quarter to eight when he put in
an appearance, and for the first time for some days
he changed into evening dress for the chief meal of
the day. He appeared to be as morose and savage
as he had been in the morning, in fact even more so
if that were possible. He answered Vera's questions
curtly, so that she fell back upon herself and ate
her soup in silence. And yet, though Fenwick was
so quiet, it seemed to Vera that he was regarding her
with a deep distrust, so that she found herself flush-
ing under his gaze. He put his spoon down presently, and pointed with his hand to Vera's swollen
fingers.

"What have you got there?" he demanded.
"How did you do that?"

"I burnt it," Vera stammered. "It was an accident."

"Well, I don't suppose you burnt it on purpose," Fenwick growled. "I don't suppose you put your hand into the fire to see if it was hot. What I asked you was how you did it. Please answer my question."

"I repeat it was an accident," Vera said, coldly. "I burnt my fingers in such a way——"

"Yes, and you are not the first woman who has burnt her fingers interfering with things that don't concern her. I insist upon knowing exactly how that accident happened."

Vera turned a cold, contemptuous face to her companion; she began to understand now that his suspicions were aroused. It came back to her vividly enough that she had dropped the hot sovereign on the floor, and that, owing to the shock and sudden surprise, she had not replaced it. It was just possible that Fenwick had gone into the little room and had missed the sovereign from the neat layer of coins on the top of the box. And then another dreadful thought came to Vera—supposing that the drugged man had not recovered from the effects of his dose by the time that Fenwick had returned? It was a point which both she and Venner had overlooked. There was nothing for it but to take refuge behind an assumed indignation, and decline to answer offensive questions put in that tone of voice. Vera was still debating as to the most contemptuous reply when the dining-room door opened and one of the newly-arrived servants announced Mr. Blossett.

Fenwick rose to his feet and an unmistakable oath escaped his lips. All the same, he forced a kind of sickly smile to his face, as a big man, with an exceedingly red face and an exceedingly offensive swaggering manner, came into the dining-room. The stranger was quite well dressed, nothing about his garments offended the eye or outraged good taste, yet, all the same, the man had "bounder" written all over him in large letters. His impudent red face, his aggressively waxed moustache, and the easy familiarity of his manner, caused Vera to shrink within herself, though she could have been grateful to the fellow for the diversion which his appearance had created.

"Well, Fenwick, my buck!" he cried. "You didn't expect that I should accept your invitation quite so promptly, but I happen to be knocking around here, and I thought I'd drop in and join you in your chop. This is your daughter, I suppose? Glad to make your acquaintance, miss. I was told there were many beauties at Merton Grange, but I find that there is one more than I expected."

Vera merely bowed in reply. The man was so frankly, hopelessly, utterly vulgar that her uppermost feeling was one of amusement. She could see that Fenwick was terribly annoyed, though for some reason he had to keep himself in hand and be agreeable to Blossett.

"Sit down," he said. "Ring the bell, and we will get another cover laid. I don't suppose you mind missing the soup."

"I have been in the soup too often to care about it," Blossett laughed. "To tell the truth, we had such a warm time last night that solid food and myself are not on speaking terms just now. Here, waiter, fill me a tumbler of champagne. I daresay when I have got that down my neck I shall be able to pay my proper attentions to this young lady."

Fenwick made no reply; he cut savagely at his fish as if he were passing the knife over the throat of the intruder. Meanwhile the stranger rattled on, doubtless under the impression that he was making himself exceedingly agreeable. Vera sat there watching the scene with a certain sense of amusement. She was still a little pale and unsteady, still doubtful as to the amount of information that Fenwick had gleaned as to her movements that afternoon. She would be glad to get away presently and try to ascertain for herself whether the drugged man had recovered or not. Meanwhile, there was no occasion for her to talk, as the intruder was quite able to carry on all the necessary conversation.

"This is mighty fine tipple," he said. "Waiter,

give me another tumbler of champagne. In my
chequered career I don't often run up against this
class of lotion. The worst of it is, it makes one talk
too fast, and seeing that I have got to run the gaunt-
let with the next little parcel of sparklers——"

"Fool!" Fenwick burst out. His face was livid
with rage, his eyes were shot with passionate anger.
"Fool! can't you be silent? Don't you see that
there is one here who is outside——"

"Beg pardon," Blossett said, unsteadily. "I
thought the young woman knew all about it. Lord,
with her dainty face and her aristocratic air, what
a bonnet she'd make. Wouldn't she look nice passing off as the daughter of the old military swell
with a fondness for a little game of cards? You
know what I mean—the same game that old Jim
and his wife used to play."

"Be silent," Fenwick thundered in a tone that
at last seemed to penetrate the thick skull of his
companion. "My — my daughter knows nothing
of these things."

Blossett stammered something incoherent, his
manner became more sullen, and long before dinner
was completed it was evident that he had had far
more wine than was good for him.

"If you will excuse me, I will leave you," Vera
said coldly. "I do not care for any dessert or coffee
to-night."

"Perhaps you had better go," Fenwick said with

an air of relief. "I will take care that this thing does not happen again."

But Vera had already left the room; she was still consumed with anxiety, and desired to know more of what had happened to the man whom Venner had drugged. She did not dare venture as far as the little room, for fear that suspicious eyes should be watching her. It was just possible that Fenwick had given his satellites a hint to note her movements. Therefore, all she could do was to sit in the drawing-room with the door open. Some of the men began to pass presently, and after a little time, with a sigh of relief, Vera caught sight of the one upon whom the trick of the snuff was played. He seemed all right, as far as she could judge, and the girl began to breathe a little more freely.

As she sat there in the silence watching and wait-ing, she saw Fenwick and his companion emerge from the dining-room and cross the hall in the direc-tion of the billiard room. Blossett was still talking lightly and incoherently; he leant on the arm of his host, and obviously the support was necessary. Vera had never before seen a drunken man under the same roof as herself, and her soul revolted at the sight. How much longer was this going on, she wondered? How much more would she be called upon to endure? For the present, she had only to possess herself in patience and hope for the best. She was longing now for something like action.

The silence and stillness of the house oppressed her; she would have liked to be up and doing something. Anything better than sitting there.

The silence was broken presently by the sound of angry voices proceeding from the billiard-room. Half-a-dozen men seemed to be talking at the same time—words floated to Vera's ears; then suddenly the noise ceased, as if somebody had clapped down a lid upon the meeting. Vera guessed exactly what had happened. The billiard-room door had been closed for fear of the servants hearing what was going on. It was just possible that behind those closed doors the mystery that had so puzzled Vera was being unfolded. She recollected now that between the dining- and the billiard-room was a fairly large conservatory opening on either side into the apartments in question. It was just possible that Fenwick and his companions might have overlooked the conservatory. At any rate, Vera determined to take advantage of the chance. The conservatory was full of palms and plants and flowers, behind which it was possible for the girl to hide and listen to all that was going on.

Vera fully understood the danger she was running, she quite appreciated the fact that discovery might be visited with unpleasant consequences. But this did not deter her for a moment. She was in the conservatory a little later, and was not displeased to find that the door leading to the billiard-room was open.

Behind a thick mask of ferns she took her stand.
Between the feathery fronds she could see into the
billiard-room without being seen. Fenwick was
standing by the side of the table laying down the
law about something, while the rest of his men
were scattered about the room.

"Why should I do it?" Fenwick was saying.
"Why should I trust a man like you? You come
down to-night on the most important errand, well
knowing the risks you are running, and you start by
getting drunk at the dinner table."

"I wasn't drunk," Blossett said sullenly. "As
to the girl, why, I naturally expected——"

"Who gave you the right to expect?" Fenwick
demanded. "Couldn't you see at a glance that
she knew nothing about it. Another word and you
would have betrayed the whole thing. You can
stay here all night and talk if you like, but you are
not going to have that parcel to take away to London
with you. In your present condition you would be
in the hands of the police before morning."

"But I haven't got a cent," Blossett said. "I
hadn't enough money in my pocket to pay my cab
fare from Canterbury; and don't you try on any of
your games with me, because I am not the sort of man
to stand them. You are a fine lot of workmen I know,
but there isn't one of you who has the pluck and
ability to take two thousand pound's worth of that
stuff and turn it into cash in a week. Now look

at the last parcel I had, I got rid of it in such a manner that no one could possibly discover that I ever handled the metal at all. Who among you could say the same thing?"

"Oh, you are right enough so long as you keep sober," Fenwick said. "But, all the same, I shall not trust you with the parcel that is waiting upstairs."

Vera listened, comprehending but little of what was going on. After all, she seemed to be having only her trouble for her pains. Beyond doubt these men were doing something illicit with the coinage of the country, though Vera could not bring herself to believe that they were passing off counterfeit money, seeing that the sovereigns were absolutely genuine

"Well, something has got to be done," another of the gang remarked. "We are bound to have a few thousand during the next few days, and, as Blossett says, there is nobody that can work the oracle as well as he can. The best thing I can do is to go to town with him and keep a close eye on him till he has pulled round once more. He can keep sober enough on occasions if he likes, and once the drinking fit has passed he may be right for weeks."

'I am going to have no one with me," Blossett roared. "Do you think I am going to be treated like a blooming kid? I tell you, I am the best man of the lot of you. There isn't one of you can hold a candle to me. Fenwick, with all his cunning,

is a child compared with Ned Blossett. Ask any
of the old gang in New York, ask the blistering police
if you like; and as to the rest of you, who are you?
A set of whitefaced mechanics, without pluck
enough to rob a hen-roost. Take that, you cur!"

The speaker rose suddenly to his feet and lurched
across the room in Fenwick's direction. He aimed
an unexpected blow at the latter which sent him
headlong to the floor, and immediately the whole
room was a scene of angry violence.

Vera shrank back in her shelter, hardly knowing
what to do next. She saw that Blossett had dis-
entangled himself from the mob about him and
was making his way headlong into the conservatory.
There was nothing for it but instant retreat. On
the opposite side was a doorway leading to the garden, and through this Vera hastily slipped and
darted across the grass, conscious of the noise and
struggle going on behind. She paused with a little
cry of vexation as she came close to a man who was
standing on the edge of the lawn looking at the house.
It was only for a moment that she stood there in
doubt; then a glad little cry broke from her lips.

"Charles," she said. "Mr. Evors, what are you
doing here?"

"We will come to that presently," Evors replied.
"Meanwhile, you can be observed from where you
are, and those rioters yonder may make it awkward
for you. When they have patched up their quarrel,

I will return to the house with you and explain. We can get in by the little green door behind the gun-room."

Vera suffered herself to be led away, feeling now utterly unable to be astonished at anything. They came at length to the secluded side of the house, where the girl paused and looked at her companion for an explanation.

"You seem to be strangely familiar with this place," she said. "You walk about here in the dark as if you had known this house all your lifetime. Have you been here before?"

"Many a time," Evors replied sadly. "Up to the time I was twenty my happiest years were spent here. But I see you are still in the dark. Cannot you guess who I really am, Vera? No? Then I will enlighten you. My name is Charles Evors, and I am the only son of Lord Merton. I was born here, and, if the Fates are good to me, some day I hope to die here."

CHAPTER XXI

The Third Finger

VERA ought to have experienced a feeling of deepest surprise, but she was long past any emotion of that kind. On the contrary, it seemed quite natural that Evors should be there telling her this extraordinary thing. The sounds of strife and tumult in the house had now died away; apparently the men in the billiard-room had patched up their quarrel, for nothing more could be heard save a sudden pop which sounded like the withdrawal of a cork. With a gesture of contempt, Evors pointed to the billiard-room window.

"I don't think you need worry about them," he said "As far as I can judge, they were bound to come to some truce."

"But do you know what they were doing?" Vera asked.

"I haven't the remotest idea," Evors replied. "Some rascality, beyond question. There always is rascality where Fenwick is concerned. Is it not a strange thing that I should come down here and find that fellow settled in the home of my ancestors?"

"Then you did not come down on purpose to see him?"

"No, I came here entirely on my own responsibility. If you have half-an-hour to spare, and you think it quite safe, I will tell you everything. But there is one thing first, one assurance you must give me, or I am bound to remain silent. The death of your poor father in that mysterious fashion—"

"Stop," Vera said gently. "I know exactly what you are going to say. You want me to believe that you had no hand whatever in my father's murder. My dear Charles, I know it perfectly well. The only thing that puzzles me is why you acted in that strange weak fashion after the discovery of the crime."

"That is exactly what I am going to tell you," Evors went on. "It is a strange story, and one which, if you read it in the pages of a book, you would be inclined to discredit entirely. And yet stranger and more remarkable things happen every day."

Evors led the way to a secluded path beside the terrace.

"You need not worry about getting to the house," he said. "I can show you how to manage that at any time of the day or night without disturbing anybody. I am afraid that on many occasions I put my intimate knowledge of the premises to an improper use, and that was the beginning of my downfall. What will you say to me when I confess to you that when I came out to Mexico I was driven out of the old country, more or less, like a criminal?"

"I understood you to be a little wild," Vera said.

"A little wild!" Evors echoed bitterly. "I behaved in a perfectly disgraceful fashion. I degraded the old name, I made it a byword in the district. As sure as I am standing here at the present moment, I am more or less answerable for my mother's death. It is a strange thing with us Evors that all the men begin in this way. I suppose it is some taint in our blood. Up to the age of five-and-twenty, we have always been more like devils than men, and then, for the most part, we have settled down to wipe out the past and become respectable members of society. I think my father recognised that, though he was exceedingly hard and stern with me. Finally, after one more unusually disgraceful episode, he turned me out of the house, and said he hoped never to look upon my face again. I was deeply in debt, I had not a penny that I could call my own, and, finally, I drifted out to Mexico with the assistance of a boon companion. On the way out I took a solemn oath that I would do my best to redeem the past. I felt heartily ashamed of my evil ways; and for six months no one could possibly have led a purer and better life than myself. It was about this time that I became acquainted with your father and your sister Beth."

Evors paused a moment and paced up and down

the avenue with Vera by his side. She saw that he was disturbed about something, so that she deemed it best not to interrupt him.

"It was like getting back to a better world again," Evors went on. "I believed that I had conquered myself; I felt pretty sure of it, or I would have never encouraged the friendship with your sister, which she offered me from the first. I don't know how it was or why it was that I did not see much of you about that time, but you were not in the mountains with the others."

"I was down in the city," Vera explained. "There was a friend of mine who had had a long serious illness, and I was engaged in nursing her. That is the reason."

"But it doesn't much matter," Evors went on. "You were not there to watch my friendship for Beth ripening into a warmer and deeper feeling. Mind you, she had not the remotest idea who I really was, nor had your father. They were quite content to take me on trust, they had no vulgar curiosity as to my past. And then the time came when Beth discovered what my feelings were, and I knew that she had given her heart to me. I had not intended to speak, I had sternly schooled myself to hold my tongue until I had completed my probation; but one never knows how these things come about. It was all so spontaneous, so unexpected—and before I knew what had really happen-

ed, we were engaged. It was the happiest time of
my life. I had rid myself of all my bad habits. I
was in the full flush and vigor of my manhood. I
did not say anything to Beth about the past, because
I felt that she would not understand, but I told your
father pretty nearly everything except who I really
was, for I had made up my mind not to take the old
name again until I had really earned the right to do
so. Of course, the name of Evors conveyed no
impression to anybody. It did not imply that I
was heir to Lord Merton. Your father was intense-
ly friendly and sympathetic, he seemed to understand exactly. We became more than friends, and
this is how it came about that I accompanied him
finally on one of his secret visits to the Four Finger
Mine. Your father's regular journeys to the mine
had resulted in his becoming a rich man, and, as you
know, he always kept the secret to himself, taking
nobody with him as a rule, with the exception of
Felix Zary. I will speak of Zary again presently.
You know how faithful he was to your father, and
how he would have laid down his life for him."

"Zary was an incomprehensible character,"
Vera said. "He was one of the surviving, or, rather,
the only surviving member of the tribe who placed
the Four Finger Mine in my father's hands. That
was done solely out of gratitude, and Zary steadfastly
declined to benefit one penny from the gold of the
mine. He had a curious contempt for money,

and he always said that the gold from the Four Finger Mine had brought a curse on his tribe. I really never got to the bottom of it, and I don't suppose I ever shall; but I am interrupting you, Charles. Will you please go on with your story."

"Where was I?" Evors asked. "Oh, yes, I was just leading up to the time when I accompanied your father on his last fatal journey to the mine. At one time I understand it was his intention to take with him the Dutchman, Van Fort, or your mother's brother, Mark Fenwick. However, your father decided against this plan, and I went with him instead. To a great extent it was my doing so that kept Van Fort and Fenwick out of it, for I distrusted both those men, and I believed that they would have been guilty of any crime to learn the secret of the mine. Your father, always trustful and confiding, laughed at my fears, and we started on that fateful journey. I don't want to harrow your feelings unnecessarily, or describe in detail how your father died; but he was foully murdered, and, as sure as I am in the presence of my Maker, the murder was accomplished either by the Dutchman or Fenwick, or between the two of them. Zary mysteriously vanished about the same time, and there was no one to back me up in my story. You may judge of my horror and surprise a little later when Van Fort and Fenwick entered into a deliberate conspiracy to prove that I was responsible for your father's death. They laid their plans with such a diabolical ingenuity that, had I been placed upon my trial at that time, I should have been hanged to a certainty. They even went so far as to tell Beth what had happened, with what result upon her mind you know. At this time Van Fort disappeared, and was never heard of again. Of the strange weird vengeance which followed him I will talk another time. I suppose I lost my nerve utterly, for I became as clay in the hands of Mark Fenwick. Badly as he was treating me, he professed to be my friend, and assured me he had found a way by which I could escape from the death which threatened me. Goodness only knows what he had in his mind; perhaps he wanted to part Beth and myself and get all your father's money into his hands. I suppose he reckoned without your brother, though the latter did not count for much just then, seeing that he was in the hospital at Vera Cranz, hovering between life and death, as the result of his accident. For my own part, I never believed it was an accident at all. I believed that Fenwick engineered the whole business. But that is all by the way. Like the weak fool that I was, I fell in with Fenwick's suggestion and allowed myself to become a veritable tool in his hands, but I did not go till I heard that you had come back again to look after Beth."

Vera recollected the time perfectly well; she was following Evors' narrative with breathless interest.

THE THIRD FINGER

How well she recollected the day of her own marriage and the receipt of that dreadful letter, which parted Gerald and herself on the very steps of the altar, and transformed her life from one of happiness into one of absolute self-sacrifice. She was beginning to see daylight now, she was beginning to discern a way at length, whereby she would be able to defy Fenwick and part with him for all time.

"It is getting quite plain now," she said. "But please go on. You cannot think how deeply interested I am in all you are saying. Presently I will tell you my side of the story. How I came to part with Beth, how I placed her in my brother's hands, how I elected to remain with Mark Fenwick, and my reasons for so doing. I may say that one of my principal reasons for staying with my uncle was to discover the real cause of my father's death. That you had anything to do with it I never really believed, though appearances were terribly against you, and you deliberately elected to make them look worse. But we need not go into that now. What happened to you after you fled from Mexico?"

"I am very much afraid that I dropped back into the old habits," Evors said, contritely. "I was reckless and desperate, and cared nothing for anybody. I had honestly done my best to atone for the past, and it seemed to me that Fate was dealing with me with a cruelty which I did not deserve. One or two of Fenwick's parasites accompanied me everywhere; there seemed to be no lack of money, and I had pretty well all I wanted. There were times, of course, when I tried to break the spell, but they used to drug me then, until my mind began to give way under the strain. Sometimes we were in Paris, sometimes we were in London, but I have not the slightest recollection of how I got from one place to another. I was like a man who is constantly on the verge of delirium. How long this had been going on I can't tell you, but finally I came to my senses in the house in London, and there for two days I was practically all right. All through this time I had the deepest horror of the drink with which they plied me, and on this occasion the horror had grown no less. For some reason or another, no doubt it was an oversight, they neglected me for two days, and I began to get rapidly better. Then, by the purest chance in the world, I discovered that I was actually under the same roof as Beth and your brother, and the knowledge was like medicine to me. I refused everything those men offered me, I demanded to be allowed to go out on business. They refused, and a strange new strength filled my veins. I contrived to get the better of the two men, and half an hour afterward I left the house in company with your brother."

All this was news indeed to Vera, but she asked no questions—she was quite content to stand there and listen to all that Evors had to say.

"I would not stay with your brother," he went on. "I went off immediately to an old friend of mine, to whom I told a portion of my story. He supplied me with money and clothing, and advised me that the best thing I could do was to go quietly away into the country and give myself an entire rest. I followed his advice, and I drifted down here, I suppose, in the same way that an animal finds his way home I did not know my father was away, and you can imagine my surprise when I discovered to whom he had left the house. I feel pretty much myself now; there is no danger of my showing the white feather again. If you are in any trouble or distress, a line to the address on this card will bring me to you at any time. In this house there are certain hiding-places where I could secrete myself without anybody being the wiser; but we need not go into that. Now perhaps you had better return to the house, or you may be missed. Good-night, Vera. You cannot tell how wonderfully helpful your sympathy has been to me."

He was gone a moment later, and Vera returned slowly and thoughtfully to the house. The place was perfectly quiet now; the billiard-room door was open, and Vera could see that the apartment was deserted. Apparently the household had retired to rest, though it seemed to be nobody's business to fasten up the doors. Most of the lights were out, for it was getting very late now, so that there was nothing for it but for Vera to go up the stairs to her own room. She had hardly reached the landing when a door halfway down burst open, and Fenwick stood there shouting at the top of his voice for such of his men as he mentioned by name. He seemed to be almost beside himself with passion, though at the same time his face was pallid with a terrible fear. He held a small object in his hand, which he appeared to regard with disgust and loathing.

"Why don't some of you come out?" he yelled. "You drunken dogs, where have you all gone to? Let the man come out who has played this trick on me, and I'll break every bone in his body."

One or two heads emerged, and presently a little group stood around the enraged and affrighted Fenwick. Standing in a doorway, Vera could hear every word that passed.

"I locked my door after dinner," Fenwick said. "It is a patent lock, no key but mine will fit it. When I go to bed I find this thing lying on the dressing table."

"Another of the fingers," a voice cried. "The third finger. Are you quite sure that you locked your door?"

"I'll swear it," Fenwick yelled. "And if one of you—but, of course, it can't be one of you. There is no getting rid of this accursed thing. And when the last one comes——"

Fenwick stopped as if something choked him.

CHAPTER XXII

"The Time Will Come"

THE startled group on the stairs stood gazing at Fenwick as if they were stricken dumb. There was not one of them who had the slightest advice to offer, not one of them but felt that Fenwick's time was close at hand. Every man there knew by heart the strange story of the Four Finger Mine, and of the vengeance which had overtaken the Dutchman. The same unseen vengeance was very near Fenwick now; he had had his three warnings, and there was but one more to come before the final note of tragedy was struck. Most of them looked with dazed fascination at the mutilated left hand of their chief.

"How did you lose yours?" somebody whispered.

"Don't ask me," Fenwick said hoarsely. "I break into a cold sweat whenever I think of it. But why don't you do what I tell you? Why don't you find Zary? Find him out and bring him down here, and then I can laugh at the vengeance of the Four Fingers. But I have my plans laid, and I shall know how to act when the times comes. Now you all get off to bed again and forget all my foolishness. I suppose I was startled by seeing that accursed thing lying on my table, and lost my nerve.

The little group melted away, and once more the house became silent. When morning came there was no sign or suggestion of the events of the night before. For the first time for many months, Vera felt comparatively happy. She felt, too, that at last she was reaping the reward of all her self-sacrifice, and was approaching the time when she would be able to throw off the yoke and take up her life at the point where she had dropped it. She could afford to wait on events now; she could afford to possess her soul in patience till the hour and the man came together.

Somewhat to her relief, Fenwick did not appear at breakfast, so that, for once, she could partake of the meal in comparative comfort. Swaggering up and down the terrace outside, with a large cigar in his mouth, was the man who called himself Blossett. He had the air of one who is waiting for something; possibly he was waiting for the parcel which had been the means of breeding last night's disturbance in the billiard-room. Anyway, Vera noticed that Fenwick was very busy up and down-stairs, and that all his parasites had gathered in the little room at the end of the corridor. For the present, at any rate, Vera's curiosity was satisfied. She had no intention of running any more risks, and as soon as she had finished her breakfast she went out into the grounds, with no intention of returning before lunch She made her way across the wood which led to the high road, on the possible chance of meeting Gerald It was not Gerald, however, who advanced from the deepest part of the copse to meet her, but the thin, cadaverous form of Felix Zary. He advanced towards the girl, and, in a giave, respectful way, he lifted her hand to his lips.

"You had not expected me, dear lady," he said.

"Well no, Felix," Vera said. "Though I am not in the least surprised. I suppose Mr. Venner has been to see you and has explained to you the meaning of that sheet of blank paper which reached you in an envelope bearing my handwriting."

"I have seen Mr Venner," Zary replied in his smooth, respectful, even voice, "and he explained to me. I did not suspect—if I had received your letter I should have come to you at once—I believe I would come beyond the grave at the call of one bearing the beloved name of Le Fenu. There is nothing I would not do for you. At this moment I owe my life to your resourcefulness and courage. Had I come in response to your letter, I should never have left the house alive. Fenwick would have murdered me, and the vengeance of the Four Fingers would have been lost."

"Why should it not be?" Vera said with a shudder. "Why extract blood for blood in this fashion?

THE MYSTERY OF THE FOUR FINGERS

Can all your revenge bring my dear father back to life again? And yet the vengeance draws nearer and nearer, as I know. I saw Mark Fenwick last night after he had received the third of those dreadful messages, and he was frightened to the depths of his soul. Let me implore you not to go any further——"

"It is not for me to say yes or no," Zary responded in the same quiet, silky manner. It seemed almost impossible to identify this man with murder and outrage. "I am but an instrument. I can only follow the dictates of my instinct. I cannot get away from the traditions of the tribe to which I belong. For two years now I have been a wanderer on the face of the earth; I have been in many strange cities and seen many strange things; with the occult science that I inherited from my ancestors, the Aztecs, I have earned my daily bread. I am what some call a medium, some call a conjurer, some call a charlatan and a quack. It is all the same what they call me, so long as I have the knowledge. For generations the vengeance of the Four Fingers has descended upon those who violate the secret of the mine, and so it must be to the end of time. If I did not obey the voice within me, if I refused to recognise the forms of my ancestors as they come to me in dreams, I should for ever and ever be a spirit wandering through space. Ah, dear lady, there are things you do not know, things, thank God, beyond your comprehension, so, therefore, do not interfere. Rest assured that this thing is absolute and inevitable."

Zary spoke with a certain gentle inspiration, as if all this was part of some ritual that he was repeating by heart. Quiet, almost timid as he looked, Vera knew from past experience that no efforts of hers could turn him from his intention. That he would do anything for a Le Fenu she knew full well, and all this in return for some little kindness which her father had afforded one or two of the now almost extinct tribe from which had come the secret of the Four Finger Mine. And Zary was absolutely the last of his race. There would be none to follow him.

"Very well," she said, "I see that anything I could say would be wasted on you, nor would I ask you what you are going to do next, because I am absolutely convinced that you would not tell me if I did. Still, I have a right to know——"

"You have a right to know nothing," Zary said, in a tone of deep humility. "But do not be afraid—the vengeance will not fall yet, for are not the warnings still incomplete? I will ask you to leave me here and go your way."

There was nothing for it but to obey, and Vera passed slowly through the wood in the direction of the high road. A strange weird smile flickered about the corner of Zary's mouth, as he stood there still and motionless, like some black statue. His lips

moved, but no words came from them. He appeared
to be uttering something that might have passed for
a silent prayer. He took a battered gold watch
from his pocket and consulted it with an air of grim
satisfaction. Then, suddenly, he drew behind a
thicket of undergrowth, for his quick ears detected
the sound of approaching footsteps. Almost immediately the big form of Fenwick loomed in the
opening, and a hoarse voice asked if somebody
were there. Zary stepped out again and confronted
Fenwick, who started back as if the slim black
apparition had been a ghost.

"You here!" he stammered. "I did not expect
to see you—I came here prepared to find somebody
quite different."

"It matters little whom you came to find," Zary
said. "The message sent to bring you here was
merely a ruse of mine. Murderer and treacherous
dog that you are, so you thought to get me here in
the house among your hired assassins by means of
the letter which you compelled my dear mistress
to write? Are you mad that you should pit your
paltry wits against mine?"

"I am as good as you," Fenwick said.

"Oh, you rave," Zary went on. "I am the heir
of the ages. A thousand years of culture, of re-
search, of peeps behind the veil, have gone to make
me what I am. Your scientists and your occult
researchers think they have discovered much, but,

compared with me, they are but as children arguing
with sages. Before the letter was written, the
spirits that float on the air had told me of its coming.
I have only to raise my hand and you wither up like
a drop of dew in the eye of the sunshine. I have only
to say the word and you die a thousand lingering
deaths in one—but for such cattle as you the vengeance of the Four Fingers is enough. You shall
die even as the Dutchman died, you shall perish
miserably with your reason gone and your nerves
shattered. If you could see yourself now as I can
see you, with that dreadful look of fear haunting
your eyes, you would know that the dread poison
had already begun its work. The third warning
came to you last night, the message that you should
get your affairs in order and be prepared for the inevitable. The Dutchman is no more, his foul wretch
of a wife died, a poor wreck of a woman, bereft of
sense and reason."

"This is fine talk," Fenwick stammered. "What
have you against me that you should threaten me
like this?"

Zary raised his hand aloft with a dramatic gesture;
his great round black eyes were filled with a luminous
fire.

"Listen," he said. "Listen and heed. I am
the last of my race, a race which has been persecuted
by the alien and interloper for the last three centuries. Time was when we were a great and

powerful people, educated and enlightened beyond the dreams of to-day. Our great curse was the possession of large tracts of land which contained the gold for which you Eastern people are prepared to barter honor and integrity and everything that the honest man holds dear. For it you are prepared to sacrifice your wives and children, you are prepared to cut the throat of your best friend. When you found your heart's desire in my country, you came in your thousands, and by degrees murders and assassination worked havoc with my tribe. It was not till quite recently that there came another man from the East, a different class of creature altogether. I am alluding to your late brother-in-law, George Le Fenu. He sought no gold or treasure; he came to us, he healed us of diseases of which we knew no cure. And in return for that we gave him the secret of the Four Finger Mine. It was because he had the secret of the mine and because he refused to share it with you that you and the Dutchman, with the aid of his foul wife, killed him."

"It's a lie," Fenwick stammered. "George Le Fenu suffered nothing at my hands. It was the young man Evors."

"It is false," Zary thundered. His eyes were dark, and in a sudden flood of fury he reached out a long thin hand and clutched Fenwick by the collar. "Why tell me this when I know so well how the whole thing happened? I can give it you now chapter and verse, only it would merely be a waste of breath. I declare as I stand here with my hand almost touching your flesh that I can scarcely wait for the vengeance, so eager am I to extract the debt that you owe to George Le Fenu and his children."

By way of reply, Fenwick dashed his fist full into the face of Zary. The latter drew back just in time to avoid a crushing blow; then his long thin arms twisted about the form of his bulky antagonist as a snake winds about his prey. So close and tenacious, so wonderfully tense was the grip, that Fenwick fairly gasped for breath. He had not expected a virile force like this in one so slender. A bony leg was pressed into the small of his back— he tottered backward and lay upon the mossy turf with Zary with one bony hand at his throat, on the top of him. It was all so sudden and so utterly unexpected that Fenwick could only gasp in astonishment. Then he became conscious of the fact that Zary's great luminous eyes were bent, full of hate, upon his face. A long curved knife gleamed in the sunshine. Very slowly the words came from Zary.

"I could finish you now," he whispered. "I could end it once and for all. It is only for me to put in action the forces that I know of, and you would utterly vanish from here, leaving no trace behind. One swift blow of this knife——"

"What are you doing?" a voice asked eagerly. "Zary, have you taken leave of your senses? Release him at once, I say."

Very slowly Zary replaced the knife in his pocket and rose to his feet. There was not the least trace of his recent passion—he was perfectly calm and collected, his breathing was as even and regular as it had been before the onslaught.

"You are quite right, master," he said. "I had almost forgotten myself. I am humiliated and ashamed. The mere touch of that man is pollution. We shall meet again, Mr. Evors."

Zary went calmly away and vanished in the thick undergrowth as quickly and mysteriously as if he had been spirited from the spot. Fenwick rose to his feet and wiped the stains from his clothing.

"I certainly owe you one for that," he growled. "That fellow would most assuredly have murdered me if you had not come up just at the right moment. It is fortunate, too, that you should have turned up here just now. Come as far as the house. I should like to say a few words to you in private."

It was well, perhaps, that Evors could not see the expression of his companion's face, that he did not note the look of mingled triumph and malice that distorted it. It never for a moment occurred to him as possible that black treachery could follow so closely upon the heels of his own magnanimity. Without the slightest demur he followed Fenwick to the house. The latter led the way upstairs into a room overlooking the ancient part of the house, murmuring something to the effect that here was the thing that he wished to show Evors. They were inside the room at length, then, with a muttered excuse, Fenwick hastened from the room. The key clicked in the door outside, and Evors knew that he was once more a prisoner.

"You stay there till I want you," Fenwick cried. "I'll teach you to play these tricks on me after all I have done for you."

"You rascal," Evors responded. "And so you think that you have me a prisoner once more. Walk to the end of the corridor and back, then come in here again and I will have a pleasant surprise for you. You need not be afraid—I am not armed."

Perhaps some sudden apprehension possessed Fenwick, for he turned rapidly as he was walking away and once more opened the door. Evors had been as good as his word—the surprise which he had promised Fenwick was complete and absolute.

"Vanished," Fenwick cried. "Gone! Curse him, what can have become of him?"

CHAPTER XXIII

Smoked Out

A feeling of helpless exasperation gripped Fenwick to the exclusion of all other emotions. Everything seemed to be going wrong just now; turn in any direction he pleased some obstacle blocked his path. Like most cunning criminals he could never quite dispossess himself of the idea that honesty and cleverness never went together. All honest men were fools of necessity, and therefore the legitimate prey of rogues like himself. And yet, though he was more or less confronted now with men of integrity, he was as helpless in their hands as if he had been a child. The maddening part of the whole thing was his inability to find anything to strike. He was like a general leading an army into the dark in a strange country, and knowing all the time that he had cunning unseen foes to fight.

Thoughts like these were uppermost in Fenwick's mind as he gazed in consternation about the little room from which Evors had vanished. So far as Fenwick knew, Evors had saved his life from Zary, but that had not prevented Fenwick from behaving in a dastardly fashion. It seemed to him as if

[258]

Fate were playing into his hands by bringing Evors here at this moment. Hitherto he had found Evors such plastic material that he had never seriously considered him in the light of a foe. Now, for the first time, he saw how greatly he had been mistaken.

"Where can the fellow have gone to?" he muttered. "And whence comes his intimate knowledge of the house?"

He tapped the walls, he examined the floor, but there was no sign whatever of the means by which Evors had made good his escape

Fenwick furiously rang the bell and demanded that the old caretaker should be sent to him at once. The man came to him, shambling unsteadily along and breathing fast as if he had been running. His aged features were quivering with some strange excitement, as Fenwick did not fail to notice, despite his own perturbation.

"What on earth is the matter with you?" he exclaimed. "You look as if you had seen a ghost! What is it? Speak up, man!"

"It isn't that, sir," the old man said in trembling tones. "It is a sight that I never expected to see again. A bit wild he was—aye, a rare handful at times, though we were all precious fond of him. And to see him back here again like this——"

"What the devil are you talking about?" Fenwick burst out furiously. "The old fool is in his second childhood."

"It was the young master," the caretaker babbled on. "Why, you could have knocked me down with a feather when he came in the house with you. As soon as I set eyes on Mr Charles——"

"Mr. what?" Fenwick asked. "Oh, I see what you mean. You are speaking of Mr. Evors, who ¡came in with me."

"That's it, sir, that's it," the old man said. "Mr. Evors, only we used to call him Mr. Charles."

Fenwick began to understand.

"Let's have it out," he said "Mr. Evors, whom you saw with me just now, is Lord Merton's only son?"

"That he be, sir, that he be. And to think that he should come home like this. It'll be a good day for the old house when he returns to settle down altogether."

Fenwick dismissed the old man with a contemptuous gesture. He had found out all he wanted to know, though his information had come to him as an unpleasant surprise. It was a strange coincidence that Fenwick should have settled upon Merton Grange for a dwelling-place, and thus had picked out the actual home of the young man who had suffered so much at his hands. But there was something beyond this that troubled Fenwick. It was a disturbing thought to know that Charles Evors could find his way about the house in this mysterious fashion. It was a still more disturbing thought to feel that Evors might be in league with those who were engaged in tracking down the so-called millionaire. There were certain things going on which it was imperative to keep a profound secret. Doubtless there were secret passages and panels in this ancient house, and Fenwick turned cold at the thought that perhaps prying eyes had already solved the problem of the little room at the end of the corridor. He lost no time in calling his parasites about him. In a few words he told them what had happened.

"Don't you see what it means?" he said. "Charles Evors is here, he has come back to his old home, and what is more he has come back to keep an eye on us. I feel pretty certain that someone is behind him. Very likely it is that devil Zary. If the police were to walk in now, guided by Evors, we should be caught like rats in a trap. I didn't want to trust that stuff to Blossett, but he must get away with it now without delay. There is a train about twelve o'clock to London, and he must get one of the servants to drive him over in a dogcart. Now don't stand gazing at me with your mouths open like that, for goodness knows how close the danger is. Get the stuff away at once."

The man Blossett came into the garden, a big cigar between his lips. He laughed in his insolent fashion when he was told of his errand. The hot blood was in Fenwick's face, but he had not time to quarrel with the swaggering Blossett.

"I thought you would come to your senses," the latter said. "Nobody like me to do a little thing of that sort. Now let me have the case and I'll be off without delay. Better put it in a Gladstone bag. If I have any luck I shall be back here to-night, and then we can share the bank-notes and there will be an end of the matter. You had better sink all the materials in the moat. Not that I am afraid of anything happening, myself."

Half an hour later Blossett was being bowled down the drive behind a fleet horse. A little later still, as the train pulled out of the station, Egan and Grady stood there watching it with rueful faces. Venner was with them, and smiled to himself, despite the unfortunate nature of the situation.

"I thought we had cut it a bit too fine," Grady said. "It is all the fault of that confounded watch of mine. Now what's the best thing to be done? Shall we telegraph to Scotland Yard and ask to have Blossett detained when he reaches Victoria?"

"I don't quite like the idea," Egan said. "If we were English detectives it wouldn't much matter, but I guess I don't want Scotland Yard to have the laugh of me like this. It may cost a deal of money, and I shall probably have to pay it out of my own pocket, but I am going to have a special train."

"My good man," Venner said, "it is absurd to think that you can get a special train at a roadside station like this. Probably they do things differently in America, but if you suggest a special to the station-master here, he will take you for an amiable lunatic. I have an idea that may work out all right, though it all depends upon whether the train that has gone out of the station is a fast or a slow one."

The inquiry proved the fact that the train was a slow one, stopping at every station. It would be quite two hours in reaching Victoria. Venner smiled with the air of a man who is well pleased with himself. He turned eagerly to his companions.

"I think I've got it," he said. "We will wound Fenwick with one of his own weapons. It will be the easiest thing in the world to get from here to Victoria well under two hours in a motor."

"I guess that's about true," Grady said, drily. "But what applies to the special equally applies to the motor. Where are we to get the machine from?"

"Borrow Fenwick's," Venner said. "I understand the working of a Mercedes, and, I know where the car is kept. If I go about this thing boldly, our success is assured. Then you can wait for me at the cross roads and I can pick you up."

"Well, you can try it on, sir," Egan said doubtfully. "If you fail we must telegraph to Scotland Yard."

But Venner had not the slightest intention of failing. There were no horses in the stable at Merton Grange, and consequently no helpers loafing about the yard. There stood the big car, and on a shelf all the necessaries for setting the machine in motion. In an incredibly short space of time Venner had backed the Mercedes into the yard; he turned her dexterously, and a moment later was speeding down a side avenue which led to the Park. The good old saying that fortune favors the brave was not belied in this instance, for Venner succeeded in reaching the high road without mishap. It was very long odds against his theft being discovered, at any rate, for some considerable time; and even if the car were missing, no one could possibly identify its loss with the chase after Blossett. It was consequently in high spirits that the trio set out on their journey. Naturally enough Venner was curious to know what the criminal charge would be.

"Though I have found out a good deal," he said, "I am still utterly at a loss to know what these fellows have been up to. Of course, I quite understand that there is some underhand business with regard to certain coins—but then those coins are real gold, and it would not pay anybody to counterfeit sovereigns worth twenty shillings apiece."

"You don't think so," Egan said, drily. "We shall be able to prove the contrary presently. But hadn't you better wait, sir, till the critical moment comes?"

"Very well," Venner laughed good-naturedly. "I'll wait and see what dramatic surprise you have in store for me."

SMOKED OUT

The powerful car sped over the roads heedless of police traps or other troubles of that kind, and some time before the appointed hour for the arrival of Blossett's train in London they had reached Victoria. It was an easy matter to store the car in a neighboring hotel, and presently they had the satisfaction of seeing Blossett swagger from a first-class carriage with a heavy Gladstone bag in his hand. He called a cab and was rapidly driven off in the direction of the city. Egan in his turn called another cab, giving the driver strict injunctions to keep the first vehicle in sight. It was a long chase, but it came to an end presently outside an office in Walbrook. Blossett paid his man and walked slowly up a flight of steps, carrying his bag. He paused at length before a door which was marked "Private," and also placarded the information that here was the business place of one Drummond, commission agent. Scarcely had the door closed on Blossett than Egan followed without ceremony. He motioned the other two to remain behind; he had some glib story to tell the solitary clerk in the outer office, from whom he gleaned the information that Mr. Drummond was engaged on some particular business and could not see him for some time.

"Very well," he said, "I'll wait and read the paper."

He sat there patiently for some five minutes, his quick ears strained to catch the faintest sound of what was taking place in the inner office. There came presently the chink of metal, whereupon the watcher whistled gently and his comrade and Venner entered the room. Very coolly Egan crossed over and locked the door.

"Now, my young friend," he said to the astonished clerk, "you will oblige me by not making a single sound. I don't suppose for a moment you have had anything to do with this; in fact, from your bewildered expression, I am certain that you haven't. Now tell me how long have you been in your present situation."

"About three months," the clerk replied. "If you gentlemen happen to be police officers——"

"That is exactly what we are," Grady smiled. "Do you find business brisk—plenty of clients about?"

The clerk shook his head. He was understood to say that business was inclined to be slack. He was so frightened and uneasy that it was somewhat difficult to discern what he was talking about. From time to time there came sounds of tinkling metal from the inner office. Then Grady crossed the floor and opened the door. He stepped inside nimbly, there was a sudden cry, and then the voice of the detective broke out harshly.

"Now drop it," he said. "Keep your hands out of your pocket—there are three of us here altogether, and the more fuss you make the worse it will be for both of you. You know perfectly well who I am, Blossett; and we are old friends, too, Mr. Drummond, though I don't know you by that name. You will come with me——"

"But what's the charge?" Blossett blustered. "I am doing business with my friend here quite in a legitimate way."

"Counterfeit coining," Grady said crisply. "Oh, we know all about it, so you need not try to bluff it out in that way. I'll call a cab, and we can drive off comfortably to Bow Street."

All the swaggering impudence vanished from Blossett. As for his companion, he had not said a word from start to finish. It was about an hour later that Venner and his companions were seated at lunch at a hotel in Covent Garden, and Venner was impatiently waiting to hear what was the charge which had laid Blossett and his companion by the heels. Grady smiled as he drew from his pocket what appeared to be a brand new sovereign.

"This is it," he said. "A counterfeit. You wouldn't think so to look at it, would you? It appears to be perfectly genuine If you will balance it on your finger you will find that it is perfect weight, and as to the finish it leaves nothing to be desired. And yet that coin is false, though it contains as much gold as any coin that you have in your purse."

"Now I begin to understand," Venner exclaimed. "I have already told you all about my discovery at the Empire Hotel, also what happened quite recently at Merton Grange. I could not for the life of me understand what those fellows had to gain by making sovereigns red-hot. Of course, I took them to be real sovereigns——"

"Well, so they are practically," Egan said. "They contain absolutely as much gold as an English coin of equal value. They are made from the metal Fenwick managed to loot from the Four Finger Mine."

"What, do you know all about that?" Venner cried.

"We know all about everything," Grady said gravely. "We have been tracking Fenwick for years, and it is a terrible indictment we shall have to lay against him when the proper time comes. We shall prove beyond the shadow of a doubt that he was one of the murderers of Mr. George Le Fenu —but we need not go into that now, for I see you are anxious to know all about the trick of the sovereigns. After Fenwick was compelled to abandon the Four Finger Mine, he found himself with a great deal less gold than he had expected. Then he hit upon the ingenious scheme which we are here to expose. His plan was to make sovereigns and half-sovereigns, and put them on the market as genuine coins. Now do you see what he had to gain by this ingenious programme?"

CHAPTER XXIV

The Mouth of the Net

"I am afraid I am very dense," Venner said, "but I quite fail to see how a man could make a fortune by selling for a sovereign an article that cost him twenty shillings, to say nothing of the trouble and cost of labor and the risk of being discovered——"

"As a matter of fact, the risk is comparatively small," Grady said. "It was only by a pure accident that we got on the inside track of this matter. You see, the coins are of actual face value, they are most beautifully made, and, indeed, would pass anywhere. Let me tell you that every sovereign contains a certain amount of alloy which reduces its actual value to about eighteen and threepence. Now you can see where the profit comes in Supposing these men turn out a couple of thousand sovereigns a day—no very difficult matter with a plant like theirs; and, of course, the money can be disposed of with the greatest possible ease This leaves a profit of a hundred and seventy-five pounds a day. When I have said so much, I think I have told you everything. Don't you admire the ingenuity of an idea like this?"

It was all perfectly plain now—indeed, the mystery appeared to be ridiculously simple now that it was explained.

"And what are you going to do now?" Venner asked.

Grady explained that the next step would be the arrest of Fenwick and his gang at Merton Grange. For that purpose it would be necessary to enlist the assistance of the local authorities. And in no case did the American detectives purpose to effect the arrest before night. So far as Venner was concerned, he was quite at liberty to accompany the Americans on their errand; at the same time they let him infer that here was a situation in which they preferred his room to his company.

"As you will," Venner smiled. "So far as I am concerned, I am going to get back to Canterbury as soon as I can. With all your preparations you have an exceedingly clever man to deal with, and it is just possible that by this time Fenwick already knows that you have laid the messenger by the heels. Men of that sort never trust one another, and it is exceedingly probable that Blossett has been watched."

Grady and Egan admitted this possibility cheerfully enough. Doubtless they had made plans which they did not care to communicate to Venner. He left them presently, only to discover to his annoyance that he had just missed a train to Canterbury, and that there was not another one till nearly six o'clock. It was quite dark when he stepped out of the carriage at Canterbury Station and stood debating whether he should walk as far as the lodgings he had taken near Merton Grange, or call a cab. As he was idly making up his mind, he saw to his surprise the figure of the handsome cripple descending from the next carriage. He noted, too, that the cripple did not seem anything like as feeble as before, though he appeared to be glad enough to lean on the arm of a servant. At the same moment Le Fenu was joined by Evors, who came eagerly forward and shook him warmly by the hand. What these two were doing here, and what they had in their minds, it was not for Venner to say. He wondered what they would think if they knew how close he was, and how deeply interested he was in their movements. He hung back in the shadow, for just then he did not want to be recognised by Le Fenu.

"What a queer tangle it all is," he said to himself. "If I spoke to Le Fenu, he would recognise me in a moment as an old friend of his father's. I wonder what he would say to me if he knew I was his brother-in-law—and Evors, too. Imagine their astonishment if I walked up to them at this moment. Still, on the whole, I think I prefer to watch their movements. If they are going to thrust their heads into the lion's mouth, perhaps I may be able to stand by and render some assistance."

[271]

It was as Venner had anticipated, for presently Le Fenu and Evors entered a cab and gave the driver directions to take them as far as Merton Grange. Venner made up his mind that he could do no better than follow their example.

The cab stopped at length outside the lodge gates, where Evors and Le Fenu alighted, and walked slowly up the drive. It was rather a painful effort for Le Fenu, but he managed it a great deal better than Venner had anticipated. They did not enter the house by the front door—on the contrary, they crept round a small side entrance, beyond which they vanished, leaving Venner standing on the grass wondering what he had better do next.

Meanwhile, Evors led the way down a flight of stairs till he emerged presently in a corridor. With his companion on his arm he walked to the little room at the end and boldly flung open the door.

The room was empty, a thing which both of them seemed to expect, for they smiled at one another in a significant manner, and nodded with the air of men who are quite pleased with themselves.

"You had better sit down," Evors said. "That walk must have tired you terribly. I should be exceedingly sorry——"

"You need not worry about me," Le Fenu said in a clear, hard voice. "I am a little tired, perhaps, but I have a duty to fulfil, and the knowledge of it has braced me wonderfully. Besides, I am so much better of late, and I am looking eagerly forward to the time when I shall be as other men. Now go and fetch him, and let us get the thing done. But for the fact that he is my mother's brother I would have had no mercy on the scoundrel. Still, the same blood flows in our veins, and I am in a merciful mood to-night."

Evors walked boldly out of the room and down the stairs into the hall—then in a loud voice he called out the name of Mark Fenwick. The dining-room door burst open and Fenwick strode out, his yellow face blazing with passion in the light.

"So you are back again," he said hoarsely. "You are a bold man to thrust your head into the lion's mouth like this."

"There are others equally bold," Evors said, coolly. "I am strong enough and able enough to take you by that fat throat of yours and choke the life out of you. You have a different man to deal with now—but there are others to be considered, so I will trouble you to come along with me. The interview had best take place in the little room at the end of the corridor. You know the room I mean. Ah, I see you do."

Fenwick started. It was quite plain that Evors' hint was not lost on him. Without another word he led the way up the staircase into the little room. He started again and half turned when he caught sight of the white, handsome face of Le Fenu. In all

18   [273]

probability he would have disappeared altogether, but for the fact that Evors closed the door and turned the key.

Fenwick stood there, his yellow face scared and terrified. Cold as it was, a bead of perspiration stood on his bulging forehead. He looked from one to the other as if he anticipated violence. Le Fenu sat up in his chair and laughed aloud.

"You are but a sorry coward after all," he said. "You have no need to fear us in the slightest. We shall leave the vengeance to come in the hands of others. And now sit down—though you are not fit to take a chair in the company of any honest men."

"In my own house," Fenwick began feebly. "you are——"

"We will overlook that," Le Fenu went on. "It is our turn now, and I don't think you will find our conditions too harsh. It is not so long ago since my friend here was a prisoner in your hands, and since you reduced him to such a condition of mind that he had abandoned hope and lost all desire to live. It is not so long ago, either, since you dared to make me a prisoner in my own house for your own ends. It was fortunate for you that I chose to live more or less alone in London and under an assumed name. But all the time I was looking for you, all the time I was working out my plans for your destruction. Then you found me out—you began to see how I could be useful to you, how I could become your miserable tool, as Mr. Evors here did. You dared not stay at your hotel—things were not quite ripe for you to come down here. Therefore you hit upon the ingenious idea of making me a prisoner under my own roof. But Fate, which has been waiting for you a long time, intervened, and I became a free man again just at the very moment when Mr Evors also regained his liberty. Since then we have met more than once, and the whole tale of your villainy is now plain before me. You might have been content with the murder of my father and the blood money you extracted from the Four Finger Mine, but that was not enough for you—nothing less than the extermination of our race sufficed. It was no fault of yours that I was not killed in the so-called accident that has made me the cripple that I am. That was all arranged by you, as I shall be able to prove when the proper time comes I escaped death by a miracle, and good friends of mine hid me away beyond the reach of your arm. Even then you had no sort of mercy, even then you were not content with the mischief you had wrought. You must do your best to pin your crime to Mr. Evors, though that conspiracy cost my sister Beth her reason Of course, you would deny all these things, and I see you are prepared to deny them now. But it is absolutely useless to add one lie to another, because we know full well——"

"Stop," Fenwick cried. "What are you here for? Why do you tell me this? A desperate man like myself——"

"No threats," Le Fenu said, sternly. "I am simply here to warn you. God knows what an effort it is on my part not to hand you over to your punishment, but I cannot forget that you are a blood relation of mine—and, therefore, I am disposed to spare you. Still, there is another Nemesis awaiting you, which Nemesis I need not mention by name. When I look at your left hand I feel sorry for you. Bad as you are, the terrible fate which is yours moves me to a kind of pity."

Le Fenu paused and glanced significantly at Fenwick's maimed hand. The latter had nothing more to say; all his swaggering assurance had left him—he sat huddled up in his chair, a picture of abject terror and misery.

"You can help me if you will," he said hoarsely. "You are speaking of Zary. That man is no human being at all, he is no more than a cold-blooded tiger, and yet he would do anything for you and yours. If you asked him to spare me——"

Fenwick broke off and covered his face with his hands. His shoulders were heaving with convulsive sobs now, tears of self-pity ran through his fingers. For the time being, at any rate, the man's nerve was utterly gone. He was prepared to make any conditions to save his skin. Agitated and broken as he was, his cunning mind was yet moving swiftly. A little time ago, these two men would not have dared to intrude themselves upon his presence, he had held them like prisoners in the hollow of his hand; and now it seemed to him that they must feel their position to be impregnable, or they would never have intruded upon him in this bold fashion.

"I am not the man I was," he gasped. "It is only lately that my nerve seems to have utterly deserted me. You do not know what it is to be fighting in the dark against a foe so cold and relentless as Felix Zary. When the first warning came I was alarmed. The second warning frightened me till I woke in the night with a suffocating feeling at my heart as if I were going to die. Against the third warning I took the most elaborate precautions; but it came all the same, and since then I have been drinking to drown my terror. But what is the good of that?—how little does it serve me in my sober moments? As I said just now, Zary would do anything for your family, and if you would induce him to forego that dreaded vengeance which hangs over me——"

"Impossible," Le Fenu said coldly. "Zary is a fanatic, a dreamer of dreams; he has a religion of his own which no one else in the world understands but himself. He firmly and honestly believes that some divine power is impelling him on, that he is merely an instrument in the hands of the Maker

[277]

of the universe. There have been other beings of the same class in a way. Charlotte Corday believed herself to be the chosen champion of Heaven when she stabbed the French monster in his bath. Nothing I could say or do would turn Zary from what he believes to be his duty. The only thing you can do is to go away and lose yourself in some foreign country where Zary cannot follow you."

"Impossible," Fenwick said hoarsely. "I could not get away. If the man possesses the powers he claims he would know where to find me, even if I hid myself in the depths of a Brazilian forest. I tell you I am doomed. I cannot get away from the inevitable."

Fenwick slipped from his chair and fairly grovelled in his anguish on the floor. It was a pitiable sight, but one that moved the watchers with contempt. They waited patiently enough for the paroxysm of terror to pass and for Fenwick to resume something like the outer semblance of manhood. He drew himself up at length, and wiped the tears from his sickly yellow face.

"I cannot think," he said. "My mind seems to have ceased to act. If either of you have any plan I shall be grateful to hear it. It seems almost impossible——"

The speaker suddenly paused, for there came from below the unmistakable sounds of high voices raised in expostulation. It occurred to Fenwick for a moment that his subordinates were quarrelling among themselves; then his quick ears discerned the sound of strange voices. He rose to his feet and made in the direction of the door. A minute later a stealthy tap was heard on the door, and a voice whispered, asking to be admitted. Evors glanced at Le Fenu in an interrogative kind of way, as if asking for instructions. The latter nodded, and the door opened. The man in the list slippers staggered into the room, his red face white and quivering, his whole aspect eloquent of fear.

"What is it?" Fenwick whispered. "What's the trouble? Why don't you speak out, man, instead of standing there like that?"

The man found his voice at last, his words came thickly.

"They are here," he said. "The men from America. You know who I mean. Get away at once. Wait for nothing. Those two devils Egan and Grady are downstairs in the hall."

CHAPTER XXV

An Act of Charity

FENWICK looked at the speaker as if he did not exactly comprehend what he had said. The man's mind was apparently dazed, as if the accumulation of his troubles had been too much for him. He passed his hand across his forehead, striving to collect his thoughts and to find some way of facing this new and unexpected peril.

"Say that again," he faltered. "I don't quite understand. Surely Egan and Grady are in New York."

"They are both down in the hall," the man said, vehemently. "And, what's more, they know that you are here. If you don't want to spend the night in gaol, get away without any further delay."

Fenwick could only look about him helplessly. It seemed to him futile to make further effort. Turn which way he would, there was no avenue open to him. He looked imploringly in the direction of Charles Evors.

"I think I can manage it," the latter said. "Now, you fellow, whatever your name is, leave the room at once and go downstairs and close the door behind you."

The man slunk away, and, at a sign from Le Fenu, Evors closed the door. Evors jumped to his feet and crossed the room to where a picture was let into the panelling. He pushed this aside and disclosed a dark opening beyond to Fenwick's astonished gaze. The latter stared about him.

"Now get through there," Evors said. "It is a good thing for you that I know all the secrets of the old house. There are many panels and passages here, for this used to be a favorite hiding-place for the fugitive cavaliers in the time of Cromwell."

"But where does it go to?" Fenwick stammered.

Evors explained that the passage terminated in a bedroom a little distance away. He went on to say that Fenwick would only have to press his hand upon the wall and that the corresponding panel of the bedroom would yield to his touch.

"It is the Blue Room," he said, "in which you will find yourself presently. Wait there and I'll see what I can do for you. I fancy that I shall be able to convey you outside the walls of the house without anybody being the wiser."

Fenwick crept through the hole, and Evors pulled the panel across, leaving the room exactly as it had been a few minutes before. He had hardly done so when there was a sound of footsteps outside, and without ceremony the American detectives came in. The occupants of the room had had ample time to recover their self-possession, so that they could look coolly at the intruders and demand to know what this outrage meant. The Americans were clearly puzzled.

"I am sure I beg your pardon," Egan said, "but I understand that Mr. Fenwick is the tenant of the house."

"That is so," Evors said. "Do you generally come into a gentleman's house in this unceremonious fashion?"

"Perhaps I had better explain my errand," Egan said. "We are down here with a warrant for the apprehension of Mark Fenwick, and we know that a little time ago he was in the house. He is wanted on a charge of stealing certain valuables in New York, and also for manufacturing counterfeit coins. We quite expected to find him here."

"In that case, of course, you have perfect liberty to do as you please," Evors said. "I may explain that I am the only son of Lord Merton, and that I shall be pleased to do anything to help you that lies in my power. By all means search the house."

Grady appeared as if about to say something, but Egan checked him. It was no time for the Americans to disclose the fact that they knew all about the murder of Mr. George Le Fenu, and how Evors had been more or less dragged into the business. Their main object now was to get hold of Fenwick without delay, and take him back with them to London.

"Very well, sir," Egan said. "We need not trouble you any further. If our man is anywhere about the house, we are bound to find him. Come along, Grady"

They bustled out of the room, and presently they could be heard ranging about the house. As the two friends discussed the situation in whispers the door was flung open and Vera came in. Her face was aflame with indignation—she was quivering with a strange unaccustomed passion.

"Charles," she cried. "I hardly expected to see you here."

"Perhaps you are equally surprised to see Evors," Le Fenu said "We have had an explanation——"

"I have already met Charles," Vera said. "But he did not tell me you were coming down here. Still, all that is beside the point. There will be plenty of time for full explanation later on. What I have to complain of now is an intolerable outrage on the part of Mark Fenwick. He has actually dared to intrude himself on the privacy of my bedroom, and despite all I can say——"

"By Jove, this is a piece of bad luck," Evors exclaimed. "My dear Vera, I had not the slightest idea that you were occupying the Blue Room. In fact, I did not know that it was being used at all.

I managed to send Fenwick that way for the simple
reason that there are two American detectives downstairs with a warrant for his arrest. It was your
brother's idea to get him away——"

"What for?" Vera asked, passionately.

"Why should we trouble ourselves for the safety
of an abandoned wretch like that? He is the
cause of all our troubles and sorrows. For the
last three years he has blighted the lives of all of us,
and there is worse than that—for, as sure as I am
speaking to you now, the blood of our dear father
is upon his head."

"Yes, and mine might have been also, but for
a mere miracle," Le Fenu said. "He tried to do
away with me—he would have done away with all
of us if he had only dared. But one thing do not
forget—he is our mother's only brother."

Vera started and bit her lips. It was easy to see
that the appeal was not lost upon her, and that she
was ready now to fall in with her brother's idea.
She waited quite humbly for him to speak.

"I am glad you understand," he said. "It would
never do for us to hand that man over to justice,
richly as he deserves his sentence. And you can
help us if you will. Those men will search every
room in the house, including yours. If you are in
there when they come and show a certain amount
of indignation——"

"Oh, I quite understand," Vera responded.

"And I will do what I can for that wretched creature."

"What is he doing now?" Le Fenu asked.

"He has huddled himself up in a wardrobe," Vera explained. "He seems so paralysed with fear that I could not get anything like a coherent account of what had happened. Anyway, I will go back to my room now. You need not be afraid for me."

As matters turned out, Vera had no time to spare, for she was hardly back in her room before the detectives were at the door. She came out to them, coldly indignant, and demanded to know what this conduct meant. As was only natural, the Americans were profoundly regretful and almost abjectly polite, but they had their duty to perform, and they would be glad to know if Vera had seen anything of Mark Fenwick, for whose apprehension they held a warrant

"Well," Vera said, loftily, "you don't expect to find him in here, I suppose? Of course, if your duty carries you so far as to ransack a lady's room, I will not prevent you."

The absolute iciness of the whole thing profoundly impressed the listeners. Astute as they were, it never occurred to them that the girl was acting a part; furthermore, with their intimate knowledge of Fenwick's past, they knew well enough that Vera had no cause to shield the man of whom they were in search.

"We will not trouble you," Egan stammered. "It is a mere matter of form, and it would be absurd to suppose that our man is concealed in your room. In all probability he received news of our coming and got away without warning his companions. It is just the sort of thing that a man of his type would do. We have the rest of the gang all safe, but we shall certainly have to look elsewhere for their chief. Will you please accept our apologies?"

Vera waved the men aside haughtily. She was glad to turn her back upon them, so that they could not see the expression of her face. She was trembling violently now, for her courage had suddenly deserted her. For some long time she stood there in the corridor, until, presently, she heard the noise of wheels as two vehicles drove away. Then, with a great sigh of relief, she recognised the fact that the detectives had left the house. She opened the door of her room and called aloud to Fenwick. She called again and again without response.

"You can come out," she said, contemptuously. "There is no cause to fear, for those men have gone."

A moment later the yellow, fear-distorted face of Mark Fenwick peeped out into the corridor. He came shambling along on tottering limbs, and his coarse mouth twitched horribly. It seemed to Vera as if she were looking at a mere travesty of the man who so short a time ago had been so strong and masterful and courageous.

"They gave me a rare fright," Fenwick said in a senile way. He seemed to have aged twenty years in the last few minutes. "That—that—was very cool and courageous of you, my dear. I couldn't have done any better myself. You dear, kind girl. He advanced now and would have taken Vera's hands in his, but she turned from him with loathing. She was wondering which she disliked most—the cold, cruel, determined criminal, or this miserable wreck of a man glad to lean on anyone for support.

"Don't touch me," she said, with a shudder. "Don't thank me for anything for I should have handed you over to those men gladly. I was ready and willing to do so, only my brother recalled to me the fact that the same blood runs in the veins of both of us. It was the remembrance of this that made me lie just now, that caused me to run the risk of a criminal charge myself. For I understand that anybody who harbors a thief for whose arrest a warrant has been issued, runs the risk of going to gaol. And to think that Le Fenu should do a thing of that kind for such a creature as yourself—it is too amazing."

"I suppose it is, my dear," Fenwick said in the same carneying voice. "I never expected to find myself shielded behind a woman. But I have lost all my nerve lately, and the more I drink to drown my troubles, the worse I get. But you must not

think too badly of me, for I am not so black as I
am painted."

"Could you be any blacker?" Vera asked.
"Could any human being have descended lower than
you have descended? I think not. You imagine
because I threw in my lot with you three years ago
that I knew nothing of your crimes. As a matter
of fact, I knew everything. I knew how you had
shifted the responsibility of that dastardly murder
on to the shoulders of the man who is in love with
my sister Beth. It was for her sake that I pretended
ignorance, for her sake that I came with you to try
to get to the bottom of your designs. What I have
endured in the time nobody but myself can know.
But it has all come out now, and here am I to-day
trying to shield you from the very vengeance that I
have been plotting for you all this time. Oh, don't
say anything, don't deny it, don't add more useless
lies to the catalogue of your vices. Go now. Let
us see the last of you, and never intrude upon us
again."

All this outburst of indignation had apparently
been wasted on Fenwick for he did not appear to be
listening at all. He had enough troubles of his own,
and, despite the fact that his nerve had failed him,
it was no feeling of remorse that left him stricken and
trembling and broken down before Vera's scornful
eyes. He could only whine and protest that he was
absolutely helpless.

[288]

AN ACT OF CHARITY

"But what can I do?" he murmured, with tears in his eyes. "I am not so young as I was, indeed I am much older than people take me for. I have no money and no friends, there is not a place I can go to. Don't turn me out—let me stay here, where I shall be safe"

"It is impossible," Vera said, coldly. "We have done enough, and more than enough for you. Now come this way, and I will hand you over to my brother and Mr. Evors. They are cleverer than I am, and may be able to devise some means for getting you out of the country. Why don't you come?"

"I can't," Fenwick almost sobbed. "There is something in my limbs that renders them powerless. If you will give me your arm, I daresay I shall be able to get as far as the little room."

The touch of the man was pollution, yet Vera bravely endured it. She could hear the excited servants talking in whispers downstairs, and one of them might appear at any moment. It would be far better for the domestic staff to assume that the culprit had vanished, otherwise their gossip would assuredly bring the detectives back again without delay. Vera was glad enough when her task was finished and the trembling form of Mark Fenwick was lowered into a seat. The cunning look was still in his eyes; the born criminal would never get rid of that expression, though for the rest he was an object now more for pity than fear.

"It is very good of you," he said. "It is far better than I deserve. You will say I can't stay here——"

"That is absolutely certain," Le Fenu said, coldly. "Most assuredly you can't remain here. You may remain for the night, and Mr. Evors and myself will try and think of a plan between us."

"And Zary," Fenwick whispered. The mention of that dreaded name set him trembling again. "Keep me away from Zary. I am afraid of a good many things, but the mere mention of that man's name stops my heart beating and suffocates me."

"You had better go away," Le Fenu said to Vera, "and leave the wretched creature to us. There will be no trouble in hiding him here for a bit. There are two rooms here that nobody knows anything about except Evors and his father."

Vera was only too glad to get away into the open air, glad to feel that at last this nerve-destroying mystery was coming to an end. She wanted to see Venner, too, and tell him all that had happened. In all probability he was waiting at the accustomed spot. With a light heart and a feeling of youthfulness upon her that she had not felt for some time, she set out on her journey.

CHAPTER XXVI

THE LAST FINGER

IN the ordinary course of things, and but for the dramatic events of the evening, it would have been about the time of night when dinner was finished and the house-party had gathered in the drawing-room. It had been somewhere about seven when the Americans reached Merton Grange, and now it was getting towards nine. It was not exactly the temperature at which one enjoys an evening stroll, but the recent events had been so exciting that Vera felt how impossible it would be to settle down to anything within the limits of the house. There was a moon, too, which made all the difference in the world. As Vera walked along, she almost smiled to herself to think how strange her conduct might look in the eyes of those formal people whose lives run in conventional channels. She told herself more than once that it would be absurd to hope to see Gerald at this time of night, but all the same she continued her journey across the park.

She had not so far to go as she expected, for presently she could see the glow of a cigar in the dis-

tance, and Venner came up. A little joyful cry came
from Vera.

"This is very fortunate," she said. "How lucky
it is that I should run against you in this fashion."

"Well, I was flattering myself that you came on
purpose," Venner said. "And, after all, it is not
so very lucky, seeing that I have been hanging about
this house on the chance of seeing you since it became dark. But you look rather more disturbed
and anxious than usual. My dear girl, I do hope
and trust that there are no new complications. I
shall really have to take you by force and carry you
out of the country. Why should we have to go on
living this miserable kind of existence when we can
take our happiness in both hands and enjoy it?
Now don't tell me that something fresh has occurred
which will keep us apart, for another year or two?
By the way, have you had any visitors to-night?"

"What do you know about them?" Vera asked.
"Have you found out anything about Mr. Fenwick?"

"Well, I should say so," Venner said, drily.
"I have absolutely got to the bottom of that mysterious coin business. In fact, I accompanied Egan
and Grady to London, and I was with them when
they arrested that awful creature, Blossett. Egan
and Grady are old friends of mine, and I told them
all about the strange coins and how you literally
burnt your fingers over them. They were coming
down here to arrest Fenwick, and I offered to accom-

pany them; but they declined my offer, so I returned
here alone, and have been hanging about the house,
curious to know what had taken place. Have they
bagged our friend Fenwick yet?"

"It is about Mr. Fenwick that I wish to speak
to you," Vera replied. "Mr. Evors is down here.
By the way, I don't know whether you are aware of
the fact that he is the son of Lord Merton."

"Perhaps you had better tell me the story," Venner said.

"I am coming to that presently. Mr. Evors is
down here, he is the man who is engaged to my
sister Beth."

Venner whistled softly to himself. At any rate,
he knew all about that, for his mind went swiftly
back to the series of dramatic events which had taken
place some time previously in the house in Portsmouth Square. He recollected now the whitefaced young man who had broken away from his
captors and joined Le Fenu, otherwise Bates, in the
drawing-room. He recollected the joy and delight
of the girl, and how she had clung to the stranger as
if he had come back to her from the other side of
the grave.

"There will be a great many things to be explained
between us, presently," he said, gravely. "But for
the present, I want to know all about Fenwick.
Where is he now?"

"He is hiding up at the house. I believe they

have put him into a secret room, the whereabouts of which is known only to Charles Evors. Of course, he will not stay."

"But why shield such a blackguard at all?" Venner asked. "Surely, after all the trouble he has caused you——"

"You must not forget that he is our own flesh and blood," Vera said, quietly. "I had almost ignored the fact—I am afraid I should have ignored it altogether had not my brother taken a strong view of the matter. At any rate, there he is, and we are in a conspiracy to get him safely out of the country. For the present the man is utterly broken down and absolutely incapable of taking care of himself I want you to do me a favor, Gerald. I want you to take a hand in this business. While the police are still hot upon the track it would not be prudent for Mr. Evors or my brother to be too much in evidence just now."

"My dearest girl, I would do anything in the world for you," Venner cried. "And if I am to take that sorry old rascal out of the country and get rid of him altogether, I will do so with pleasure and never count the cost. If I could see your brother——"

"Then why not come and see him now?" Vera said. "You will have to meet sooner or later, and there could be no better opportunity for an explanation."

THE LAST FINGER

To Le Fenu and Evors smoking in the dining-room came Vera and Venner. Le Fenu looked up with a sort of mild surprise and perhaps just a suspicion of mistrust in his eyes.

"Whom have we here, Vera?" he said.

"This is Mr. Gerald Venner," Vera said. "You know him perfectly well by name—he was with us, on and off, for a considerable time before our poor father died. Father had a great regard for him, and I hope you will have the same, for a reason which I am just going to mention."

"I am sure I am very pleased to meet you," Le Fenu said, politely. "This is my friend, Mr. Charles Evors, the only son of the owner of the house. When I come to look at you, Mr. Venner, I confess that your appearance pleases me, but I have had to deal with so many suspicious characters lately that really——"

"Don't apologise," Venner laughed. "You will have to make the best of me. I came here to-night with Vera to have a thorough explanation of certain matters."

"Oh, indeed," Le Fenu responded with uplifted brows. "My sister and you appear to be on very familiar terms——"

"It is only natural," Vera laughed. A vivid blush flooded her face. "Charles, Mr. Venner is my husband."

"I am not in the least surprised to hear it," Le

[295]

Fenu said. "In fact, I am not surprised at anything. I have quite outgrown all emotions of that kind, but perhaps you will be good enough to tell me how this came about, and why I have not heard it before. As your brother, I am entitled to know."

"Of course, you are. It was just after our father died that I promised myself to Gerald. I had my own ideas why the marriage should be kept a secret. You see, I had more or less thrown in my lot with my uncle, Mark Fenwick, because I had determined to get to the bottom of the business of our father's death. I felt certain that Charles here had nothing to do with it; though, owing to his folly and weakness, he played directly into the hands of the man who was really responsible for the crime."

"We all know who is responsible for the crime," Le Fenu said. "There is no necessity to mention his name."

"Oh, I know that," Vera went on. "The explanation I am making now is more to my husband than either of you. He has been goodness and kindness itself, and he is entitled to know everything. It was within a few minutes of my being married that I learned something of the dreadful truth. I learned that Fenwick had conspired to throw the blame of the tragedy upon Charles Evors. I found out what an effect this conspiracy had had on our poor Beth. There and then I came to a great resolution. I wrote to my husband and told him that in all probability I could never see him again—at any rate, I could not see him for a long space of time. I implored him to trust me in spite of all appearances, and he did so. Now he knows the reason why I acted so strangely. I can see that he has a thousand questions to ask me, but I hope that he will refrain from doing so at present. The thing that troubles me now is what has become of poor little Beth."

"Oh, she is all right enough," Le Fenu said. "I thought of that before I came down. I have left her in the safe hands of the very clever doctor who has my case under his charge, and Beth is with his family. We can have her down here to-morrow if you like."

"Nothing would please me better," Vera said, fervently. "And now, I want to know if you have done anything or formed any plan for getting rid of Mark Fenwick. I shall not be able to breathe here until he is gone."

Le Fenu explained that they had come to no conclusion at present. He was quite alive to the fact that delay was dangerous, seeing that Lord Merton's agents would have to communicate with him by telegram, and that the owner of the house might be back again at any moment. Therefore, it was absolutely necessary that something should be done in the matter of Mark Fenwick without loss of time. Vera indicated her companion.

"That is why I brought Gerald here," she said.

"I thought he might be able to help us. He knows all sorts and conditions of people, and it is probable that he may be able to find an asylum in London where the wretched man upstairs can hide till it is quite safe to get him out of the way."

"I think I can manage that part of the programme," Venner said. "There is an old servant of mine living down Poplar way with his wife who will do anything I ask him. The man has accompanied me all over the world, and he is exceedingly handy in every way. Those people would take a lodger to oblige me, and when you come to think of it, Poplar is not at all a bad place for anybody who wants to get out of the country without being observed. It is close to the river, and all sorts of craft are constantly going up and down. What do you think of the idea?"

"Excellent," Evors cried. "Couldn't be better. Do you think those people would mind if you looked them up very late to-night?"

"Not in the least," Venner said. "There is only one drawback, and that is the danger of traveling."

Le Fenu suggested that the difficulty could be easily overcome by the use of Fenwick's motor, which, fortunately, the detectives had brought back with them when they came in search of the culprit. It was an easy matter to rig Fenwick up in something suggestive of a feminine garb and smuggle him out into the grounds, and thence to the stable, where the motor was waiting Fenwick came downstairs presently, a pitiable object. His mind still seemed wandering; but he braced himself up and became a little more like his old self when the plan of action was explained to him. Vera drew a deep breath of relief when once the man was outside the house.

"Thank God, we shall never see him again," she said, fervently. "And now, I believe I could eat something. It is the first time that the idea of food has been pleasant to me for days."

Meanwhile, Venner and Fenwick were speeding along in the car towards London. Perhaps it was the knowledge that safety lay before him, perhaps it was the exhilaration caused by the swift motion of the car, but Fenwick became more and more like himself as they began to near the Metropolis.

"This is very kind of you," he said, "considering you are a stranger to me. If you only knew my unfortunate story——"

"I know your story perfectly," Venner said, coldly. "You see, I had the pleasure of the friendship of the late Mr. George Le Fenu, and Mr Evors and the younger Mr. Le Fenu are also known to me. Not to be behindhand in exchanging confidence for confidence, I may also say that your niece, Vera, is my wife."

Fenwick said no more, for which Venner was profoundly grateful. They came at length to the little house in Poplar, where Fenwick was smuggled in, and a certain part of the story confided to a seafaring man and his comfortable, motherly wife, who professed themselves ready and willing to do anything that Venner asked them.

"Give him a sitting-room and a bedroom," Venner said; "and take this ten-pound note and buy him a rough workman's wardrobe in the morning as if you were purchasing it for yourself. Let him lie low here for a day or two, and I will write you instructions. As to myself, I must get back to Canterbury without delay."

Trembling with a sort of fearful joy, Fenwick found himself presently in a comfortable sitting-room at the back of the house. He noted the cleanliness of the place, and his heart lightened within him. Something of his own stern self-reliant courage was coming back to him; his busy mind began to plan for the future. Presently he was conscious of a healthy desire to eat and drink. In response to his ring, the landlady informed him that she had some cold meat in the house, and that it was not yet too late to send out for some wine if he desired it.

"Very well," Fenwick said in high good-humor. "Give me the cold meat, and ask your husband to get me a bottle of brandy. I shall feel all the better for a thorough wash, and don't be long, my good woman, for I have never been so hungry in my life as I am now."

Fenwick returned to the sitting-room a few minutes later to find a decent meal spread out for him. There was cheese and butter and some cold meat under a metal cover. A bottle of brandy stood by the side of Fenwick's plate, with a syphon of soda-water. He took a hearty pull of the mixture. The generous spirit glowed in his veins. He would cheat the world yet

"And now for the food," he said. "I trust it is beef. Nothing like beef on occasions like this. Also——"

He raised the cover from a dish. Then he jumped to his feet with a snarling oath. He could only stand there trembling in every limb, with a fascinated gaze on the dish before him.

"God help me," he whispered. "There is no getting away from it. The last warning—the fourth finger!"

CHAPTER XXVII

Nemesis

For a long space of time Fenwick stood there, his head buried in his hands. All the way through, he had never been able to disguise from himself the feeling that, sooner or later, this dread thing must happen. Years ago he had taken his life in his hands in exploring the recesses of the Four Finger Mine; he had more or less known what he had to expect, for the mine had been a sacred thing, almost a part of the religion of the diminishing tribe which had imparted the secret to Le Fenu, and any intruder was bound to suffer. So far as Fenwick knew, the last survivor of this tribe was Felix Zary. Leaving out of account altogether the latter's religious fanaticism, he had been deeply and sincerely attached to the family of Le Fenu, and now he was playing the part of the avenging genius. All these things came back to Fenwick as he sat there.

He knew full well the character of the man he had to deal with; he knew how clever and resourceful Felix Zary was. Hitherto, he had scorned the suggestion that there was some mysterious magic behind Zary's movements, but now he did not know what to think. All he knew was that he was doomed, and that all the police in the Metropolis could not shield him from the reach of Zary's long arm.

And here, indeed, was proof positive of the fact. Two hours before, nobody, not even Fenwick himself, knew that he would spend the night at the little house in Poplar. And here was Zary already upon his track, almost before he had started on the long journey which was intended to lead to the path of safety. Fenwick never troubled to think what had become of the meal prepared for him, or how the extraordinary change had been brought about. Gradually, as he sat there, something like strength and courage came back to him. Come what might, he would not yield, he would not surrender himself into the hands of the foe without a struggle. He replaced the cover on the dish, and rang the bell for his landlady. She came in a moment later, comfortable and smiling, the very picture of respectable middle-age. As Fenwick glanced at her, he at once acquitted her of any connection with his final warning.

"I am sorry to trouble you," he said, "but I should like to know if you have any other lodgers. You see, I am rather a bad sleeper, suffering a great deal from nightmare, and I should not like to alarm your other lodgers in the middle of the night."

"Lord bless you, sir," the woman said, "we haven't any lodgers at all. We don't need to take them, seeing that my man is comfortably fixed. Of course, we are pleased to do anything we can for you, but we shouldn't have had you here at all if it hadn't been to please Mr. Venner. We'd do anything for him."

"No doubt," Fenwick said, hastily. "I suppose your husband sees a good many of his old friends occasionally?"

"No, he doesn't," the woman replied. "I don't suppose we have had anybody in the house except yourself for the last two months. I hope you have enjoyed your supper, sir?"

"Oh, yes," Fenwick stammered. "I finished all the meat. There is one thing more I should like to ask you. I may have to go out presently, late as it is. Do you happen to have such a thing as a latchkey? If you haven't, the key of the front door will do."

The latchkey was forthcoming, and presently Fenwick heard his landlord and his wife going upstairs to bed. He did not feel comfortable until he had crept all over the house and seen that everything was made secure. Then he sat down to think the matter out. Twice he helped himself liberally to brandy, a third time his hand went mechanically to the bottle—then he drew back.

"I mustn't have any more of that," he said. "It would be simply playing into the hands of the fiend who is pursuing me."

NEMESIS

With a resolution that cost him an effort, Fenwick locked the brandy away in a cupboard and
threw the key out of the window. In his present
state of mind he dared not trust himself too far.
Partially divesting himself of his clothing he drew
from about his waist a soft leather belt containing
pockets, and from these pockets he produced a
large amount of gold coins and a packet of bank-
notes. Altogether there were some hundreds of
pounds, and Fenwick congratulated himself on the
foresight which had led him to adopt this plan in
case necessity demanded it. He had enough and
more than enough to take him to the other side
of the world, if only he could manage to get rid of
Felix Zary.

His mind was made up at length; he would creep
out of the house in the dead of the night and make
his way down to the Docks. At every hour ships of
various size and tonnage put out of the port of London, and, no doubt, the skipper of one of these for a
consideration would take him wherever he wanted
to go; and Fenwick knew, moreover, that there were
scores of public-houses along the side of the river
which are practically never closed, and which are
run entirely for the benefit of seafaring men. It
would be easy to make inquiries at some of these
and discover what vessels were leaving by the next
tide, and a bargain could be struck immediately.
So far as Fenwick was concerned, he inclined to-

wards a sailing ship bound for the Argentine. His spirits rose slightly at the prospect before him; his step was fairly light and buoyant as he proceeded in the direction of his bedroom. There was no light in the room, so that he had to fumble about in his pockets for a box of matches which fell from his fingers and dropped on to the floor.

"Confound it," Fenwick muttered. "Where are they?"

"Don't trouble," a calm, quiet voice said out of the darkness. "I have matches, with which I will proceed to light the gas."

Fenwick could have cried aloud, had he been physically able to do so. There was no reason for a light to be struck or the gas to be lighted so that he might see the face of the speaker. Indeed, he recognised the voice far too well for that. A moment later, he was gazing at the impassive face of Felix Zary.

"You did not expect to see me," the latter said. "You were under the impression that you were going to get away from me. Never did man make a greater mistake. It matters little what you do, it will matter nothing to you or anybody else in twelve hours from now. Do you realise the fact that you have but that time to live? Do you understand that?"

"You would murder me?" Fenwick said hoarsely.

"You may calm yourself on that score. You are

unarmed, and I have not so much as a pocket knife in my possession. I shall not lay a hand upon you— I shall not peril my soul for the sake of a creature like you. There are other ways and other methods of which you know nothing."

"How did you get here?" Fenwick asked hoarsely. "How did you put that dreadful thing on my table?"

Zary smiled in a strange, bland fashion. He could have told Fenwick prosaically what a man with a grasp like his could do in connection with a water pipe. He could have told, also, how he had dogged and watched his victim within the last few hours, with the pertinacity of a bloodhound. But Zary could see how Fenwick was shaken and dazed by some terrible thing which he could not understand. It was no cue of Zary's to enlighten the miserable man opposite.

"There are things utterly beyond your comprehension," he said, calmly. "If you look back to the past you will remember how we laid our mark upon the man who stole the Four Finger Mine. That man, I need not say, was yourself. To gain your ends you did not scruple to take the life of your greatest friend, the greatest benefactor you ever had. You thought the thing out carefully. You devised a cunning scheme whereby you might become rich and powerful at the expense of George Le Fenu, and scarcely was the earth dry upon his coffin before your warnings came. You knew the legend of the Four Finger Mine, and you elected to defy it. A week went by, a week during which you took the gold from the mine, and all seemed well with you. Then you woke one morning to find that in the night you had lost your forefinger without the slightest pain and with very little loss of blood. That was the first sign of the vengeance of the genius of the mine. Shaken and frightened as you were, you hardened your heart, like Pharaoh of old, and determined to continue. Another week passed, and yet another finger vanished in the same mysterious fashion. Still, you decided to stand the test, and your third warning came. With the fourth warning, your nerves utterly gave way, and you fled from the mine with less ill-gotten gain than you had expected. It matters nothing to me what followed afterwards, but you will admit that at the present moment you have not benefitted much by your crime. I have nothing more to say to you. I only came here to-night just to prove to you how impossible it is for you to hide from the vengeance of the mine. In your last bitter moments I want you to think of my words and realise——"

As Zary spoke he moved across the room in the direction of the gas bracket; he laid his hand upon the tap, and a moment later the room was in darkness. There was a sound like the sliding of a window, followed by a sudden rush of cold air, and by

the time that Fenwick had found his matches and
lighted the gas again there was not so much as a
trace of Zary to be seen

"I wish I hadn't thrown away the key of that
cupboard," Fenwick said, hoarsely. "I would give
half I possess for one drop of brandy now. Still,
I won't give in, I won't be beaten by that fellow.
At any rate, he can't possibly know what I intend
to do. He could not know that I shall be on board
a vessel before morning"

Half an hour later, Fenwick left the house and
made his way straight to the Docks. At a public-
house in the vicinity he obtained the brandy that he
needed so badly, and felt a little stiffened and braced
up by the spirit. He found presently the thing he
wanted, in the shape of a large barque bound for the
River Plate. The skipper, a burly-looking man
with an enormous black beard, was uproariously
drunk, but not quite so intoxicated that he could
not see the business side of a bargain.

"Oh, you want to go out with me, mister?" he
said. "Well, that's easily enough managed. We've
got no passengers on board, and you'll have to rough
it with the rest of us. I don't mind taking you on
for fifty pounds."

"That's a lot of money," Fenwick protested.

The black-bearded skipper winked solemnly
at the speaker.

"There's always a risk in dealing with stolen

goods," he said. "Besides fifty pounds isn't much for a man who wants to get out of the country as badly as I see you do, and once I have passed my word to do it, I'll see you safe through, and so will my crew, or I'll know the reason why. Now, my yellow pal, fork out that money, and in half an hour you'll be as safe as if you were on the other side of the herring-pond and not a policeman in London will know where to find you. Now, is it a bargain or not?"

Fenwick made no further demur; he accepted the conditions there and then. There was nothing to be gained by affecting to pose as an honest man, and he was a little frightened to find how easily this drunken ruffian had spotted him for a fugitive from justice.

"I can't give you the money just now," he whispered. "I've got it concealed about me, and to produce a lot of cash in a mixed company like this would be too dangerous."

The skipper nodded, and proposed further refreshment. Fenwick agreed eagerly enough; he was feeling desperate now, and he did not seem to care much what happened to him. He could afford to place himself entirely in the hands of the black-bearded skipper, who would look after him closely for his own sake. After all said and done, he had no cause to doubt the honesty of the seaman, who appeared to be fairly popular with his companions and well-known in the neighborhood. It was the best part of an hour before the commander of the

barque staggered to his feet and announced in an
incoherent voice that it was time to get aboard.
Presently they were straggling down to the dock,
Fenwick propping up his companion and wondering
if the latter was sober enough to find his way to his
ship. It was very dark; a thin rain had begun
to fall, and the waters of the river were ruffled by
an easterly breeze. The skipper stumbled down a
flight of steps and into a roomy boat, which was
prevented from capsizing by something like a miracle.
Presently they came alongside the black hull of a
vessel, and Fenwick found himself climbing up a
greasy ladder on to a dirty deck, where two seamen
were passing the time playing a game of cards.
Down below, the skipper indicated a stuffy little bunk
leading out of his own cabin, which he informed Fenwick would be placed at his disposal for the voyage.

"If you don't mind I'll turn in now," the latter
said. "I'm dead tired and worn out. My nerves
are all jumping like red hot wires. Do you think
I shall be safe here?"

"Safe as houses!" the skipper said. "And,
besides, we shall be dropping down the river in about
an hour."

Just as he was, Fenwick rolled into the bunk,
and in a moment was fast asleep. When he came
to himself again, the vessel was pitching and rolling;
he could hear the rattling creak of blocks and
rigging; there was a sweeter and fresher atmosphere

in the little cabin. A sense of elation possessed the fugitive. It seemed to him that he was absolutely safe at last. The skipper had evidently gone on deck after having finished his breakfast, for the plates lay about the table and some tepid coffee in a tin had apparently been left for the use of the passenger.

"I don't think much of this," Fenwick muttered. "Still I daresay I can better it if I pay for it. I'll go on deck presently and see what the black-bearded pirate has to say. At any rate, I am absolutely safe now, and can afford to laugh at the threats of Felix Zary. If that man thinks——"

Fenwick paused, and the knife and fork he was holding over the cold bacon fell from his hands. It was too cruel, the irony of Fate too bitter, for there, just in front of him, propped up by the sugar basin, was a cabinet photograph of the very man who was uppermost in his thoughts. It was Felix Zary to the life; the same calm, philosophic features, the same great round eyes like those of a Persian cat. It all came back to Fenwick now, the whole horror of the situation. His head whirled, and spots seemed to dance before his eyes; a string snapped somewhere in his brain. Zary was behind him, he thought, close behind him like an avenging fury.

With a horrid scream, Fenwick tumbled up the stairs on to the slippery deck. All round him was a wild waste of white waters. The ship heeled over as Fenwick darted to the side . . .

CHAPTER XXVIII

EXPLANATIONS

NIGHT was beginning to fight with morning by the time that Venner returned to Merton Grange. There was no one to be seen; the house was in total darkness, so that Venner placed the motor in the stable and returned to his own rooms. On the whole, he was disposed to congratulate himself upon the result of his night's work. It mattered very little to himself or anybody else what became of Fenwick, now he was once out of the way. He was never likely to trouble them again, and as far as Venner could see, he was now in a position openly to claim his wife before all the world

Despite his feeling of happiness, Venner slept but badly, and a little after ten o'clock the next morning found him back at Merton Grange. Evors greeted him cordially, with the information that he alone was up as yet, and that the others had doubtless taken advantage of the opportunity to get a good night's rest.

"And you will see, my dear fellow," he said, "how necessary such a thing is. Goodness knows how long it is since I went to bed with my mind absolutely at rest. The same remark applies with equal force to Miss Le Fenu—I mean your wife."

"I can quite understand that," Venner said. "It has been much the same with me, though I must confess that I was so happy last night that I could not sleep at all. By the way, have you any information as to your father's movements? He probably knows by this time that his house has been given over to a gang of swindlers."

"He does," Evors said. "I have had a telegram from him this morning to say that he will be home some time in the course of the day; and, to tell the truth, I am looking forward with some dread to meeting my father. But I think I shall be able to convince him now that I am in earnest and that I am anxious to settle down in the old place and take my share in the working of the estate. When my father sees Beth and knows her story, I am sanguine that he will give us a welcome, and that my adventures will be over. I want him to meet Beth down here, and last night after you had gone, and we were talking matters over, Vera promised to go up to town to-day and fetch her sister. By the way, what has become of your friend—Gurdon, I think his name is? I mean the fellow who very nearly lost his life the night he fell down the cellar trap and found himself landed in the house in Portsmouth Square."

"Oh, Gurdon's all right," Venner laughed.

EXPLANATIONS

"I hope you will have the chance of making his acquaintance in the course of the day. You seem to have been in Charles Le Fenu's confidence for some time—tell me, why all that mystery about the house in Portsmouth Square? Of course, I don't mean Le Fenu's reason for calling himself Bates, and all that kind of thing, because that was perfectly obvious. Under the name of Bates he was lying low and maturing his plans for crushing Fenwick. As a matter of fact, Fenwick was almost too much for him. Indeed, he would have been if Gurdon and myself had not interfered and given both of you a chance to escape. It was a very neat idea of Fenwick's to kidnap a man and keep him a prisoner in his own house."

"Yes," Evors said. "And he used his own house for illegal purposes. But before I answer your question, let me ask you one. Why was Gurdon prowling about Portsmouth Square that night?"

"That is quite easily explained," Venner replied. "I sent him To go back to the beginning of things, I have to revert to the night when I first saw Mark Fenwick at the Great Empire Hotel, posing as a millionaire, and having for company a girl who passed as his daughter. Seeing that this pseudo Miss Fenwick was my own wife, you can imagine how interested I was She has already told in your hearing the reason why she left me on our wedding day, and if I am satisfied with those reasons it is nothing

[315]

to do with anybody. As a matter of fact, I am
satisfied with them, and there is no more to be said;
but when I ran against Vera again at the hotel I
knew nothing of past events, and I made an effort
to find out the cause of her apparently strange conduct. In a way, she was fighting against me; she
would tell me nothing, and I had to find out everything for myself. On the night in question I sent
Gurdon to Portsmouth Square, and he had the misfortune to betray himself."

"It nearly ended in his death," Evors said, sober-
ly. "Charles Le Fenu was very bitter just about
that time. You can quite understand how it was
that he mistook Gurdon for one of Fenwick's spies.
But why did he go there?"

"He followed my wife, and there you have the
simple explanation of the whole thing. But you
have not yet told me why those two or three rooms
were furnished in the empty house."

"Who told you about that?" Evors asked.

"What a chap you are to ask questions! We got
into the empty house after the so-called Bates was
supposed to have been kidnapped, and to our surprise we found that all that fine furniture had
vanished. There was no litter of straw or sign of re-
moval outside, so we came to the conclusion that it
had been conveyed from one house to the other.
After a good deal of trouble, we lit upon a moveable
panel, and by means of it entered the house where

you and Le Fenu were practically prisoners. We
were on the premises when you managed to get the
better of that man in the carpet slippers and his
companion; we heard all that took place in the
drawing-room between Fenwick and Beth and Le
Fenu. In fact, we aided and abetted in getting the
police into the house. You will recollect how
cleverly Le Fenu managed the rest, and how he and
you got away from the house without causing any
scandal That was very smartly done. But come,
are you going to tell me the story of the empty house,
and why it was partly furnished?"

"I think I can come to that now," Evors said.
"The whole thing was born in the ingenious brain
of Felix Zary. He was going to lay some sort of
trap for Fenwick, but we shall never know what it
was now, because Fate has disposed of Fenwick in
some other way. Now, won't you sit down and
have some breakfast with me?"

At the same moment Vera came in. Familiar as
her features were and well as Venner knew her,
there was a brightness and sweetness about her now
that he had never noticed before. The cloud seemed
to have lifted from her face; her eyes were no longer
sad and sombre—they were beaming with happiness.

"I am so glad you have come," she said. "We
want you to know all that happened last night after
you had gone."

Venner explained that he knew pretty well all

that had taken place, as he had been having it all out with Evors. What he wanted now was to get Vera to himself, and presently he had his way.

"We are going for a long walk," he said, "where I have something serious to say to you. Now that you have no longer any troubles on your shoulders, I can be very firm with you——"

"Not just yet," Vera laughed. "Later on you can be as firm as you like, and we are not going for a long walk either. We shall just have time to get to the station and catch the 11.15 to Victoria. I am going up to London to-day to bring Beth down here. I think the change will do her good. Of course, we can't remain in the house, so I have taken rooms for the three of us at a farm close by. When Beth has had everything explained to her and knows that the man she loves is free, you will see a change for the better in the poor child. There is nothing really the matter with her mind, and when she realises her happiness she will soon be as well as any of us. You will come with me to London, Gerald ?"

"My dearest girl, of course I will," Venner said. "I will do anything you like. Let us get these things pushed through as speedily as possible, so that we can start on our honeymoon, which has been delayed for a trifling matter of three years, and you cannot say that I have been unduly impatient."

Vera raised herself on her toes and threw her arms round her husband's neck. She kissed him twice—

there were tears in her eyes, but there was nothing but happiness behind the tears, as Venner did not fail to notice.

"You have been more than good," she whispered. "Ah, if you only knew how I have missed you, how terrified I was lest you should take me at my word and abandon me to my fate, as you had every right to do. And yet, all the time, I had a curious feeling that you trusted me, though I dared not communicate with you and tell you where you could send me so much as a single line. I was fearful lest a passionate appeal from you should turn me from my purpose. You see, I had pledged myself to fight the battle for Beth and her lover, and for the best part of three years I did so. And the strangest part of it all is that you, my husband, from whom I concealed everything, should be the very one who eventually struck straight to the heart of the mystery."

"Yes, that's all right enough," Venner smiled, "but why could not you have confided in me in the first instance? Do you think that I should have refused to throw myself heart and soul into the affair and do my best to help those who were dear to you?"

"I suppose I lost my head," Vera murmured. "But do not let us waste too much time regretting the last three years; and do not let us waste too much time at all, or we shall lose our train."

"That is bringing one back to earth with a vengeance," Venner laughed. "But come along and

let us get all the business over, and we can look
eagerly forward to the pleasure of afterwards."

It was all done at length—the long explanation
was made in the West End doctor's drawing-room,
and at length Beth seemed to understand the
complicated story that was told her. She listened very carefully, her questions were well chosen;
then she flung herself face downwards on the couch
where she was seated and burst into a passion of
weeping. Vera held her head tenderly, and made a
sign to Venner that he should leave them together.

"This is the best thing that could happen," she
whispered. "If you will come back in an hour's
time you will see an entirely different girl. Don't
speak to her now."

It was exactly as Vera had predicted, for when
Venner returned presently to the drawing-room,
he found a bright, alert little figure clad in furs and
eager for her journey. She danced across the room
to Venner and held up her lips for him to kiss them.

"I understand it all now," she cried. "Vera has
told me absolutely everything. How good and
noble it was of her to sacrifice her happiness for the
sake of Charles and myself, and how wicked I must
have been ever to think that Charles could have
been guilty of that dreadful crime. Ever since then
there has been a kind of cloud over my mind, a certain sense of oppression that made everything dim
before my eyes. I could not feel, I could not even

shed a tear. I seemed to be all numb and frozen, and when the tears came just now, all the ice melted away and I became myself again. Don't you think I look quite different?"

"I think you look as if you would be all the better for a lot of care and fussing," Venner said. "You want to go to some warm spot and be petted like a child. Now let us go and say good-bye to these good friends of yours and get down to Canterbury. There is somebody waiting for you there who will bring back the roses to your pale cheeks a great deal better than I can."

"Isn't Mr. Gurdon coming with us?" Vera asked.

"He can't" Venner explained. "I've just been telephoning to him, and he says that he can't come down till the last train. He will just look in presently after dinner—he is sharing my rooms with me. But hadn't we better get along?"

Canterbury was reached at length, and then Merton Grange, where Le Fenu and Evors were waiting in the portico. Lord Merton had not yet arrived; indeed, Evors explained that it was very uncertain whether he would get there that night or not.

"Not that it makes much difference," he said, eagerly. "Of course, you will all dine with me. For my part, I can't see why you shouldn't stay here altogether."

"What?" Vera cried, "without a chaperon?"

"I like that," Le Fenu exclaimed. "What do

21   [321]

you call yourself? Have you so soon forgotten the fact that you are a staid married woman? What do you think of that, Venner?"

Vera laughed and blushed softly; she was not thinking so much now of her own happiness as of the expression of joy and delight on the face of her sister. Beth had hung back a little shyly from Evors as they crossed the hall, and he, in his turn, was constrained and awkward. Very cleverly Vera managed to detach her husband and her brother from the others.

"Let them go into the dining-room," she whispered. "It doesn't matter what becomes of us."

"But is she really equal to the excitement of it?" Le Fenu asked, anxiously. "She must have had an exceedingly trying day."

"I am quite sure that she is perfectly safe," Vera said. "Of course, she was terribly excited and upset at first, but she was quite calm and rational all the way down, as Gerald will tell you. All Beth wants now is quiet and change, and to feel that her troubles are over. Let's go and have tea in that grand old hall. If the others don't care to come in to tea we will try not to be offended."

The others did not come in to tea, neither were they seen till it was nearly time to dress for dinner. Assuredly Vera had proved a true prophet, for Beth's .shy, quiet air of happiness indicated that she had suffered nothing through the events of the day. It was a very quiet meal they had later on, but none the less pleasant for that. Dinner had come to an end and the cigarettes were on the table before Gurdon appeared. He carried a copy of an evening paper in his hand, and despite his usual air of calmness and indifference, there was just the suspicion of excitement about him that caused Venner to stand up and reach for the paper.

"You have news there for us, I am sure," he said. "I think we are all in a position to stand anything you like to tell us."

"You have guessed it correctly," Gurdon said. "It is all here in the *Evening Herald*."

"What is all here?" Le Fenu demanded.

"Can't you guess?" Gurdon asked. "I see you can't. It is the dramatic conclusion, the only conclusion of the story. Our late antagonist, Fenwick, has committed suicide!"

CHAPTER XXIX

This Mortal Coil

It cannot be said that Gurdon's announcement caused any particular sensation. To all of those who knew anything about the inner history of the Four Finger Mine the conclusion appeared to be perfectly logical. It was Venner who mentioned the secret of the mine before anybody had even the curiosity to ask to see the paper.

"Do you think that this has been the outcome of anything that Zary did?" he asked Le Fenu. "You see, as far as I am concerned, I was only in the mine once or twice, and before your father's death my knowledge of its romantic history was limited I can't altogether bring myself to believe that the mine was haunted by avenging spirits and all that kind of thing. In this twentieth century of ours, one is naturally very cynical about such matters."

"I really cannot tell you," Le Fenu replied. "Of course there must be human agency afoot. Zary always declared that he was the last of his tribe, and when he died the secret of the mine would belong to our family alone. As a matter of fact, my father died first, so that Zary alone is in possession of the strange secret of that dread place. One thing is very certain. It was none of us who took vengeance on the Dutchman who murdered my father. Who was responsible for that I do not know. Still, there was something very terrible and awe-striking about the way in which the Dutchman's fingers returned to his wife, one by one I should like to have known, also, how Fenwick lost his fingers. But Zary would never tell me. I think he professed that it had been done through the agency of the spirits of his departed ancestors, who guarded the mine. Mind you, I don't say that it is impossible, for we are beginning to understand that there are hidden forces in Nature which till quite recently were a sealed book to us. It is no use speculating about the matter, because we shall never know. Zary has been always fond of us, but I have a feeling now that we shall never see him again. I believe he came to England on purpose to accomplish the death of Mark Fenwick, and you may rely upon it that he will vanish now without making any further sign."

"That is more than possible," Gurdon said, thoughtfully; "but so far as I can judge from what this paper says, Fenwick's death seems to have been prosaic enough. Perhaps I had better read you the account in the newspaper."

Without waiting for any further permission, Gurdon began to read aloud:—

THE MYSTERY OF THE FOUR FINGERS

"Strange Suicide in the Channel.

"Death of Mr. Mark Fenwick.

"Late this afternoon the barque *British Queen*
put back into the Port of London with the schooner
Red Cross in tow. It appears that the barque in
question was bound for the River Plate, and had
dropped down the river with the morning tide.
Outside the mouth of the Thames she had encountered exceedingly squally weather, so much so that she
had lost a considerable amount of running gear
owing to the gusty and uncertain condition of the
wind. About eleven o'clock in the morning an
extra violent squall struck the vessel, and the skipper,
Luther Jones, decided to put back again and wait
till the next tide. It was at this point that the *Red
Cross* was sighted making signals of distress. At
considerable hazard to himself and his crew the
skipper of the *British Queen* managed to get the
schooner in tow, and worked her up the river on a
short sail. This in itself is simply an incident il-
lustrating the perils of the sea, and merely leads up
to the dramatic events which follow. It appears,
according to Captain Jones' statement, that very
early this morning a man called upon him in a
public-house and demanded to know what he would
require for a passage to the River Plate. Satisfactory terms having been arranged, the stranger
came aboard the *British Queen* and immediately

[326]

repaired to his bunk. So far as the captain could see, his passenger was exceedingly reticent, and desirous of avoiding publicity; in fact, the skipper of the *British Queen* put him down as a fugitive from justice. All the same he asked no questions; presumably he had been well content to hold his tongue in return for a liberal fee in the way of passage money. So far as Captain Jones knows, his passenger slept comfortably enough, and it is quite evident that he partook of breakfast in the morning. What happened subsequently, it is somewhat difficult to say, for Captain Jones was busy on his own deck looking after the safety of his ship. These events took place shortly before the *Red Cross* was sighted.

"It was at this time that Captain Jones believes that he heard a shrill scream coming from the cabin, as if his passenger had met with an accident, or had been frightened by something out of the common. He came on deck a moment later, looking like a man who had developed a dangerous mania. He seemed to be flying from some unseen terror, and, indeed, gave every indication suggestive of the conclusion that he was suffering from a severe attack of *delirium tremens*. Captain Jones does not share this view, though it is generally accepted by his crew. Before anybody could interfere or stretch out a hand to detain the unfortunate man, he had reached the side of the vessel and thrown himself into the tre-

mendous sea which was running at the time. It
was absolutely out of the question to make any attempt to save him, though, naturally, Captain Jones
did what he could. Then occurred one of the strange
things which so frequently happen at sea. Five
minutes later a great wave breaking over the fore-
deck cast some black object at the feet of Captain
Jones, which object turned out to be the body of the
unhappy suicide. The man was quite dead; indeed, he had sustained enough bodily injuries to
cause death, without taking drowning into consideration.

"As before stated, Captain Jones came in contact
with the *Red Cross* a little later, and on reaching the
safety of the Pool he immediately communicated with
the police, who took possession of the body of the
suicide. On Scotland Yard being communicated
with, a detective was sent down and immediately
recognised the body as that of Mr. Mark Fenwick,
the American millionaire.

"No doubt is entertained that the police officer is
right, as Mr. Fenwick was well-known to thousands
of people in London, not only on account of his
wealth, but owing, also, to his remarkable personal
appearance. At the present moment the body lies
in a public-house by the side of the Thames, and an
inquest will be held in the morning.

"Later.—Since going to press, we hear that
startling developments are expected in the matter

of the suicide of Mr. Mark Fenwick. On excellent authority we are informed that the police hold a warrant for the arrest of Fenwick and others, on a series of criminal charges, among which that of uttering counterfeit coin is not the least prominent. If these facts prove to be correct, it will be easy to see why Mr. Fenwick was attempting to leave the country in fugitive fashion. Further details will appear in a later edition."

"That is the whole of the story," Gurdon said when he had concluded. "On the whole, I should say that Mark Fenwick is very well out of it. He has had a pretty fair innings, but Fate has been too strong for him in the long run. It is just as well, too, that he has escaped his punishment—I mean, for your sakes, more than anything else. If that man had been put upon his trial, a charge of murder would have been added sooner or later, and you would have all been dragged from police court to criminal court to give evidence over and over again. In fact, you would have been the centre of an unpleasant amount of vulgar curiosity. As it is, the inquest will be more or less of a formal affair, and the public will never know that Fenwick has been anything more than a common swindler."

Venner was emphatically of the same view; personally, he was exceedingly glad to think that the knot had been cut in this fashion and that the unpleasant business was ended. He discussed the matter thoughtfully with Gurdon as he and the latter walked in the direction of his rooms, for he had refused to spend the night at Merton Grange, though Vera, of necessity, had arranged to stay there.

"I suppose one ought to be thankful," he said, "that matters are no worse. Still, at the same time, I must confess that I should like to have a few words with Zary. I wonder if we could get him to take us back to Mexico with a view to exploring the Four Finger Mine. After all said and done, it seems a pity that that rich treasure house should be lost to the world."

"Better leave it alone," Gurdon said. "It makes me creep when I think of it. All the same, I am with you in one thing. I should certainly like to see Zary again."

Gurdon and his companion were destined to have their wish gratified sooner than they had expected. They let themselves into the farmhouse where they were staying, and Venner turned up the lamp in the big rambling sitting-room. There, half-asleep in a chair before the fire, sat the very man whom they had been discussing. He appeared to be heavy with sleep—his melancholy eyes opened slowly as he turned to the newcomers.

"You have been thinking about me," he said—"you have been wondering what had become of me. We are strangers, and yet we are not strangers.

Mr. Venner is known to me, and Mr. Venner's wife also. I was aware that my dear young mistress was his wife when it was still a secret to everybody else. You are puzzled and mystified over the death of Mark Fenwick. Mr. Gurdon has been reading an account to you from a newspaper."

"You are certainly a very remarkable man," Gurdon said. "As a matter of fact, that is exactly what I have been doing. But tell me, Zary, how did you know?"

"You have a great poet," Zary said, calmly and deliberately. "He was one of the noblest philosophers of his time. I have read him, I hope to read him again many times. His name is Shakespeare, and he says 'there are more things in Heaven and earth than are dreamt of in our philosophy.' Gentlemen, that is so, as you would know if you possessed the powers that I do. But I could not explain— you would not understand, for your minds are different from mine. I am going away; I shall never see my dear friends again—for the last time we have met. And because I could not endure a formal parting I have come to you to give them all a message from me. It is only this, that I shall never cease to think of them wherever I may be—but I need not dwell upon that. As to Fenwick, I did not design that he should die so peaceful a death. I had gauged his mind incorrectly; I had goaded him into a pitch of terror which drove him over the border-

land and destroyed his reason. Therefore, he committed suicide, and so he is finished with."

There was a pause for some time, until it became
evident that Zary had no more to say. He rose to
his feet, and was advancing in the direction of the
door when Gurdon stopped him.

"Pardon me," the latter said, "but like most
ordinary men, I am by no means devoid of my fair
share of curiosity. What is going to be done in
the matter of the Four Finger Mine?"

Zary's large round eyes seemed to emit flashes of
light. His face had grown hard and white like that
of a statue.

"Well," he demanded, "what about the mine?"

"Why, you see, it practically belongs to Mr.
Le Fenu's children," Gurdon said. "In which
case it should prove an exceedingly valuable property."

"The mine belongs to us, it belongs to me,"
Zary cried. "I am the last of my tribe, and the secret
shall die with me. Man, do you suppose that
happiness lies in the mere accumulation of money?
I tell you that the thing is a curse, one of the greatest
curses that ever God laid on humanity. To hundreds and thousands of us this life of ours on earth
is a veritable hell through the greed for gold. Of
all the wars that have brought pain and suffering
to humanity, none has done a tithe of the harm
wrought by the incessant battle for the yellow metal

which you call gold. If there had been no such thing on earth, the tribe to which I belong would to-day walk as gods amongst ordinary men. No, I shall do nothing to pander to this disease. When I die the secret of the mine perishes with me. Never more will man work there as long as I have the health and strength to prevent it."

The latter part of Zary's speech had sunk almost to a whisper; he made a profound bow to Venner and Gurdon, then left the room softly. He seemed to vanish almost like the spirit of one of his departed ancestors, and his place knew him no more.

"Curious man," Gurdon said, thoughtfully. "Very quiet and gentle as a rule, but not the kind of person you would care to have as a foe. I have a very strong feeling that none of us will ever see Felix Zary again. Now, don't you think we can begin to forget all about this kind of thing? Surely we have had enough horrors and mysteries, and I can only wonder at the way in which those girls have borne up against all their troubles. Tell me, what are you going to do? I mean as to your future."

"Upon my word, I really haven't given it a thought," Venner said. "It is not very often that a man has the unique experience of being married three years without a honeymoon, and without more than half an hour in his wife's company. You can but feebly guess, my dear fellow, how terribly I have suffered during the time to which I refer. Still, I trusted my wife implicitly, though all the dictates of common-sense were against me, and I am sincerely and heartily glad now that I took the line I did. As soon as possible, I intend to take Vera away for a long tour on the Continent. When I come back I shall have the old house done up again, and, I suppose, settle down to the life of a country gentleman. But, of course, I can't do anything till Beth's future is settled. I suppose, for the present, she will go back again to Le Fenu's doctor friends, pending her marriage with Charles Evors."

"The programme is all right," Gurdon said. "But suppose Lord Merton objects to the arrangement?"

"I don't fancy that he will do that, from what I hear," Venner said. "All the Evors have been wild in their youth, and the present lord is no exception to the rule. Depend upon it, he will be very glad to have his son back again, happily married, and eager to become domesticated. Besides, from what I understand from Vera, her father worked the Four Finger Mine to considerable advantage during his lifetime, and Beth is something quite considerable in the way of an heiress. On the whole, I am not disposed to worry. Now let us have one quiet cigar, and then go to bed like a pair of average respectable citizens."

CHAPTER XXX

A Peaceful Sunset

"Upon my word," Evors was saying to Beth, "I feel as nervous as an Eton boy sent up to the head for a flogging. It is just the same sensation as I used to enjoy in my schooldays; but I don't care what he says, I am going to marry you whether he likes it or not, though, of course, he is bound to like it. No one could look at that dear sweet little face of yours without falling in love with you on the spot."

Beth demurely hoped so; she pretended an easy unconcern, though, on the whole, she was perhaps more anxious than Evors, for the latter had written to his father at some length explaining how matters stood, and Lord Merton had telegraphed to say that he would be at home the following afternoon. The afternoon had arrived in due course, and now the wheels of his carriage might be heard at any moment. Vera and her husband were not far off; they had promised to come in and give their moral support if it became necessary.

"I don't see how he can possibly help liking you," Evors went on. "Thank goodness, we shall be spared the trouble of making a long explanation.

If my father had been against the arrangement he probably would have done something else besides telegraphing that he was coming; but I don't care, it doesn't matter what he says, I have quite made up my mind what to do."

"But you couldn't go against your father," Beth said, timidly.

"Oh, couldn't I? My dear girl, I have been doing nothing else all my lifetime. I have been a most undutiful son, and I have no doubt that I have come near to breaking my father's heart many a time, as he nearly broke the heart of his father before him. In common fairness he will have to admit that we Evors are all alike as young men; and, in any case, I couldn't give you up, Beth. Just think how faithful you have been to me all these years, when all the time it has seemed as if I had a terrible crime on my conscience. Your father's death——"

Beth laid her little hand upon the speaker's mouth.

"Oh, hush, hush," she whispered. "I implore you never to speak of that again. They told me, or, at least, that dreadful man told me, that you had committed that awful deed. He gave me the most overwhelming proofs, and when I demanded a chance to speak to you and hear from your own lips that it was all a cruel lie, you were nowhere to be found. This, Fenwick told me, was proof positive of your guilt. It was such a shock to me that, for the time being, I lost my reason—at least, I did not exactly lose my reason, but my brain just seemed to go to sleep in some strange way. And yet, from first to last, I never believed a word that Mark Fenwick said. There was always present the knowledge that your name would be cleared at last, and the most gratifying part of it all is the knowledge that there can be no scandal, no slanderous tongues to say that there is no smoke without fire, and those wicked things that sound so small and yet imply so much."

"Don't let us think of it. Let our minds dwell only on the happy future that is before us. We shall be able to marry at once, then we can go and live in the old Manor House by the park gates. The place is already furnished, and needs very little doing up. Sooner or later you will be mistress of this grand old home, though I hope that time may not come for many years. It seems to me——"

But Beth was not attending. She seemed to be listening with more or less fear to the sound of wheels crunching on the gravel outside. Evors had hardly time to reassure her, when the door opened and Lord Merton came in. He was a tall man of commanding presence, a little cold and haughty-looking, though his lips indicated a genial nature, and he could not altogether suppress the grave amusement in his eyes.

"This is an unconventional meeting," he said. "I received your letter, Charles, and I am bound to say the contents would have astonished me exceedingly had they been written by anybody but an Evors. But our race has always been a law unto itself, with more or less disastrous consequences. We have been a wild and reckless lot, but this is the first time, so far as I know, that one of the tribe has been accused of murder."

"It is a wicked lie," Beth burst out, passionately. She had forgotten all her fears in her indignation. "My father was killed by the man Fenwick and his colleagues. That has all been proved beyond a doubt!"

Lord Merton smiled down upon the flushed, indignant face. It was quite evident that Beth had made a favorable impression upon him.

"I admire your loyalty and your pluck," he said. "My dear child, many a woman has risked her happiness by marrying an Evors—not one of them did so except in absolute defiance of the advice of their friends. In every case it has been a desperate experiment, and yet, I believe, in every case it has turned out perfectly happily. It was the same with Charles's mother. It was the same with my mother. No Evors ever asked permission of his sire to take unto himself a wife, no Evors ever cared about social position. Still, at the same time, I am glad to know that my boy has chosen a lady. When he was quite a young man, I should not have been in the least surprised if he had come home with a flaunting barmaid, or something exquisitely vulgar in the way of a music hall artiste."

Beth laughed aloud. She had quite forgotten her fears now; she was beginning rather to like this caustic old gentleman, whose cynical words were belied by the smile in his eyes.

"I am very glad to know that you are satisfied with me," she said, timidly. "It is good to know that."

"I suppose it would have been all the same in any case," Lord Merton replied with a smile. "You would have married Charles and he would have had to have earned his own living, which would have been an excellent thing for him."

"Indeed, he wouldn't," Beth laughed. "Do you know, Lord Merton, that I am quite a large heiress in my way. I am sure you won't mind my speaking like this, but I feel so happy to-day that I hardly know what I am saying. If you only knew the dread with which I have been looking forward to meeting you——"

"Oh, they are all like that," Lord Merton laughed. "To strangers, I am supposed to be a most terrible creature, but everybody on my estate knows how lamentably weak I am. They all take advantage of me and bully me, even down to the lads in the stable, and I won't disguise from you the satisfaction I feel in the knowledge that you have money of your own. For some considerable time past I have been

severely economising with a view to paying off some
alarming mortgages on the estate, so that I should
not have been in a position to allow Charles much in
the way of an income. It will be my ambition when
my time comes to hand you over the property without
a penny owing to anybody."

"May that day be a long way off, sir," Charles
said, with feeling. "I hope to assure you how I
appreciate the noble manner in which you have
forgiven——"

"Say no more about it, say no more," Lord Merton said. He seemed to have some little difficulty
in the articulation of his words. "Let us shake
hands on the bargain and forget the past. I was
profoundly interested in your long letter, and I must
confess to some little curiosity to see your other
friends, especially Mrs. Venner, who seems to have
played so noble a part in the story. I understand
that she and her husband are down here. I suppose
you made them more or less comfortable, which
must have been a rather difficult undertaking in the
circumstances. However, I have arranged to have
all the old servants back to-morrow, and it will be
some considerable time before I let the old house
again. Now run away and enjoy yourselves, and
let us meet at dinner as if nothing had happened.
I don't want it to appear that there has been anything like a quarrel between us."

So saying, Lord Merton turned and proceeded

to his own room, leaving Beth in a state of almost
speechless admiration. It was so different from
anything she had expected, that she felt as if she
could have cried for pure happiness. The sun was
shining outside; through the window she could see
the deer wandering in the park. It was good to
know that the old dark past was gone, and that the
primrose path of happiness lay shining before them.
Presently, as they wandered out in the sunshine,
Vera came on the terrace and watched them. There
was no need to tell her that the interview with the
master of the house had been a smooth one. She
could judge that by the way in which the lovers were
walking side by side. Venner came and stood by
his wife's side.

"So that's all right," he said. "As far as one can
judge, they have managed to propitiate the ogre."

"What do you mean by calling a man an ogre
in his own house?" the voice of Lord Merton asked
at the same moment. "For some few minutes I
have been keeping an eye on you two, but I suppose
I must introduce myself, though you will guess who
I am. Mr. Venner, will you be good enough to do me
the honor of introducing me to your wife? I have
heard a great deal of her from my son. Mrs. Venner, if you will shake hands with me I shall esteem
it a great favor."

"Then you are not annoyed with us?" Vera
asked. "You are not displeased at the way we have

taken possession of your house? I am afraid that indirectly we have been the cause of a great scandal."

"Oh, don't worry yourself about that," Lord Merton, said breezily. "There have been far worse scandals than this in great houses before now; and, at any rate, it does not touch us. I am afraid you have been rather inconvenienced here, and that the Grange has not upheld its reputation for hospitality. Still, I hope it will be all right to-morrow, and I sincerely trust that you can see your way to stay here for some little time to come. I am going to ask my sister, Lady Glynn, to come down and act the part of hostess. Somebody will have to introduce Beth to the county as my future daughter-in-law."

"You are pleased with the arrangement?" Vera asked, demurely.

"Indeed, I am," Lord Merton cried. "You do not know what an eccentric lot we are. I should not have been at all surprised if Charles had come home with some curiosity in the way of a bride, and I am only too profoundly grateful to find that he has made so sweet a choice. But, tell me, you will stay here some little time——"

"I am afraid not," Venner, said regretfully. "If you will allow us to come back a little later on, I am sure that my wife and myself will be very pleased. I have no doubt that Evors will be impatient to claim his bride, but I hope he will wait for a month or two

[342]

at least. You see, I have a bride of my own, though, in a way, we are old married people. I don't know whether Charles told you anything of our story, but if you would like to hear it——"

Lord Merton intimated that he had already done so. He expressed a hope that Venner and his wife would return again a little later on; then, making some excuse, he returned to the house, leaving Venner and Vera together. For some little time they wandered across the park very silently, for the hearts of both were full, and this was one of those moments when words are not necessary to convey thought from one mind to another Presently Evors and Beth appeared in the distance and joined the others.

"Well," Venner said with a smile, "it is some time since I saw two people look more ridiculously happy than you two. But I am sincerely glad to find that the ogre is only one in name. My dear Charles, your father is quite a delightful person. I quite understood from what you told me that we had a lot of trouble in store for us. On the contrary, he seems to be as pleased with the course of events as we are."

"He seems to have altered so much lately," Evors said. "At any rate, he has been particularly good to me, and I am not likely to forget it. Behold in me a reformed character, ready to settle down to a country life with Beth by my side——"

"Not quite, yet," Venner said, hastily. "You will have to curb your impatience for a bit; you must not forget how Vera has suffered for the sake of you both, and how patiently I waited for my happiness. You must promise us that the marriage will not take place under two months, or I give you a solemn warning that we shall not be there. Our own honeymoon——"

"Of course Charles will promise," Beth said, indignantly. "Oh, I could never dream of being married unless Vera were present And, after all, what are two months when you have a whole lifetime before you? I am sure that Charles agrees with me."

"I don't, indeed," Evors said, candidly. "Still, I am not going to be disagreeable, and Beth knows that she has only to look at me with those imploring eyes of hers to get absolutely her own way."

They left it at that, and gradually drifted apart again. When Vera and her husband returned to the Grange, the setting sun shone fully in their faces, flinging their shadows far behind. Venner paused just for a moment under the sombre shadow of a clump of beeches, and drew his wife to his side.

"One moment," he said. "We have not yet decided where we are going. I have everything in readiness in London, and I suppose that you are not lacking in the matter of wardrobe Don't tell me, while having everything that woman can want in the way of dress, that you have nothing to wear."

"I won't," Vera said, softly. "My dear boy, cannot you see how glad I shall be to be alone with you at last? Everything is going well here, and Beth is entirely happy. You have been very good and patient, and I will keep you waiting no longer. If you so will it, and I think you do, let it be to-morrow."

Venner stooped and kissed the trembling lips held up to his. Then very silently, their hearts too full for further speech, they turned towards the house.

THE END

Lightning Source UK Ltd.
Milton Keynes UK
UKHW020637090223
416652UK00001B/262